HOW TO BE A BADASS DETECTIVE

HOW TO BE A BADASS DETECTIVE

HOW TO BE A BADASS DETECTIVE™ BOOK THREE

MICHAEL ANDERLE

This book is a work of fiction. All of the characters, organizations, and events portrayed in this novel are either products of the author's imagination or are used fictitiously. Sometimes both.

Copyright © 2021 Michael Anderle
Cover copyright © LMBPN Publishing
A Michael Anderle Production

LMBPN Publishing supports the right to free expression and the value of copyright. The purpose of copyright is to encourage writers and artists to produce the creative works that enrich our culture.

The distribution of this book without permission is a theft of the author's intellectual property. If you would like permission to use material from the book (other than for review purposes), please contact support@lmbpn.com. Thank you for your support of the author's rights.

LMBPN Publishing
PMB 196, 2540 South Maryland Pkwy
Las Vegas, NV 89109

Version 1.00, June 2021
ebook ISBN: 978-1-64971-874-7
Print ISBN: 978-1-64971-875-4

THE HOW TO BE A BADASS DETECTIVE
BOOK THREE TEAM

Thanks to our Beta Team

Kelly O'Donnell

Thanks to our JIT Readers

Veronica Stephan-Miller
Daryl McDaniel
Deb Mader
Wendy L Bonell
Dave Hicks
Rachel Beckford
Zacc Pelter
Deb Sateren

If We've missed anyone, please let us know!

Editor
The Skyhunter Editing Team

*To Family, Friends and
Those Who Love
To Read.
May We All Enjoy Grace
To Live The Life We Are
Called.*

CHAPTER ONE

His name was Viator Psellus, and although he was one thousand six hundred and forty-eight years old, he still lived within the book that bore his name. The tome was the body that clothed and housed his immortal spirit.

But soon, he felt—no, he *knew*—there would again be an opportunity to have a real human body. And then he could achieve things beyond what any human being alive today could conceive.

He was born in the ancient city of Adana in what is now Turkey in the year 374 CE. At the time of his birth, Adana lay within the Eastern Roman Empire. When he was twenty-one years old, the Empire split in two. Thereafter he lived in the land called Byzantium.

It was around the time this great civilizational shift occurred that Psellus began his study of the arts of magic. He had continued his studies, had continued his pursuit of the craft, his *magnum opus*, continuously until the present year of 2022.

Resting within the book, he waited and his mind wandered, then focused, then wandered again. His thoughts were never far from what would happen when he once again had a mortal body.

So much had changed since the last time he'd had what most people would recognize as a "life." It had been but a single century, only one out of the sixteen he had lived, but the pace of social and technological advancement had increased to a staggering degree. The world of today was scarcely recognizable compared to the world of 1919, when he had last possessed flesh and blood.

During those years of the early twentieth century, he had seized control of two bodies in quick succession. The first had been a member of a Serbian secret society called the Black Hand, which was notorious for its role in starting World War One. Viator Psellus, in the guise of a young and fanatical Bosnian, had been among those who pushed for the killing of Archduke Franz Ferdinand. He had personally spoken to Gavrilo Princip, the chief assassin, urging him to greater heights of fervency.

The man he had possessed had seemed insignificant at the time. Psellus had desired to be involved in great events, the better to showcase his magic and learn new things from the strife and flux that would result. However the man and his comrades had proven to be more important than the sorcerer had expected.

And so, after the Great War began and things became too difficult for him to handle, he had migrated again. The second time, he had seized the body of a middle-aged Italian woman shortly before her departure to the United States. With him directing her mortal form, she had brought his grimoire on her voyage.

Thus, Psellus had come to America, and there he had remained for over a hundred years.

The Italian lady had died unexpectedly of cholera in 1919, and Psellus had no choice but to return to the book, his immortal safe haven in times of trouble and uncertainty, and to wait. His last host had willed her possessions to a niece, who had no interest in them.

And so *The Grimoire of Viator Psellus*, one of the greatest albeit most obscure tomes of magical knowledge in the world, had languished in a vault for decades, unread and sealed away from mankind.

Until 2020. The niece passed away, and her inherited treasure trove had found its way to an auction house. Psellus could have taken control of any of the individuals who had handled the book or dared to open its pages, but he did not. He sensed that it would be better and smarter to wait for the right host to appear.

The world was much different now. To understand it and take advantage of it, he would need the help of someone who was not only well-versed in the magic of the twenty-first century but was considered the first among equals of its sorcerers.

When he had taken the Bosnian man and the Italian woman, he had deliberately chosen individuals who were humble, insignificant. The former had been a fanatic and the latter a moderately wealthy person, but otherwise, they were unremarkable. Humbled by the Industrial Revolution, Psellus had thought it best to lie low until he could learn more about how technology could be combined with magic.

Now, as he and the grimoire had emerged again into the light of another century, he grasped that he had been wrong to take such a strange detour. His usual approach, throughout all of history since his first life had neared its end, was to possess people who were *important.* Not overly visible, perhaps, but persons who were close to the world's centers of power.

It was only fitting for a mage of his stature.

Viator Psellus had waited and watched. The auction house had retained him, safe within his book, and he'd obscurely perceived that someone of significance would purchase him soon. Knowing this, he reposed in silence and reflected on all he had learned about the present day.

The Industrial Age had come and gone with what would have been shocking rapidity in earlier times, but the pace of history had quickened. The world had moved on to the Digital Age, and technology was almost indistinguishable from magic.

Though physically trapped within the tome he had written and consecrated, Psellus' mind was capable of following obscure chains of connection to other things and seeing far beyond the confines imposed by his current circumstances. As soon as the executors of the Italian lady's estate took him out of his vault, his consciousness had flowed through and beyond them to other people they knew, and he had been able to see fleeting images of the world beyond.

He had heard things and made deductions based on the available evidence. The world's wealthiest and most powerful countries these days—the United States, the United Kingdom, Germany, Russia, China, and Japan—owed enormous amounts of their power to their investiture in "computers" and "the Internet," which stored and transmitted information in ways that put the most skilled scryers and diviners in history to shame.

Grasping this, Viator Psellus had summoned what magical resources remained to him, drawn upon his vast astral reserves as well as the energies woven into the pages of the book, and cast a spell.

It was a call, a signal—a cry to be noticed by people who might wish to read his grimoire and would find it interesting, particularly if they were sorcerers skilled in the magic of the digital era.

He could not yet be certain the spell had succeeded. More time would be needed to see who answered the call, but, he felt certain, not much more.

Soon. Someone would come; someone with access to the milieu of modern technology, with means and resources that would quickly become Psellus' own.

Then he would become a magician unlike any in history. Perhaps the greatest of all time.

Of course, he would try to avoid starting a war this time around.

But mistakes sometimes happened.

Kera and Chris had flipped a coin to determine who had to drive the rented car back to downtown Los Angeles. The SUV was smaller than Chris' Jeep but a lot larger than (and much different from) Kera's motorcycle. He had done all of the driving in the damn thing already so far.

It was only fair.

"Dammit," Kera had said, then climbed behind the wheel.

Chris got into the passenger's seat and buckled in. "It's not that long a drive, dear. Granted, everything takes twice as long in LA traffic, but you'll be fine. I can take over around Pomona if you can't deal with it, but it'll be nice to have a short break."

Scowling, she shifted to drive and pulled out on the road.

Once Kera had gotten into a groove on the highway, quickly adjusting to operating the vehicle, Chris tried to make conversation. He had drunk two full cups of coffee with their breakfast, whereas Kera had limited herself to one, so of the two of them, he was feeling more animated.

"So," he began, "did you hear anything from Lia? Like, any texts or emails? I didn't see anything, but usually if there's agency business, you're the one she contacts. After all, you're technically the CEO."

Kera raised an index finger. "Not *technically*. I *am* the CEO, but it's a small enough company that I consider everything a group effort. Ugh, I don't even want to think about how badly we would have flubbed all of this stuff recently if it had been just me on my own. Or if I had like one or two employees, but they were people I didn't know, didn't trust, and who were incompetent morons in general. With you and Lia and Steph as my crew, we function a hell of a lot better."

"Agreed." Chris stretched his arms and rolled his head around on his neck. "That doesn't answer my question, though. *Did* you hear from her?"

"Oh, right. No," said Kera. "She kept quiet all through our little vacation-from-vacation. That probably means either that nothing is happening or that a bunch of stuff has gone down, but none of it was drastic or weird, so she's just chugging along without us until we get back."

It occurred to her also that Lia might be worried about disturbing her and Chris after their ordeal. Lia had driven out to Jurupa Valley to help with the assault on the Orthodoxy's safehouse, but she'd gone straight back home to Long Beach once it was over. Kera hadn't given her instructions on whether or not to contact her if something came up.

Chris shrugged. "Well, she usually does fine. Serious workaholic, though."

"You should talk," Kera observed.

He chortled and rubbed one eye. "Yeah, yeah, sometimes I can be. But hey, I accompanied you on *two consecutive vacations* and only worked when I had to. I'd allege that it's fair to say I'm not *addicted* to work. I merely get deep into it when I have a good reason."

"Right." She frowned as traffic thickened; they were getting into the urbanized part of the Inland Empire by this point. "And I appreciate it. If anything, the biggest slacker at our company is me. Stephanie doesn't count since she still works at the Mermaid. When is she going to quit?"

Chris squinted into the distance. "I believe the arrangement was that once we started getting a steady and reliable flow of cases, she would join full-time. Notwithstanding the size of your inheritance, it helps for a business to have actual customers to be able to pay its employees."

"True."

Kera sat in silence for a moment or two. Other thoughts had been churning within her mind over the last couple of days, things she knew were important and would need to be addressed when the time was right. Until this morning, they had not yet found expression in spoken words.

"I wish," she began, "we knew who that woman we took out was—the lead witch from the train, who was trying to sacrifice me and the little girl. Pavla seemed pretty sure it was Milena, who was one of the most senior and powerful members of the Orthodoxy if so. But I'm not positive, and I don't feel great about it."

Chris listened, looking at her face as she spoke, and taking in her words with his usual mixture of deep thought and caring acceptance.

"Kera," he replied, "it's a *good* thing you don't enjoy killing people. It's too bad you've had to do it as many times as you have, but from everything you've told me, as well as everything that I've seen, it was necessary and justified in each case. When you take on bad people and try to save innocent lives, you're going to end up in situations where the choices aren't easy."

She knew all that; he hadn't told her anything new. It was nice to hear him say it out loud, though.

He went on, "I *might* have killed one person, but I'm not sure. When we were staking out El Peluquero at the wharf, remember? Lia and I were in the Jeep, and I had to ram that one SUV. One of the guys popped out and tried to shoot us, and we both shot back. I don't know which of us dropped him since we fired at the same time. Part of me hopes it wasn't me, though I'm sure Lia doesn't want the responsibility either."

Kera nodded. Chris' sidearm of choice was a .357 Magnum revolver, whereas Lia's was a little .380 pistol. Chris' would have been the deadlier if he had hit his mark, but gunshot wounds were strange things, and in the darkness and chaos, there was no way to make sure.

"Yeah," she said. "I'm just glad all of us are still alive. And that girl Jessica. The thing is, it isn't only the morality of having had to kill her—Milena or whoever she was. There's something else."

Chris blinked, surprised. "Oh? You can tell me about it if you want."

Her nostrils flared as she breathed in and out. Around her, the city buzzed and shone and honked. Traffic was bad but no worse than usual for the SoCal road system.

"When I took her down," Kera explained, "I felt a lot of magic *release*. That might not make sense to someone who doesn't have the gift. For one thing, there was the spell she was trying to cast, where as soon as she performed the sacrifice, all my power would have been transferred to her godawful friends. That one dissipated as soon as she died. But there was more. It was as though a bunch of other enchantments had been buzzing along in the background, and they all fizzled out with her death. I think that by removing her from the picture, I screwed the Orthodoxy pretty badly."

Everything she had seen so far suggested that the members of the Orthodoxy were awful people. The coven operated more like an organized crime ring than a society of casters, and yet...

"So?" Chris inquired. "Why do you feel bad about *that?* Not trying to, like, invalidate your feelings; I ask because I'm confused. It seems like screwing them over would be a *good* thing."

Kera grimaced, staring straight ahead. "In most regards, yes, but remember, they're at war with a certain *other* group. I'm worried that by weakening them, I handed an advantage to those fucking council people."

Her hands tightened on the wheel, her knuckles turned white, and she clenched her jaw.

"You know," she added, "the ones who were hunting me. The

bastards who stole the Kims' magic from them and would have done the same thing to me unless I had agreed to bow down before them."

Chris quipped, "Ah, I remember. Makes more sense now."

"I hope they both lose," Kera snapped, not trying to hide her bitterness. "The world might be a better place if all of them shut the hell up and went away and left everyone else the fuck alone."

CHAPTER TWO

Stephanie inhaled deeply, and when she let the breath out, it took the form of a sigh. She leaned back in her chair and stared at the ceiling. It was only early afternoon, but it had already been a long day.

She was at Lia's house in Long Beach, which was a decent drive from her home near downtown, not to mention from Kera's place. They had been talking about having Lia move closer to the center of the city or perhaps renting a company office equidistant from all of them so that no one had to fight LA traffic for an extended period to come to work.

So far, they were making do.

Steph turned her eyes and hands back to the laptop's keyboard to resume her work. A moment later, the door rattled, then someone turned a key in the knob, opened it, and stepped in.

"Hi," she called. "Lia?"

A soft voice responded, "Yes, of course. Thank you for covering for me." Her heels clacked on the floor as she walked into the kitchen, out of Stephanie's line of sight. It sounded like she was carrying a big paper bag, presumably filled with food.

Steph had only had a banana for breakfast, and she admitted to herself that there was no way she would skip lunch. "No problem. Usually you're the one who works all day, right? You can take a break once in a while."

"I suppose." Lia opened the bag. "But I feel mildly ashamed, as ridiculous as that might sound. I got us some sandwiches if you're interested. Since you said you didn't want a break today, you might as well eat something on the job."

Steph figured there was no point in disguising her enthusiasm. "Damn, Lia. You didn't have to do that, but I'm not complaining. Thanks. What kind?"

She got up, went to the kitchen, and saw that her friend had purchased a tray of miniature sub sandwiches with a variety of meat, cheese, and vegetable options. Steph, not being a picky eater, sampled a little of everything.

"To be honest," she confessed, "I was reconsidering the whole 'not taking a break today' thing just based on caloric needs or whatever. I haven't been using magic much, but I think my metabolism's still higher than it used to be."

Lia poured herself a glass of juice to go with her light meal. "That could be. From what you and Kera have said in the past, I gather that as you advance as a caster, you begin to subconsciously run passive magical processes that consume a small amount of your energy, like how a computer still draws a little bit of power when you leave it idling or in Sleep mode."

Steph nodded. "Something like that. I feel like my mind wanders, only it *gets places*, instead of just running in circles in my head if that makes sense. Makes me suspect that I'll be at Kera's level eventually in terms of all the stuff I can do with my mind. I think she's still stronger than me overall, though, so maybe not."

"I wouldn't know," Lia replied. "Still, you both have extraordinary talents. Now, back to work. Have we gotten more requests? That's a stupid question. Of course, we have. It's only a matter of how many and how serious they are."

Stephanie shuddered. It was true.

At some point in the recent past, neither of them was sure when, word about their agency and its exploits had spread on the Internet and attracted the wrong sort of attention. It was not merely that they had been involved with two separate serial killing sprees as well as a major art theft and a child abduction. No, those things, as sensational as they might be, were still within the realm of normality.

The problems had begun when someone put out the word that MacDonagh Investigations dealt with paranormal matters. The crazies had all come out of the woodwork, along with the spammers and trolls.

"Yeah," said Steph, "plenty of bullshit." She sat down at her laptop, which was on a table a short way from Lia's desk in the front corner of the living room. Then she checked her email. "Ugh, this is the eighth yeti-related request I've gotten today. Can't be more than one or two of those the work of legitimate wackos. The rest are probably kids on the Internet who think it's hilarious to waste our time."

Lia balked. "*Yetis?* Abominable snowmen? In Los Angeles? People are even stupider than I thought."

"Or think they're clever." Stephanie sifted through the results. "Oh, and here's one asking if we can clairvoyantly—his word, not mine—kill his ex-wife by causing her car to crash or something like that. I didn't know detective agencies hired out hitmen, psychic or otherwise."

Lia munched a sandwich and washed it down with juice. "I and Johnny and Sven could provide him with contacts who might be useful to him, but let's not. We need to stay on the right side of the law. Especially me, given my history."

"Right." Steph kept her eyes on the screen. "Hmm, this one is kind of interesting. Something about a magical book at an auction. It belonged to a dead lady..."

Lia snapped her fingers as she struggled to finish chewing. "Mark that one," she said after swallowing. "It sounds like something Kera would be into. And if it involves a book, particularly one that is confirmed to exist, it might take us in the direction of high-class stolen property. Those are the cases we need to pursue. Maximum profit and prestige, minimum danger and shady reputation."

Stephanie had bookmarked it by the time Lia finished speaking. "I was thinking the exact same thing."

The two women shared the task of filtering the remainder of the emails and phone messages their business had received. In addition to the mountainous piles of spam, there was a smattering of legitimate requests for help from people who seemed serious and would likely be able to pay for the agency's services.

When Lia took over the job of evaluating the remainder of the missives, Stephanie shifted her focus to determining when they might be able to speak to each customer to discuss their case.

At first, it was a rote act of examining their schedule, trying to guess how much time it would take to consult with each person, and placing things in a sensible order. After she took a minute to sit back, finish her lunch, and examine the big picture, something clicked in her mind.

Damn, we're turning out to be a solvent business after all. We've got, like, ten or so good customers lined up. It will be up to Kera to decide how much we charge them and that sort of thing, but I think we're over the line as far as knowing we can succeed at this.

Which means I can start working for Kera full-time. No more waiting tables, even though the Mermaid ain't all bad.

She rubbed her eyes and looked sidelong at her co-worker. "Hey, Lia."

Lia raised her eyebrows and responded, "Yes?" without looking away from her PC.

"So far, I'm counting ten cases that seem legit. If you remember what we talked about before, when Kera was asking when I was gonna quit my day job? I'd say the time has come. We got enough customers to turn a profit for at least the next few months, and that will give us enough of a reputation to get more. Right?"

Lia stopped typing and turned to her friend. "I hadn't thought of it that way, but yes, I believe you're right. When making a major decision, if you have a gut feeling that it's the *correct* decision, sometimes it's better to finalize it right away instead of waffling over the details and allowing inertia to keep you where you are. If you want my advice, compose your two weeks' notice today and turn it in next time you're at work. Insofar as Kera wouldn't refuse to hire you, you could technically quit on the spot, but..."

"But that," Steph finished for her, "would be a bitch-ass move. Cevin's a good guy to work for, and I wouldn't do that to him. Not to mention Jenn and the newer folks would get screwed over and have to pick up the slack until they found someone else."

Lia nodded and turned back to her screen and keyboard. "It's up to you, but it sounds like you have the right idea."

Okay, then, Stephanie concluded. *As soon as I finish this itinerary, I'll type up my formal letter of resignation. Guess I could call the bar and accomplish the same thing, but I'm moving up in the world, so I might as well start doing things the professional way.*

Ten minutes later, she opened a word processor program, found a template online for the type of letter she was aiming for, and got to work. She snickered to herself as she opened with *To Whom It May Concern*, feeling vaguely ridiculous for using such a pretentious phrase.

It sounded nice, though. She wondered if Cevin would be impressed or flattered that she was treating his humble business as though it were a large, respectable company.

Toward the end of the composition, Lia interrupted her to

ask, "Could you send me the link to that book case? I'm caught up with everything else, and I'd like to review the information before we present it to Kera. She and Chris are supposed to be back sometime today."

"Sure." Steph paused in her writing and sent the link to Lia via email. While her co-worker perused the info, she finished her letter, skimmed it for errors, saved it, and sent it to the printer.

As she was returning to her seat with the freshly printed sheet of paper, Lia said, "Huh. This is interesting."

Stephanie diverted from her path and stopped behind Lia's shoulder. "Yeah, seemed like it. I didn't have time to read everything, though. What all did you find?"

Lia had three tabs open, one her email. The one displayed on the screen was from a message board.

"Here," she indicated, pointing, "we have the handle of the guy who sent the email. He said that his mother used to talk about her friend, a Mrs. Manfredini, who supposedly possessed an ancient, or possibly medieval-era, spellbook she swore was haunted. She kept it in a vault and died not too long ago. He emailed me, saying he probably can't afford to purchase the book, but he might be able to pay us to investigate the matter. He claims to have no real agenda; it's just something he's always been curious about. He made this post on a discussion board over two years ago, so he's consistent, and he did not just make the story up yesterday as a prank."

Steph nodded. "Yeah, that's the impression I got. Still, do we have independent verification that the thing exists?"

"Yes." Lia clicked on the third tab. "Here we have an auction site which is offering the book in question. I checked them out, and they're a very staid, prim establishment with a good reputation, so it's not as though it's only listed on a snake-oil phishing site that delivers cheap Chinese knock-offs four months later than scheduled or anything like that."

Laughing, Stephanie responded, "Well, glad you did your homework. What does it say?"

The book, they saw, was called *The Grimoire of Viator Psellus*. It had been up for auction previously but had not found a buyer. It would be available for sale starting tomorrow evening. The starting price was set at five thousand dollars. It was considered a rare collectible, and the auction house did not expect it to sell for any less than ten thousand.

"Gah." Steph was aghast. "I mean, Kera has that kind of money, doesn't she? Still a hell of an operating expense, seeing as how the guy who wants us to check it out probably can't pay more than that."

Lia ran her fingers through her long black hair. "Yes, if Kera decides to take the case, we may end up having to wait for someone to buy it and then approach the new owner the right way to get them to allow us to examine it. However, there's one further wrinkle, which is alluded to here."

The book's listing politely avoided any lurid details, but it mentioned that it had a "history" and that rumors about its supposedly supernatural qualities had circulated over the years. Naturally, the auctioneers played that up as part of the item's mystique and as an element of its historical significance.

"There's more, though." Lia went back to the forum and scrolled down to reveal more of the conversation beyond the one guy's introductory post. "It seems that a couple other people have heard of the grimoire, and here's where it starts to get weird. The legends have it that the book is a conduit for malevolent spirits that can possess anyone who reads it."

Steph gave an appreciative nod. "Shit. Possess, as in, like, demonic possession, taking over their body?"

"Apparently." Lia scrolled onward. "There are other fairly ridiculous stories we can likely dismiss, such as that the book was involved in setting off World War I in Europe. As for the possession thing, I'm inclined to be skeptical, but being around you and Kera has, shall we say, opened my mind to new possibilities."

That, Steph thought, *is a mild way of putting it. Most people aren't ready for how many things in the world are real that they always figured were made-up or something crazy people hallucinated. Hell, it took* me *a while to accept it all.*

She shook her head and waved a hand. "Well, Kera can review it herself when she's back. Sounds a little spicier than what she wants to move toward since we've gotten caught up in a lot of difficult, nasty stuff lately, but you know how she is. Can't stay away from trouble, like she thinks she's the only one who can deal with it."

Lia said nothing, but the faint wry smile on her face suggested she understood completely.

Both women returned to their separate endeavors. About ten minutes later, someone knocked on the door. Steph rose first to answer it and recognized the familiar figures of Kera and Chris on the doorstep.

She opened the door and smiled. "Hey there, strangers! Welcome back."

"Hi." Kera's voice was ragged and she gave off a definite air of grumpiness, as though something was bothering her. "Long drive. I had to do most of it myself, but Chris took over after we stopped at my place."

"Yeah," her boyfriend confirmed. "I probably shouldn't have put it up to a coin toss. Kera's more out of practice than I am when it comes to driving things that have more than two wheels."

Stephanie gestured at the sandwich tray, telling them to help themselves to the leftovers if they wanted, then told them there were business updates to discuss once they were ready.

"Great," Kera muttered.

Chris gave her an odd look; he had heard enough of her concerns that he understood why she might still be dealing with a mixture of stress and guilt, but it bothered him that she was being so crabby at a time when all was well.

As the couple entered the living room, Lia pushed back in her chair and stood up. "Hello, Kera. Hello, Chris. I hope you're both well-rested after everything that happened. Stephanie and I have been working on a glut of new queries from prospective clients."

"Oh?" Chris responded. "A *glut*, you say? When did we get famous?"

Kera crossed her arms. "Yeah, that's interesting. What the hell happened?" She sounded tired and annoyed despite her second vacation.

Stephanie laughed as Lia explained. "Word got out that we were involved in paranormal research, so some teenagers on the Internet thought it would be amusing to ask us to investigate yeti sightings in their backyards and that sort of thing."

Chris cracked up, but Kera was irritated. "Cute. We finally start to build a reputation and promptly turn into the butt of bad jokes. I bet there are memes circulating online using our logo."

"Perhaps," Lia conceded, "but amidst all the dross, there were a surprisingly large number of requests that we think might be legitimate. Eleven or twelve, I believe?"

Stephanie clarified, "Yeah, twelve. Used to be ten. I have the people lined up over the course of the next two and a half weeks, but nothing's set in stone yet. We wanted your approval before we call them back and set anything up."

"Thanks." Kera strolled toward the two computers. "Can I have a look at them? We want to prioritize, um, whichever one will be quickest so we can get to the others, or possibly if there's one that stands out as having a lot of potential, we should focus on that."

Chris remarked, "I vote for quickest, but Kera has the final say. Especially if one would shower us with vaster sums of money than the others."

Lia cleared her throat. "Actually, there *is* one that we thought you would find interesting since it involves a rare piece with an unusual history, which is being auctioned off for a substantial sum."

Everyone waited as Kera ran her index finger over her lips and chin, thinking it over. "Hmm. That does sound intriguing. Tell me the details."

CHAPTER THREE

John C. Brimes had nothing better to do that morning, so he hacked into a database in the National Security Agency that housed data they'd aggregated over the last fifteen to twenty years. It was one of the few he hadn't tried before.

He doubted it would be difficult to get in, and indeed it wasn't. They did not even know he had poked around in the others, after all, so they had not updated their security protocols or otherwise done anything that would confound his usual methods.

A mug of coffee sat on the desk in front of him. He'd drunk about half of it so far—the equivalent of a quarter cup of regular coffee since he had switched to half-caff about two months ago. Too much caffeine overstimulated his brain and made him jumpy, erratic, and irritable. That kind of mood caused him to do stupid things.

He had gotten this far in life primarily by doing *smart* things and minimizing the effects of his dumber moments. He chuckled, recalling incidents from the past in which, while being an utter moron, he had stumbled onto a new insight that had led him to his next breakthrough in the theory and practice of computer software.

John took a sip of his weak coffee and stared at the screen before he resumed his work. Midway into the next step of the process, his phone rang.

He typically kept it on the desk, arranged so that if someone called, he could easily set it to speakerphone and thereby keep both hands free for his computer. Which was what he did now.

"Yello?" he said. He had a thin, nasally voice that, combined with his nerdy appearance, tended to disarm people, though it didn't win their instant respect. He had to work for that.

A woman's voice replied, "Mr. Brimes, good afternoon. It's Leila. If you're available for a minute or two, I have an update on the auction situation."

John stopped typing and minimized the screen showing his endeavors. No one else was in the house at present, but it was an old habit that died hard. "Oh, really? Yes, tell me about it."

Leila went on to inform him that of the four auctions he had told her to watch, one would be going live tomorrow at 5 p.m. Pacific Time. The one for a book called *The Grimoire of Victor Pisellius*.

John laughed, though it was good-natured. Mockery was not his intent. *"Viator Psellus,"* he corrected. "I looked it up. Very old Greco-Roman name, I believe. But yes, that was perhaps the most interesting of them all. Ping me about it tomorrow at, oh, say, 4:30 before you leave. If I'm not available, I would appreciate it if you would stay a little late and place a starting bid of," he paused, inhaling and contemplating the matter, "thirty thousand dollars and six cents. The six cents is to offset any of the smartasses who think they can defeat me by offering one cent, or five cents, over my bid. After that, I'll handle things myself."

"Yes, sir," Leila agreed. "You'll hear from me at 4:30 tomorrow. Let me know if you need anything else."

Smiling, John turned back to his hacking. "Thanks. I'm good."

Leila hung up, leaving him to the hobby that had made him a wealthy, important, and well-respected individual.

The current treasure trove, he saw, was not very interesting. Typically, they weren't. Lots of banal web searches for banal mail-order products or banal types of pornography. Emails between parents and children arguing about the meals at family holidays. Phone calls between employers and employees full of dull tension and dislike, or people trying to set up arrangements to buy drugs without being blatant about it.

None of it interested him, and he doubted the majority of it interested the NSA either. No, the fun part was cracking their security. The journey was more important than the destination.

John sighed and stretched. His study on the third floor of the mansion contained a vast window that encompassed the whole south-facing wall, which looked out upon the rolling tree-covered hills and showed the rooftops of other houses and buildings. They rambled downward until, in the distance, the community stopped at the edge of the ocean. Sea and sky were both an endless field of deep blue.

He scratched himself, wondering if it was worthwhile to change out of his bathrobe and into proper clothes, but there wasn't much point. He didn't feel like going out today. Why bother?

He ran his business from his home most of the time, and the feds didn't request his presence as often as they used to. Then again, the NSA would probably need to speak to him after he presented them with his findings on the laughable weaknesses in their security.

John refilled his mug, calculating that the second cup of coffee would still only equate to *maybe* one full serving of regular-strength stuff. He would be more animated than usual, but everything should be fine.

The NSA would be angry and suspicious, of course. Someone's head would roll once they knew someone had pored over their semi-legally harvested data.

John would disguise the specifics. He would say he had noticed a chink in the armor and run an analysis comparing it to similar systems that had suffered breaches in the recent past. He would present them with the *possibility* that they *could* be hacked. It would soften the blow while still getting their attention.

They would hire him to repeat what he'd just done, pay him, and continue trusting him. He had never abused his security clearance, after all.

He frowned. By nature, he was not a malicious person, and though he did not feel any particular guilt about accumulating wealth, he had tried to avoid doing anything egregiously cruel or unethical in the course of his rise to the top. There were undoubtedly other individuals who were not as scrupulous, and some of them might possess hacking skills comparable to his.

He wondered, *What if some of those nasty people inhabited the government? The NSA could do a lot of damage and impinge upon a lot of Constitutional protections with all that information. Worse yet, hostile foreign governments might use it to blackmail citizens into their service.*

He shook his head. It was useless to dwell on such things. Important though he was, the decisions involved in data harvesting were over his head.

Furthermore, the wheels of bureaucracy were slow to grind, so he would have some time to devote to other pursuits such as making sure he won his auction on that book.

It was strange; he had woken up one morning at his usual rising time of 11:30 a.m. with an irresistible compulsion to investigate matters pertaining to the paranormal, the occult, the alchemical, and the thaumaturgic. He recalled having a vague interest in such things when he was younger, but he had shoved them aside in favor of focusing on the more tangible and useful fields of computer science and cybersecurity.

But he was now in early middle age, and it was time for him to start developing a hobby on the side. Magic seemed like it would be fun.

Mother LeBlanc stared into the depths of the Chalice. Around her, the dining room of the old Louisiana manor was quiet and empty.

The cup was not large, and she could scarcely have fit one of her slim dark hands, balled into a fist, inside it, yet it had depth. Looking into it, one first had the impression of seeing an optical illusion whereby some material used in the Chalice's construction was refracting the light. After a moment of study and concentration in which the cup seemed to draw the viewer in, the illusion became more like a hallucination.

Within it, LeBlanc saw centuries of history and untold depths of power that could be drawn upon by those with righteous cause to do so. Those who had no other option and were unwilling to sacrifice the lives of others to save themselves.

When Old Jack had bequeathed it to humanity, he'd had in mind exactly the sort of scenario that LeBlanc and the rest of the North American Council of Thaumaturgy now faced. LeBlanc was beginning to unlock its secrets. Soon, its properties would serve her and her friends in their deadly conflict with the coven that sought to wipe them out and rule North America through force and fear.

Hugh Buchanan, who was the oldest member of the council after LeBlanc, wandered into the dining room. "Hello there, Mother. Are you making progress with that thing? It belongs to a magical tradition that I'm afraid I do not know much about, but perhaps I might be of some help, regardless."

She looked away from the cup's interior for the first time in at least an hour to give him a warm yet subdued smile. "Thank you,

Hugh, but I believe I have figured it out myself. The Chalice gathers and stores excess magical energy, you see, allowing it to be saved for later and distributed to its caretakers in times of need to augment their strength."

"Ah." He nodded, pulled out a chair, and gradually settled into it. He looked nearly as old as he truly was, unlike LeBlanc, who could easily pass for twenty-five, and though tough enough when he had to be, his body did not serve him as well as it used to. "That is fascinating and sounds eminently useful, if I may say so."

LeBlanc returned her gaze to the artifact. "You may. And yes, the, ah, *entity* who created it did so in response to humanity's need for such power under desperate circumstances, but in accordance with certain ethical standards."

Hugh flexed his hands as he got comfortable. "No sacrifice of living things required, you mean?"

"Exactly," LeBlanc confirmed. "Normally, augmenting one's strength in that fashion requires the blood sacrifice of a human being, ideally one who possesses the gift, and the stronger their magic is, the better. The cruelty involved in such practices raises grave concerns and was repulsive to Old Jack, so he created the Chalice and gave it to a trusted magician who dwelled in this swamp long, long ago. It has been kept here ever since and used occasionally, but not often. Since I was able to remove it from its hiding place and bring it to this house, we have the entity's blessing to use it."

Hugh was deep in thought as he listened. He was both wise and intelligent, but like many smart people, he knew enough to keep his mouth shut when he encountered things he did not understand. "I see," was all he said. "Although I'm curious, I won't inquire as to the specifics. I trust your judgment, and if it works, it works."

He frowned. "And we could use a miracle these days. I'm amazed we've found as much peace here as we have. It won't last, of course. The Orthodoxy will hunt us down soon."

"I know," LeBlanc conceded. "We cannot run from them indefinitely. Another confrontation is brewing, and this time we must win. It won't be easy, but we have a chance—particularly with this in our possession." She flourished her hand toward the Chalice.

The old man examined the relic. "Is it truly so powerful that we might be able to end the war here and now?"

The bayou woman shrugged. "I don't know, to be honest, but I consider it, shall we say, *highly possible*. Anyway, half our number are out on errands or scouting missions, but I asked the others who are still here to join us momentarily. We will talk it over and go from there."

Hugh did not object. Within the next five minutes, the two of them were joined by James, Samantha, Mary, and Ezeudo. Everyone said their greetings and hurried through the rote pleasantries before settling in. They knew what was coming.

LeBlanc pursed her lips. "It would be better to wait for everyone to be present before we discuss our collective strategy, but our time is sufficiently limited that half of us speaking amongst ourselves will have to suffice. We can update the others when they return while we make the necessary preparations. Yes, that is how we will do it unless anyone objects."

Mary commented, "I too would rather have the whole council together, but you're right; we might not have time for another formal meeting later. Let's hash things out now and solicit feedback from the others later."

Samantha was next to speak. "As I understand it, the plan was to lie low here, recover our strength, and get hold of the artifact, then flee to the West Coast. Do we still intend to do that? It presents both advantages and disadvantages, and there are arguments both for and against it. Lots of bad things could happen if we cross another half a continent. Then again, the Orthodoxy might spread themselves thin in pursuing us, making it easier to defeat them piecemeal."

She, James, and Ezeudo stayed silent as they waited for the senior members to offer their two cents. Mary and Hugh hesitated, and LeBlanc seemed distracted by her ruminations.

James coughed. "LeBlanc, you're the one with inside knowledge about how the Holy Grail there works, and you know this house as well. With you more or less leading the defense, we would have the home-field advantage if we lure the Orthodoxy here and make them fight on our turf."

Mary folded her hands. "That is true, but it also means they would know to prepare for a siege. We might have the advantage in terms of choosing our battlefield, but they would possess the initiative. It has long been said that the best defense is a good offense. By leading them on another wild goose chase, we might be able to create a situation where the Orthodoxy blunders into an ambush by us they can't prepare for. Amanda would agree with me, no doubt."

No one challenged her last assertion. Amanda had become borderline vindictive since the death of Zacharia McConnell, her close friend, at the rival coven's hands. She had continuously been the one who advocated hardest for striking back, and the sooner, the better.

LeBlanc turned to their newest member—not a full initiate of the council, but a friend, with bonds forged in the fires of their strife and shared troubles.

"Ezeudo," she inquired, "what do you think? No false humility, please. You may be a novice in the magical arts compared to us, but your experience with human conflict means we value your opinion."

The tall Nigerian blinked; he had not expected anyone to call upon him for advice.

"Ah, well," he began, "my specialty was stopping or avoiding wars, not fighting them, but I naturally learned how other people fought in my work. I would say that it all depends on strength. You told me yesterday that you perceived the Orthodoxy was weaker now than when they first invaded. They lost someone, or something, that had been benefiting them. If the Chalice is as mighty as you say, we might be better off staying here to fight. But if they can replenish their strength, for example by calling up reserves from Europe or hiring mercenaries, we might do better to stay on the move and make them divide their forces, defeating one group at a time."

He sniffed, and for a couple of seconds, the humidity of the bayou reminded him of his homeland, which he had not seen in many years. "But do not take my advice as the only piece of information you consider."

"Of course," said LeBlanc. "And thank you. Well, allow me to propose a partial measure that will serve us well and also buy time for us to confer with the others later today. We should begin fortifying the house in a superficial way by moving things to secure positions and mapping out how we would defend it against an assault. Creating a safe room to which we might retreat if our outer and intermediate defenses are breached. This can be done while simultaneously making cursory preparations for leaving New Orleans behind, should we decide to do so."

Mary pointed out that burrowing into a hole would allow the Orthodoxy to pin them in, call in reinforcements, and defeat them by attrition.

LeBlanc's smile was disturbingly enigmatic. "I know, but the safe room would still have an emergency exit of sorts. Within the cellar, there is a vault, and within the vault, there is a secret passage through a grotto-tunnel that leads into the swamp. In fact, it leads to a part of the swamp where our enemies might have great difficulty pursuing us. Then again, anyone but me might find it equally unpleasant, so it would be best to save that for the last resort. Still, it means that we could escape and flee again if we must."

The discussion continued. Virtually everyone assumed in the

back of their mind that LeBlanc would have the final say, but they approached the problem of what to do next from all angles.

James was supporting himself on the table with his elbow. He looked healthier and stronger than ever in the physical sense, closer to being fully recovered from his battle injuries than he had been since his home had first been overrun by their enemies.

But something else was wrong with him. He seemed lackluster and depressed. Everyone knew their crushing defeat, combined with his near-death and the long, arduous cross-country journey, had taken a massive toll on him.

That wasn't it, though. There was more; LeBlanc was sure of it.

"James," she began and looked him directly in the eyes. "What is wrong? Please talk to us. I'm frankly amazed it took you as long to recover as it did. To put it in a blunt way, it is as though you had lost the will to live and only survived because we forced you to. Have you given up hope? All is not lost. We still have a chance."

His face turned sour at that, but everyone's gaze was upon him. Clearly, he had hoped to avoid a discussion of his mental or emotional state.

Samantha lay a hand atop his. They had been lovers if only briefly, and it had been a good ten years since then. She had done more than any of them to look after him and try to heal him during his lengthy convalescence. "It's okay, James. We only want to help."

He let out a sigh that was as heavy with sadness as his usual cynical exasperation. "All right, then. You're going to make me say it out loud, aren't you? I can't just wait around and assume you all get it. No, I have to be the asshole who ruins the mood by blurting out the shit you're not supposed to blurt out."

Brows furrowed in concern and confusion.

He breathed in, then stated, "I didn't expect to live. I did not feel like I *deserved* to survive, okay? All of this—*all of it*—is my fault because it all goes back to that fucking book, which was my brilliant idea. Damian and Zacharia would still be alive if I hadn't made the smooth-ass argument that we should advertise for apprentices by going public. I was *trying* to die in battle so you guys could think of me as a martyr instead of, like, the guy everyone blames for all of this happening."

He closed his eyes and rubbed his temples once the words were out. His face flushed pink but returned to its normal color after a few seconds.

When he opened his eyes, LeBlanc was staring at him sharply. "Oh, for goodness' sake, James," she snapped, and everyone started in shock at the harshness of her tone. "You are being *ridiculous*. Get up off your proverbial ass and stop moping. It's not as though *you* killed Damian and Zacharia, and the book was almost as much my doing as yours. Stop this nonsense immediately. You did not die; therefore, you still have work to do and things we need you for. Start acting like it."

James stared dumbly back, his mouth opening and closing without words managing to come out since he had no idea how to respond.

Mary looked amused. "Well, that is one way of putting it. There might have been gentler ways as well."

Hugh Buchanan shook his head; it was obvious that he intended to practice his usual philosophy of keeping quiet when in doubt.

Samantha's brow furrowed, and she moved closer to James, not bothering to speak but adding a gentle grip on his shoulder to the one she had on his hand.

Ezeudo broke the awkward silence, and though his dark face was solemn and even stern, his words were surprisingly kind.

"James," he began, "I think Mother LeBlanc meant to shock you out of your gloomy state, but you must understand that all of us care for you and want you back. We are glad you didn't die. You took a wound that could have been fatal to save my life. This was while those people, the Orthodoxy, were ruthlessly sacrificing their own servants to destroy us. You showed me what is important and why we have to maintain our rule in this country with fair laws that respect human life and dignity."

Hugh nodded. James grimaced but listened earnestly.

"This fight," the Nigerian went on, "is not only about you, or me, or the council. It is about all the people of this continent. We have not only heard but seen how the Orthodoxy behaves when they are in power. They harvest people's lives to fuel their power. They will not allow any opposition or disloyalty and will crush and destroy those who displease them. Rather than practicing magic according to ethical standards, they use even the most evil of spells if it serves their agenda. Other people are depending on all of us to prevent this. That includes you. It even includes me. Not one of us is…what is the word that means 'unnecessary?'"

LeBlanc told him, "Well, 'unnecessary' is perfect for your purposes, but perhaps you meant 'superfluous?'"

"Yes," he affirmed. "None of us is superfluous. We all matter to the outcome."

James felt like a fool, and there was no way for him to escape the necessity of admitting he was wrong. But acknowledging his past wrongdoings was why he'd held such a dismal attitude to begin with.

He sat up straighter. "Okay, fine, I get it," he responded. "By half-assedly hoping to die, I have arguably made things even worse. But what if I finish healing and we win, and then I screw everything up *again*? I haven't steered us to where we need to be for the present. I don't trust myself in the future. Why should any of *you* trust me, then? If I can't do things right, you might be better off without me."

To the surprise of everyone else, the first to respond was Mary Mitchell.

"You are one of us, James," she pointed out. "We all agreed to make you a full thaumaturge of the council despite your status as a greenhorn." He was their youngest member, and one of the youngest ever admitted to their table. "As much as I might have wished to blame you for everything when this first happened since that would have kept things simple, it is, in truth, far more complicated than that. You merely nudged things in a direction whereby problems that had existed for a long time were brought to the forefront. Sooner or later, with or without errors committed by you or anyone else, we would have had to deal with something like this."

Hugh gave a low grunt. "Hrrm, yes. I would say that's accurate."

Mary spread her hands. "We all rule together," she concluded. "That is the source of our strength, and it is part of why the lesser covens respect us. You might not have been aware when your condition was worse, but some of them have finally begun to aid us or pledge to help us as things worsen. They are afraid of the Orthodoxy, but it has dawned on them that they risk no more by opposing them than they do by submitting to their tyranny. If we are to lead the forces of magic on this continent, we have to fix our problems the way we always have. To do that, we need you and everyone else."

James adjusted his glasses. "Well, you've successfully humbled me with flattery. And if LeBlanc has faith in her sacred cup, then I have faith in her. Let's do this."

CHAPTER FOUR

Anezka had a spare moment in which to relax. The rigors of leadership, particularly during something as strenuous as all-out combat between major covens, left her with little time to herself. For the most part, she did not mind. She thrived in conditions of conflict that proved too taxing for most people.

But things had grown far more taxing recently. She stared at her black fingernails, smoothing them around the edges with a mundane steel file and allowing the dust to pile upon the ebony wood of the table. She would have to refinish the lacquer to account for the damage done by the act of filing, but she was so skilled at maintaining her nails that other people would have to examine them closely to notice.

If all else failed, there were always glamours or spells to deflect attention. Magic could, as per all of her long lifetime's experience, achieve *anything.*

Milena was dead and gone, along with all the magic she had woven to support their war effort.

As though a bolt of lightning had struck her mind, Anezka let out a barking roar and stabbed the nail file into the table, splitting the finely aged and finished wood. The blade went halfway in and stuck it there. She stared at it, shuddering with rage.

Someone knocked on the door. "Grandmistress?" a voice asked in Russian. "Is everything all right?" It was a young man; if Anezka recalled correctly, his name was Alexei. He had risen to the middling ranks of the coven in a mere six years and was considered promising.

He also was mistrusted by his fellow witches and warlocks, however, due to his propensity for reporting to his superiors on any and all wrongdoings of which they might have been guilty.

Anezka cleared her throat, and though he could not see her, made a beckoning motion with her hand. "Yes. Come in."

The door opened and in stepped the young lieutenant, wearing a nondescript semi-formal outfit the color of ash. He was burly and had reddish-blond hair. His face was blank, and he stood ramrod-straight.

Anezka smiled. "Come here, Alexei. We have another ten minutes before the rest of the elders return, and I wish to discuss something."

She could feel his uncertainty. It was unusual for the grandmistress to engage her underlings in casual, familiar conversation, and even more so if they were males, as she tended to trust her subordinate witches more than warlocks. The one exception was Vassily, her right-hand man among the senior members of the coven.

He presented himself beside the table, a bit more than arm's reach from her. His eyes flicked toward the nail file embedded in the table, then returned to looking at nothing. "Yes?"

Anezka inhaled lazily and curled and uncurled her fingers, curious if he would notice the slight damage to her nails. Men were astonishingly obtuse about such things. "Tell me," she began, "how is morale among the lower-ranking members lately?"

Alexei's face darkened, and the muscles along his jaw grew tighter.

"Do not lie," Anezka informed him in a soft voice. "I must know the truth if I am to lead us. You do nothing wrong by answering my question honestly and accurately."

He sniffed. "Lying did not cross my mind, Grandmistress. I hesitated only because the news is...mixed. From the one side, everyone looks forward to destroying the council. Some are growing weary—I told them to marshal their strength until the end and not to waver, of course—but everyone, as far as I can tell, is eager to fight again."

Anezka responded with a slow nod. "And the other side of the story?"

"Everyone," Alexei admitted, and now it seemed to pain him to speak, "is concerned about the extent of the losses we suffered after Milena's death. Hana and Daniela have been rightfully scorned and mocked for running away, yet there is a mood of fear as to what could have made them do so. They were never considered cowards. And many spells do not work as well. There is talk that Milena was like a generator and that without her, we have lost power."

The grandmistress drummed her nails on the surface of the table. Her nostrils expanded and contracted. "Yes, I see. Our people are observant. It is good to know that I am not leading an army of fools who cannot deduce the obvious. But we must not have contagious fear spreading amongst them. Our coven has suffered a setback, yes, but not a *defeat*. We must simply use more drastic methods. Victory is well within our grasp. I and the other elders have a plan which is unlikely to fail."

Alexei puffed out his chest. "That is good to hear, madam."

She smiled. "Thank you. You may return to your duties."

He gave her a curt bow and marched out of the conference room. Anezka knew that when his guard shift was over, he would spread what she had said and also identify anyone who was consumed by doubts and defeatism. Such people would have to be dealt with.

Not by killing them, of course. Anezka would *like* to simply eliminate anyone who undermined their objective, but she could not afford to reduce the number of her forces. Hence, Hana and Daniela were still allowed to serve, albeit in demoted positions and under the burden of shame.

Once the war was over—if they survived the coming battle—Anezka would have both of them executed. But not yet. Not while they could still help destroy the council.

They had failed at their task, which was the aid and protection of Milena—miserably so. Much had depended upon Milena's success; Anezka had not realized the full magnitude of the loss the Orthodoxy had suffered when Kera had killed her.

As their specialist in blood sacrifice and the incredibly powerful charms of augmentation that could be derived from it, Milena had been responsible for keeping the coven's troops operating at peak efficiency. And not only in terms of raw strength on the battlefield. She had, of her own volition, directed some of the power she'd harvested toward bolstering the Orthodoxy's communications networks, their run-of-the-mill scrying endeavors, their healing spells, and their cloaking enchantments.

The "generator" analogy Alexei had mentioned was apt. Without Milena, the Orthodoxy was possibly twenty-five percent weaker than it had been mere days ago. Maybe more. The loss of a full squad of low-level troops would have been less of a problem than the collapse of Milena's network of magic.

Anezka pulled the file out of the wood. She did nothing to repair the ragged hole it left, just slipped the little blade back into her black dress.

"But," she told herself, speaking in a barely audible whisper, "all is not lost. There is still the matter of the local hedge witches. They will serve their purpose. And we have eliminated nearly all doubt about our foes' approximate location."

New Orleans. Of course, New Orleans—the home of Mother LeBlanc, the council's oldest and most powerful member. Anezka still didn't know *exactly* where they were, but her soldiers were closing in around the Mississippi Delta and checking the bayous. The council would not be able to escape to another region without the Orthodoxy discovering it instantly.

Shortly thereafter, the door opened again, and in streamed three of the other senior witches. The full membership of the coven's high table was not present since more than half of them were out leading the war effort, but enough of them were around for Anezka to manage a serviceable conference and continue their important work at their current base of operations.

Anezka greeted each in turn. "Vassily. Izabella. Evgenia. Welcome back. Tell me how things are proceeding."

They took their seats and gave their reports. Nothing they had to say about troop movements or resource management was surprising or particularly significant.

Anezka reflected on their overall situation, placing the new facts into the ever-evolving mental framework she used to assess the entire operation.

They had spent two days in Knoxville, Tennessee, a location chosen for its relatively equal distance from all the points to which they expected to send troops if necessary. Despite the terrible setback of Milena's demise, they had narrowed their search. The grandmistress had moved her army southeast, closer to what they were all but certain was their final destination.

The Orthodoxy now ran its campaign out of a hotel in Jackson, Mississippi. New Orleans lay a mere three hours to the south.

It was tempting—so terribly, incredibly tempting—to move upon the bayou city at once. To surround it and have their witches swarm through the streets, sweeping every district and neighborhood. To fly over the nearby countryside and loudly announce to the council that doom had come for them and they should surrender now, or at least come out and fight.

But Anezka was smarter than that. She had to allow for the possibility that not all of them were gathered in one place or that there might be some other minor mistake in their intel. They needed to finish their plan and gather their strength before at last the axes fell upon the council's thin and quivering necks.

Evgenia was still finishing her report. "...is a slim chance that the majority of the council has remained in New Orleans, but that one, two, or three of their number has slipped away to the West Coast or some other place, perhaps to request help from unknown allies. But we doubt they would want to divide their forces when their numbers are so inferior to ours."

Vassily pointed out, "It would be unwise to commit our entire organization to an assault on New Orleans if LeBlanc has reinforcements set to arrive from Los Angeles or Vancouver or who knows where else. We need better actionable intelligence."

"I agree," said Anezka. "We shall spend the next day gathering further information on the one hand and continuing to bolster our forces with conscripts on the other."

Izabella queried, "I have not received a full briefing on who these conscripts are. Locals?"

Anezka flexed her hands and brushed a lock of black hair behind her ear. Since Milena's death, she had been pondering what her greatest strengths were. She knew her abilities. She was considered one of the most powerful witches in the world, both in overall magical ability and because of the authority she wielded. She lacked the hyper-specialized talent some other casters displayed, sadly. Pavla was a greater tracker, and Milena had been more skilled in the arts of sacrifice and augmentation. But when it came to commanding others, Anezka had no equal. That was why she ruled them from the very pinnacle of their ancient hierarchy.

With this in mind, she spoke.

"Correct. There has been word that some of the council's former vassals decided to enter the fray, after all. Why, I ask, should only a portion of them participate? They all should fight in this war on one side or another. Allow me to demonstrate."

She clapped her hands, at the same time sending a psychic signal to her two jailers. A moment later, four pairs of footsteps came down the hallway. Alexei met the pair of witches who escorted the prisoners and led them all into the conference chamber.

The other elders nodded their heads in approval. Anezka looked at the captives with eyes that seemed lazy and uninterested but were alert to every detail. They looked like perfectly normal Americans, and with a couple of minor changes, might have passed for perfectly normal Ukrainians or Russians. Their clothes, now tattered, consisted of t-shirts and jeans—the standard dress of the lower classes.

They were, if the grandmistress remembered right, a couple but not married. Both were in their thirties. Her rear-echelon troops had scooped them up in West Virginia a day before she had moved everyone toward New Orleans.

"Good day," she said in English. "Tell me your names, please. Someone told them to me before, but I have forgotten since I have more important things to focus on."

The statement was meant to disarm and humiliate them. Not that it was difficult, since their magic, paltry as it was, was being blocked. As was the usual procedure with such people, they had been forced to drink a tonic of colloidal silver and nutritional iron dissolved in water, which disrupted any attempt at spellcasting, and further, they had been hexed.

There was also the damage to their bodies. All of the fingers on the man's left hand were broken and twisted, though his thumb had been spared. Lacerations ran across his face and chest. The woman was in a similar state, minus the hand trauma.

Half her hair had been burned off, and parts of her scalp showed damage as well.

The woman swallowed. "Mindy."

The man sniffled. "Dan."

"Yes. Of course." Anezka nodded. "I am told you helped the council escape from us. You interfered with our tracking efforts and aided them in getting a vehicle to take them away. Why did you do that? All the lesser covens of North America assured us they would remain neutral and take no part in the fighting. You broke your promise to us. That was especially foolish of you after we won the battle in New York. Why on earth would you wish to join with the side that is *losing?*"

She spoke as if asking a pair of children why they had broken an antique toy after an adult had forbidden them to play with it. Their motives made about as much sense to her as those of children.

Mindy coughed, then said, "We never made any such agreement. The head of our coven spoke for us without asking our opinions, and we had no choice but to pretend to agree. When your coven came to America, you said nothing about killing everyone who stood in your way. Do you expect us to just roll over and submit to people like you?"

Dan's face was drawn with concern; he probably feared his girlfriend would die for what she had just said. When Anezka did nothing, he stated, "Yes. We saw how ugly the future would be under your leadership. We did what we thought was right."

Vassily, off to the side, let out a dry, rustling chuckle. "What was *right*. Clearly, it was not right for *you*."

"Indeed," Anezka agreed. "You condemned yourselves to punishment without succeeding at what you set out to do—a most foolish waste of your time and your lives. We are not done with you yet, though. You shall be permitted to continue living a little longer. We have need of you."

Mindy's eyes flashed with hatred. "We refuse. Just kill us if that's what you want."

Anezka ran the fingertips of her left hand over the edges of her nails on her right hand. "It is not as simple as that, I'm afraid. You see, some other of the hedge covens have declared loyalty to the council recently, betraying their word to us, just as you did. But we do not have the time to punish all of them; we first must destroy the council. You will help us do that."

Dan snorted. "If you use compulsion magic, everyone will know. There is no caster who can make compelled actions look natural to anyone with the gift. You might succeed at using us as cannon fodder, but you will fail if you try to use us as propaganda to show how much 'support' you have from the locals, if that's your plan."

The grandmistress had been patient and professional with these people, but their combination of arrogance and naïveté was stunning. She stood up with startling abruptness, and the room grew colder.

"Do you think we *care?*" she barked, and her voice echoed. Despite their attempts at defiance, the captives flinched. "We do not abide by the rules you people cherish. We do not seek or even *expect* the love or admiration of your fellow lowly trick-performers. We will have your obedience, *and that is all.* We require no more. We *do not care* if you hate us as long as you fear us enough to acknowledge that we rule this country now. You, idiots, think everything is a...popularity contest. You are utterly lost when all things are reduced to their primal essence. All that matters is power and the respect it deserves."

She raised her hand, black-nailed fingers splayed, then twisted it in an odd circular motion.

Mindy and Dan hopped and contorted in place as though they were marionettes on strings being manipulated by a clumsy puppeteer. Then they turned away from the table, marching with awkward, unnatural steps toward the wall. Both of them crashed into it but continued grinding against its surface and flailing their limbs as though trying to walk through solid matter, confused as to why they could not.

Alexei snickered. He was normally composed, so the spectacle must have been unusually hilarious to him.

Anezka did not find it funny, but she appreciated how well it made her point. Mindy, Dan, and everyone else under her rulership would do as she bade them.

"You see?" she crowed. "If I command you to keep walking until the wall collapses a month from now, you shall do it. Do you think I care how you *feel* about it? Now, stop. Turn around. Stand still, and listen."

They obeyed; it was impossible for them to do otherwise.

"You two," the grandmistress continued, "shall be examples. Your wounds will be cursed to prevent them from healing so everyone can see the tortures you suffered for defying us. The *fear* your fellow lesser-coven types will experience is all we require. They will be afraid of suffering in the same way. They will be afraid of being compelled to fight against their former masters until they die, which is exactly how we will use you.

"And finally, we shall receive the one element of their individual free wills we *do* desire, which is their intentional obedience. It is easier to have them do as we command without needing to compel them by magic. But if we must compel every last one of them to march into the sea and drown to rule this continent, *we* will not care what you think of us. Is that clear?"

She did not compel their voices or use any form of magic to influence their answers.

Dan stared at the floor. "Yes."

Mindy was trying desperately not to weep, and her eyes were red. "Yes."

CHAPTER FIVE

Kera put her hands on her hips. "You know, this is nice in a way. It's like old times again. And by 'old,' I mean, uh, a few months ago. I can't believe how long it *hasn't* been since all this started."

Stephanie laughed. It was unnecessary to clarify what she meant by "all this." They had both been immersed in it; it was the basic stuff of their lives now. It formed the new world in which they lived.

They had met at Kera's place, the warehouse in downtown LA she had converted into an apartment she had lived in since leaving college. Just the two of them. Going back over the basics of magic, training and drilling and helping one another for the sake of learning more.

They had even broken out the book that started it all—Kera's copy of *How to Be a Badass Witch*, purchased via the mundane channel of Amazon before its mysterious authors had unpublished it. Having the damn thing open on the couch where both could see it or run over to thumb through its pages was bizarrely nostalgic.

"Shit," Steph remarked. "If we wanted it to be exactly like not-so-old times again, though, we'd have to go back to our metabolism being out of control and ordering enough food for six or seven people between us. Can you unlearn that? Like, is there a way to go back to sucking at managing our energy expenditure so we need to eat that much now?"

Kera bit her tongue to keep from cracking up at the thought. "No. Well, um, I have no idea. Maybe there is, but why would you *want* that? You were the one who was always complaining about how expensive it was to consume five and a half meals per day. Plus, it's undignified. Not ladylike, har har."

"Hah! Ladylike. Neither of us worried much about that. But yeah, the grocery budget being manageable again is the good part. Still, everybody loves food, and it's nice to be able to put away a ridiculous amount of it and still *lose* weight."

Her friend shrugged. "I guess. But I'm happy with the way things are. Mentioning that, though, puts in perspective the time-honored maxim that 'nostalgia ain't what it used to be' or however it goes."

"I never heard that one," Steph observed. "I'll have to keep that in mind. I bet my parents would think it's funny as hell."

Kera groaned. "I believe it qualifies as a 'dad joke,' so my father almost certainly would as well. My mom, on the other hand, might not get it and would use it as a springboard to start talking about something she did at my age that I'm not... Ugh, what am I saying? Forget about that. Let's focus on magic, shall we?"

"Sure." Steph took a deep breath, and they began.

At no point had they agreed on a specific reason they wanted to review their magic skills and perhaps progress in their respective careers as thaumaturges. The idea had arisen in both their minds at more or less the same time. They wanted to, so they did.

But as they began their training session, Kera wondered if it was something subconscious. It was making her worry.

"Okay," Kera said and tossed a potato into the air. "Catch."

Her friend caught it, though not with her hands. Staring directly at the vegetable while speaking a brief incantation and raising her fingers, she suspended it in midair, holding it magically so it floated about four and a half feet off the ground.

Steph grinned. "Done. Okay, now cook the damn thing."

Kera interlocked her fingers, turned her palms away from her face, and flexed. Then, shaking her arms as if she were about to go for a jog and was trying to get her circulation up, she focused on the potato and cast the necessary spell to bake it. Instantly.

The air around the vegetable shimmered. A reddish glow appeared as heat spontaneously gathered in a spot approximately a foot square, encasing the potato in the equivalent of a small disembodied oven.

Kera struggled, and her face contorted in annoyance. She had come a long way and was a far better spellcaster than she had been mere months ago, but it had been a while since the last time she had imposed such tight control on an evocation of heat. Usually, when she needed to burn something, it was in the thick of combat, when excess was better than restraint.

Dammit. The warmth ebbed and then increased erratically. *I've been neglecting the ways in which magic is good for basic, banal household tasks. I'm overly accustomed to using it to blow things up or fend off small armies of witches, gangsters, and God knows who else.*

Stephanie could not help laughing when the potato blackened in some places but was more or less raw in others. "Hoo boy, this isn't working out so well. We gonna feed this one to the homeless afterward? I'm not sure they would want it after you're done with it."

"Yeah, yeah, shut up." Kera grunted and tried to distribute the flow of heat more evenly. After another minute of concentrated channeling, she succeeded—sort of.

The potato was now "well done," though parts were burned. At least she hadn't left any of it raw or turned the entire thing into a lump of charcoal. "See?" she asserted. "Not a complete fiasco. I'll eat the parts of it that are, um, edible just to prove it."

Steph released the vegetable from suspension as Kera plucked it out of the air, tossing it between one hand and the other since it was blazing hot. "Should have had you float it over to the freezer," she muttered.

The non-crispy parts were decent enough, she decided as she forked them into her mouth. While she ate, Stephanie practiced a series of water spells. She had an affinity for that element to the point that she was an expert at water evocation and manipulation even if she was—in Kera's opinion—an amateur at lots of other things.

"Hey," Steph exclaimed as she gathered moisture out of the air and formed it into a perfect sphere, "looks like I still know what I'm doing." She spun it on her fingertip like a basketball, then tossed it into the sink, where it collapsed into a foamy mass atop a pile of dirty dishes.

Kera smiled and nodded. "Yeah, that was the only thing you were really good at. Hmm, next up, we should—"

"Hold on," her friend interrupted, and there was an edge to her voice Kera didn't much like. "What do you mean, the only thing I was good at?"

Oh, fuck, Kera thought. *That was a poor choice of words. Though in all honesty, Steph has never been on the same level as me, and there's not much point in pretending otherwise, is there?*

She began, "That's not what I said, exactly. I said it was the only thing you're *really* good at. The qualifier is important. You're pretty good at lots of other things as well, just less so." She cleared her throat. "Or, um, to put it another way, that's what you're best at. That's all I meant."

Stephanie stared at her for five or ten seconds, hands on her hips, then countered with, "Oh, all right. You've been doing this for longer than I have, and maybe the magic is stronger in you; I don't claim to know. But if we're gonna train together and work together and maybe fight together, we should be acting like equals."

"Yeah, I agree," said Kera. "I mean, technically, you're my

employee now, but, um, let's forget about that. This was supposed to be us messing around like friends again, not anything to do with business."

Steph turned away from her and picked up the book, browsing through a couple pages. "That's right. It was supposed to be."

It occurred to Kera why they were doing this, and why she was tenser than she was letting on, and why she had inadvertently criticized her friend.

They needed to get back in fighting shape, magically speaking, and soon. What had happened on the train was not the last they would see of the Orthodoxy, and they both knew it. What looked like a couple of girls amusing themselves with an old hobby was, in fact, a prep session for a battle they might not be able to win.

She was coming down hard on Stephanie because deep down, Kera wasn't sure her friend had the power or skill to prevail against someone like Milena. Or worse, a small army of Milenas, or whoever Milena's boss was.

Kera had barely managed to defeat the sorceress and her henchwomen, and she had an unfair advantage. Milena had been too busy preparing her sacrificial spell to focus on combat.

Kera reminded herself, *Stephanie and I managed to beat Pavla, and we were not as good then as we are now. Wait, no, we didn't. Shit, shit, shit! We held out, but Pavla did win in the end. The only reason we're still alive is that she had a change of heart at the last second.*

I wish I hadn't remembered that.

Stephanie set down the book. "Okay, sleep spell. Wanna be my guinea pig?"

Kera squinted. "Sure, but I'm not going to make it easy. That would be pointless. I won't go all-out, but I'm going to try to resist it since you have to be able to cast a spell like that under duress. If you can't knock someone unconscious while they're coming at you, determined to cave your head in, it isn't much good."

Before responding, Stephanie looked off to the side as though distracted. Kera realized she was pissed off and was trying to clamp down on blurting a comment that might start a fight.

"Kera," she began, speaking slowly, "I've been in the same dangerous situations you have, and I've come out more or less unscathed, okay? I may not have as much pure power as you do or as much training yet, but I can handle myself. There's no reason to act like I'm a little kid who has no idea what they're doing."

It had not occurred to Kera that she was acting that way. "I'm not, and I know that. I'm only making sure you're aware of the realities of the situation. It's how the pros talk to people when they want to make sure they're getting the point."

Steph sighed. "Okay, I guess you qualify as a pro by this point, but if that's the case, I'm not far from being one either, right?"

"Right," Kera agreed and tried to smile. "So, go for it. Try to knock me out. I won't resist using full power. More like, uh, medium power. It won't be easy, but I think you can do it. Just do me a favor and wake me up right away if it works, all right? I don't feel like sleeping through the whole afternoon."

To her relief, her friend's usual good cheer came back. "Ha, deal."

Stephanie raised her hands, shut her eyes, and began the incantation after she opened them again, fingers contorting in the required arcane gestures. Kera could feel the other witch's power marshaling itself, then being released against her.

At first, it was like one of those random attacks of drowsiness she occasionally experienced in the late afternoon, usually when she hadn't eaten recently or had not slept well. She perceived it as a wave washing over her—not an irresistible tidal wave, but strong enough to disrupt her peace of mind. Stephanie was probably channeling as much power into the spell as she could.

Kera marshaled her reserves of mental, physical, and magical fortitude. She did not push back with *all* her might, but her effort was more than cursory; it was analogous to how she would have resisted a spell by a lower-level Orthodoxy witch.

And the sleepy sensation weakened, wavered, and faded.

Stephanie, her hands trembling as she strained against Kera's defenses, exhaled sharply and then slumped in place. "Damn. I tried, but I just can't do spells like you can. I don't think I was born with as much of the gift. Maybe you're a prodigy, and that's the problem."

Kera shrugged. "Pavla said I probably was, but you did pretty well. Against someone with no magic, or very little, I think it would have worked."

"You *think?*" Her friend's tone sharpened, and Kera reminded herself that she would have to tread carefully.

She held up a palm. "Hey, I'm not trying to disparage you. I just don't know what it's like to be anyone but me, okay? And it's mostly a mental effect. I can't see into other people's heads well enough to determine if they would have resisted it the same way I did or slumped unconscious instantly. It depends on a lot of factors."

Steph frowned. "Fine, but just remember—"

A miracle happened; they were saved from continuing the argument when Kera's phone rang.

Scowling and turning away, she slipped the device out of her pocket and looked at the screen. It was Lia. Social calls were extremely rare for her, so it was almost certainly something to do with business.

"Hi, Lia," Kera greeted her, raising the phone to her ear. "What's up?"

Lia did not waste time on pleasantries. "Hello. I'm sure you're busy, so I'll cut right to the chase. The grimoire just sold. That spellbook we were looking at, the one by the Byzantine sorcerer our prospective client expressed an interest in. The auction site closed the bidding on it an hour and a half ago while I was taking my lunch break. I found out five or ten minutes ago."

Kera raised her eyebrows. Something deep in her stomach tingled. "Oh, really? That could be promising, or it could be bad, I guess. Who's the buyer?"

"I'm not sure yet," she confessed. "Of course, I'll be looking into it so we can arrange a meeting, formal or informal. By 'informal,' I mean you sneaking into their house to confront them with the aid of whatever magic you need to pull something like that off. Well, a normal, friendly chat would be the better option."

"Of course," Kera agreed. "But yeah, keep on it. There's no reason to assume we can't solve this guy's case by pretending to be scholars and examining the book under perfectly legitimate circumstances. Um, I think. Unless it turns out that the ghost story about it possessing people is true. Have you found out anything else about the grimoire's history? Anything to suggest it's the real deal?"

Lia drew a breath. "Yes, I've been studying its past. I am not an expert on that, but there are enough stories and reports of owners behaving strangely after purchasing it and things like that to suggest the rumors didn't come out of nowhere. I'm putting together a file I'll send you shortly. You would know better than I do how real the gossip is and how to parse the good from the bad. Interestingly, Viator Psellus and his collected works are mentioned in a couple of occult sources, one of which is pretty highly regarded. And there are a handful of historical records of a person by his name existing in the fourth-century Byzantine Empire. While it's beyond me to determine the legitimacy of his spellbook, he seems to have been a real person."

And that, Kera surmised, *is a good start. It counts for a lot. Real people have thaumaturgic power. Who's to say the casters of the past didn't get involved with traditional societies that practiced ceremonial magic?*

Lia wasn't finished, though. "I added commentary on how

much support there is for a given story or rumor. For example, some of them have evidence to back up their basic existence in the timelines as we know it. Like, we can verify the book was where it was supposed to be and in the possession of the recorded owner at that time. Others do not, and I made notes as to all of that."

Stephanie had been listening, and she nodded in approval.

Kera chuckled. "What would I do without you?"

"Well," Lia replied, "Chris' new database helped. Make sure to thank him, too."

They said their goodbyes and hung up. When Kera turned to Steph, her animosity seemed to be gone.

Why the hell is she so touchy today? Kera wondered. *I'll try to not be as dismissive of her abilities, I guess. Still, if there's a rift between us, we cannot have it getting in the way of the job.*

CHAPTER SIX

Stephanie glanced in the rearview mirror to examine her hair and makeup before she got out of the car, taking her purse with her. She locked the door, checked the parking lot for suspicious-looking characters, an old habit, and strode across the asphalt toward the restaurant.

It was half an hour past dark. The place where she had agreed to meet Regina and Ted was an Indian eatery they had both recommended, though she hadn't tried it. She was only occasionally in the mood for Indian food, but it hit the spot once in a while.

She was nervous, but it had nothing to do with cuisine. Rather, she had barely spoken to her sister for months, and she did not know Ted well. He was Chris' friend from work, but she had gotten the impression that he was obnoxious. Not to the point of being a genuine asshole, but he tested a lot of people's patience.

Makes sense, she mused, *that he'd end up with Regina. Her taste in men is weird as hell, but she's young yet. Maybe we'll all get lucky and she'll end up being one of those women who matures as she gets older.*

This would be easier if Kera hadn't been a bitch earlier.

As she approached the front doors, she chided herself for thinking about her best friend that way. Kera had made one or two stupid choices of wording, but she wasn't *trying* to be condescending.

It's in my head, she told herself. *I'm worried I don't have what it takes after all the doom-and-gloom stuff recently, not to mention that embarrassing-ass incident with the trap at the Orthodoxy's safehouse. Magenta spots all over my field of vision. Stupidest curse ever.*

After she sprang the trap, she'd been unable to remove the hex. It had taken Kera helping her with the counterspell for her sight and senses to return to normal.

Still, most people would have been killed by the other stuff the Orthodoxy witches had rigged the house with. At least she had shown enough skill to avoid the worst of it.

Shaking her head to clear it of such thoughts, which weren't important in a relaxed social occasion like this, she pushed her way into the restaurant.

It was as thick with customers as the parking lot was with cars. Only two tables were empty. She found Regina and Ted at a small table on the east side, around the corner from the main entrance. They noticed her at once and waved her over.

"Hi, girl," Regina opened.

Ted echoed her. "Hi, Girl. Is that your name? I thought your name was Stephanie."

Regina elbowed him. "Shut up, boy. That's a dad joke, and you ain't anywhere near that old."

Steph allowed herself a slight chuckle. "Ha, ha. Yeah, I'm Steph; we met once or twice before. Not for very long since you were just there to pick up Chris. Still, nice to meet you formally."

She pulled out a chair, sat down, and began looking at the menu. A waiter appeared just as she decided what she wanted to drink, a lime drop martini. The place's drink selection did not seem to have anything to do with its food menu.

"Okay," the man, who was not Indian, said. "We'll have that out for you in a minute."

Stephanie held onto her menu. "I'll probably order food after you're back with it if that's okay."

It was, and he hurried off.

Stephanie turned to the happy couple, who were teasing each other and laughing at one another's jokes nonstop. They were not paying much attention to her.

"So," Steph began, "you two have been together for what, three months now? That's not bad." She had to admit, she was envious. They seemed to be crazy about one another.

Ted squinted at her as he racked his brain. "Umm, something like that. I forget. I mean, who remembers the exact day they started dating someone?"

"Hey!" Regina protested. "I'm gonna remember that if I don't get anniversary flowers next month."

Ted held up his hands and wiggled his fingers. "Oooh, I'm really scared."

"You better be," she warned. "Anyway, Steph, how are things going with Kera and Chris and the agency? You said before you were finally quitting your job at the bar."

Steph nodded. "Yeah, long overdue, even though Cevin's a good guy to work for. But we got a ton of customer requests after some online forum started talking about the stuff we did a few weeks ago. We'll be solvent for months, so Kera will be able to pay me, no problem."

Ted coughed. "Well, wouldn't that have been the case regardless? Based on what Chris said, she's, like, *loaded.*"

"Yeah," Stephanie confirmed with a sour expression. "I don't know how much money she has, but it's a lot. She's...a good friend, though I liked it better when we were both the same rank at the Mermaid. Now she's *the boss,* you know?"

Regina nodded. "Well, don't take any shit from her. You two helped each other out a lot, right?"

The waiter returned with Steph's martini. She thanked him and ordered a platter of chana masala with puris.

"Good choice," Ted opined. "First time I tried that stuff, I was like, 'Wow, it's basically chili, only with more curry!'"

Steph laughed. "Yeah, true. And Regina, yes, I've saved Kera's ass a couple times, truth be told."

Her little sister's face took on an expression of serious concern. "You ain't been getting into anything dangerous, have you?"

Damn, Steph cursed herself, *said too much. Should have known I'd end up doing that if I didn't get my head on straight before I came here.*

"Not dangerous," she lied, feeling guilty, "but just, like, I stopped her from doing some shit that might have messed up her business ideas. When we first talked about forming the agency, the idea was we'd be equal partners, but she's acting like I'm, I don't know, her apprentice or assistant."

Ted, too, had stopped joking. "Chris told me she gets really fixated on whatever her main goal is. I don't think it's personal. It's probably just her obsessing over getting the job done. Still, Chris was losing a lot of sleep for a while there just from helping her. It was always push, push, push everything forward as fast and hard as possible, like tunnel-vision workaholic stuff. At the same time, she wasn't talking to him about everything. He made a deal that they have to share stuff with each other and be more open, and she agreed."

Steph paused to consider what he said.

"And," Regina added, snapping her fingers, "if you talked her out of bad decisions, that right there means you're just as good at this stuff as she is. Don't let her put you on the sidelines. Tell her what's up and show her you deserve to be treated as an equal so she's got no choice."

Stephanie did not talk much for the next ten minutes, mostly just sipped her drink since the couple had gone back to bantering and snarking and laughing at everything. She was deep in thought but also feeling a little better.

Okay, then, she told herself. *When we're next out in the field, Kera and me are going to take care of business together like we should.*

Kera gazed at Zee. "God, you're beautiful," she told him. "A little dusty and grimy, but true beauty cannot be tarnished by minor stuff like that. Here, let me wipe you off, okay? I want you to look nice before we go out in public."

As she fetched a semi-clean rag from the small pile she had accumulated in the corner of her garage area, it occurred to her how much she had missed him during her lengthy vacation.

He was a Kawasaki Z900, black with faint greenish piping, and she had purchased him after graduating from college. He had accompanied her on nearly every fucked-up adventure she'd had since then, as well as on banal errands.

Wiping him off only took a couple of minutes. Ideally, he could use a thorough cleaning inside and out, but for now, he'd suffice. She was only hopping over to the Kims' place for the evening.

Kera put on her leathers and her black helmet, wondering vaguely if people in Los Angeles were still talking about Motorcycle Man—or Motorcycle Woman—the mysterious vigilante who had captured the city's imagination before fading into the mists of time. These days, people's attention spans were short. The talk would fade with time.

It was cool being an anonymous local celebrity, she admitted as she wheeled the bike out of her warehouse, closed the door, and started the engine. But a big hassle. Better to be a legitimate businesswoman.

It was about an hour past dark. Traffic was still dense on the brightly lit streets, though the worst of rush hour was over. The short drive to the Kims' convenience store took mere minutes. She could have walked if she had wanted to.

When she pulled into the side lot adjacent to the property, the store was still open for business. Attached to and looming behind and over it on the second floor of the structure was the family's living quarters. In the rear, across from a small partially hidden courtyard, was the outbuilding where they had a humble private dojang. Kera had trained there many times.

She parked Zee in an empty space and placed a light enchantment over the bike to protect him from being closely examined or stolen. Then she walked through the front door of the shop.

There were a couple of customers browsing the aisles to the left. Straight ahead and to the right was the counter, behind which stood Mr. Kim.

He looked at the newcomer. "Kera, hello. I have not seen you for too long, but I know you've been busy. We will be closing soon if you'd like to stay." He was, she realized, trying to act professional and impartial, but she could tell he was happy to see her.

The feeling was mutual, and she grinned. "Not too busy to stop by. It just took a while. I need to buy some groceries anyway."

He waved her off, and she selected an armload of food before getting in line behind the two people who had been in before her. Once they were gone and she set her choices on the counter, Mr. Kim snuck over to the door.

"Hmm, no one else coming. I think we're closed now." He turned the *Yes, We're Open!* sign to *Sorry, We're Closed*. "Okay, now I will ring you up, and we can go in back. You can put this stuff in our fridge if you plan to stay long."

She paid for her purchases, and after bagging them, Mr. Kim picked them up and led the way into the hall behind the counter, flipping off the main front light on his way.

Kera followed him to a stairwell beyond the hallway, where a door on the first floor led out to the courtyard and the staircase led up to the family's humble yet cozy living quarters. As they ascended, Mr. Kim asked, "Did that book help? The one on sacrificial magic. My friend said he delivered it to you in person."

"Yes," Kera confirmed. "Pretty grim stuff, but it was useful for, um, research. That reminds me, I'm done with it now, so I need to send it back to him."

Mr. Kim nodded as they reached the landing. "Good, good. He is a collector and would appreciate that greatly. Of course, you have to tell us everything that has happened to you lately. You have no choice in the matter, ha."

Kera sighed in fake exasperation. "Aw. All right, if I *have* to."

From the kitchen, Mrs. Kim and the couple's son Sam emerged.

Sam waved. "Hi, Kera. Good to see you back." He seemed more relaxed and confident than he had in the past, Kera thought. He'd had a crush on her, but maybe he was making progress with girls his own age lately. He was halfway through high school, and from what she recalled, getting past secondary education was always good for one's romantic life.

She waved back. "Hi, Sam. Hope all is well. If you guys have time, we can talk about what's been happening."

She walked up to Mrs. Kim and hugged her. Although the older woman was often indisposed from cancer treatments and her English was limited, there was a bond between them that transcended words.

"Happy you are back," said Mrs. Kim. "We worried."

"I know. Sorry." Kera let the embrace linger. "We had trouble, but not too much."

Mr. Kim waved them toward the living room. "Well, come sit down and talk about it. We had dinner already, I am sorry to say, but there are leftovers if you want. And tea, of course. Oh." Remembering the bag of groceries in his hand, he put them in the refrigerator while his wife made tea.

A few minutes later, the four of them were seated. Kera made them talk first and found that little of note had happened. That was good to know since she hated the thought of anything bad—especially anything bad caused by her—threatening or befalling them. Quiet and boring was best.

The shop was doing well financially. Sam's grades were slipping a little, but he had promised to get back on track. He was also starting on the track team, which explained his newfound physical confidence. Most importantly, Mrs. Kim's treatments were coming along well enough that they expected her to be cancer-free in a couple more months.

Kera's heart leaped. Recalling all the pain and worry they had shared and her efforts to magically heal her friend despite the dangers involved, it was tough not to cry. "That's great. Damn. I'm really happy for you. That sounds cheesy, sorry. But I mean it."

Mrs. Kim smiled. "We know."

"Now," her husband went on, "tell us about you, and how your vacation went, and the trip back. And don't try to pretend that something weird *didn't* happen when you returned to LA. We don't know what it is, but we know that everything was not as smooth as you would like to pretend. No offense, but you are very obvious, ha-ha. Something is bothering you."

Shit, she lamented. *I knew this would happen. I only came over here to get some food, say hi, and catch up. Consciously, anyway. I should have known they would pry every last detail out of me. They're even better at it than my mother.*

Inhaling deeply, Kera started at the beginning. She summed up how surprisingly pleasant her and Chris' trip to New England had been, only for it to turn sour at the end when the volcano in Iceland grounded all flights and they had to take a train back home.

She glossed over the shenanigans on the train when she became aware of the Orthodoxy witch Milena and her two minions. She admitted they had encountered other magic users who had malevolent intent and were connected to the people who had once threatened the Kims.

A dark mood settled over the gathering. Kera almost wished she had lied to spare her friends.

"But," she added, "after we got back to California, I brought the leader to justice and drove the other two off. No one else was hurt, and Chris and I are okay."

She had, in fact, *killed* Milena but did not want to admit it.

Mr. Kim nodded and made a low throaty sound. "Hmm, yes. We sensed something strange going on to the east. Did this happen in the Inland Empire?"

"Yes," Kera admitted. "Jurupa Valley. I don't like making you guys worry, but I feel I owe it to you to warn you that I don't think all the trouble is past yet. Problems keep following me around, and I keep getting involved in them. I'll do everything I can to keep them away from you." She clenched a fist; she meant it. "But I can't be everywhere at once, so please be careful, and let me know if you see or hear anything strange. I'll warn you if something happens on my end, also."

They nodded solemnly. Previously, they had had to take a brief "vacation" to Sacramento to get away from trouble—trouble with the Orthodoxy.

Mr. Kim remarked, "That was not what we wanted to hear, but I'm glad you gave us a heads-up. Remember that we are not defenseless. And we support you."

The old couple had the gift too. They were not as strong in it as Kera was, but they could perform magic at a respectable level. Enough to see problems in advance and give themselves an edge if things went bad.

"But," Mr. Kim continued, "we must protect our family first and foremost. You can come to us, but if things become too dangerous, we will leave town until the worst is over."

Kera nodded. "Good." Thinking of the Kims' abilities

reminded her of the fight with Steph, and she briefly summarized what had happened, concluding that she was perplexed about the whole thing.

Mrs. Kim looked Kera in the eyes. "You have trust problems," she pointed out. "With Chris. With Steph."

Kera's gut tightened, but she knew the woman was correct. "Yeah, I suppose I do."

"So," Mr. Kim suggested, "try trusting her. Put her in a situation where you know you *can* trust her, and when she comes through, you will feel better about trusting her other times. See how it works?"

She began to feel better. "Yeah, okay. Thanks, as usual."

But, she added to herself, *the goal, the mission, the job has to come first. I'll do whatever I can to prove to Steph and myself that she's up to the task, but not if there's a serious risk of failure. Too much is at stake.*

CHAPTER SEVEN

Lia raised and stretched her arms, then flexed her hands as though she was preparing for a fight. "No more delays. Onward to business. Finding out who the buyer was might take some work, but I'm sure we can handle it."

"Right," Chris agreed. "Given the amount of money they paid for it, we can probably start by looking at places where the activities of rich people get discussed. That might narrow it down."

He paused and frowned vaguely into space. "In California, it won't narrow it down *much,* but hey, it's a start."

"Yes." Lia sat down in front of her laptop, and her fingers whizzed across the keyboard. "I'll check the gossip rags and social event invites since the wealthy like to show off their new purchases to their friends at swanky occasions."

Chris nodded and booted up Kera's desktop. "Noted. I, meanwhile, will deep-dive into forums discussing occult and paranormal stuff since there might be people who are sufficiently interested in the book to keep tabs on where it is at any given moment. They're wrong half the time, of course, but they might point us in the right direction if nothing else."

"Oh," Lia added, "I just remembered. I contacted Johnny and

asked him to keep an ear open as well. He's glad we're not pestering him with quasi-legal activities anymore, but he's willing to help once in a while. He still has contacts. I told him to let us know if he runs across any buzz about weird people interested in rare occult books or things of that nature."

"Good." Chris was halfway into his cup of coffee, which boded well for his work performance throughout the day to come.

Kera sat on the couch, watching them. "If we had three computers, I'd help. Chris, next time you should bring your own instead of using mine. Moocher."

"Yeah, yeah, whatever," he shot back. "My laptop is fucked right now, something to do with the display. I can probably fix it, but I haven't had time yet. And my desktop is too damn big and bulky."

Kera scoffed. "So? You drive a Jeep. It's not like you'd be trying to cram it into a tiny Japanese or European car."

He shrugged. "Next time, I'll keep that in mind."

As the pair became absorbed in their searches, Kera got up and began pacing the warehouse, waiting for updates. She felt useless. Once Steph arrived, they could work on their overall plan in more detail—and hopefully, patch up the animosity that had arisen between them. For the moment, Kera had to wait for info.

She wandered over to her makeshift gym. After a couple of minutes of stretching, she fell into a fighting stance facing the punching bag and attacked it.

Chris looked up from the PC as the sounds of his girlfriend kicking, punching, and elbowing the heavy bag echoed through the building. "Uh-oh, she's at it again. You okay, dear? I know that compulsively wanting to pound on a sack is not *always* a cry for help, but sometimes it is. If so, let me know, so I can put on a cup."

To his surprise, Lia snickered. "That was pretty funny."

Kera called, "Sure it was. *Really* funny." She front-kicked the bag at about hip level. "But no, I'm fine. I just want to warm up and get back in practice while I have the time."

"Fair enough," Chris replied and returned to his forum-scanning.

Fifteen minutes later, just as Kera was getting into the zone and beginning to enjoy her workout, someone knocked at the side entrance. "I'll get it." She hopped over, peeked out the window, and opened the door. "Hi, Steph. Glad you could make it."

Stephanie stepped in, smiling gently. She seemed to be in good spirits. "Likewise. Did I interrupt your workout?"

"Yes," said Kera, "but it's okay. I was killing time while waiting for you to get here. Lia and Chris are handling the geek stuff."

Chris protested, "Hey! You have a computer science degree, same as me. You're just out of practice since you got a job in the science of mixing alcoholic beverages, which was probably a better choice than the crap I did for that godawful office."

Kera waved a hand. "He's front-loading himself with coffee. Pay no heed. Anyway, when we make our next move, you and I will be the ones on the ground." She made sure to look into Steph's eyes when she said it so her friend got the point. "You've backed me up before, and I trust you with that as much as I trust Chris and Lia with the research and communications side of things."

Steph looked mildly uncomfortable, as though she were being put on the spot, but it vanished. "Sounds good. And that's true; we've worked together as equals many times before. No reason this should be any different. Of course, I have to ask, what the hell *are* we doing? Stealing the book? Or are we gonna wait for the buyer to receive it and then ask him politely if we can have a look?"

Kera grimaced. "Have a seat. I came to a conclusion or two earlier that you haven't heard yet. By the way, congrats on your pending resignation. Once you don't have a second job, it will be easier to stay in the loop at this one."

"No kidding," Steph agreed. She sat down on the couch on which Kera had reclined not long ago. "Okay, what's the deal?"

Kera went over everything in her mind before she spoke. "I reviewed the info we have so far on the grimoire, and while I can't be certain... Well, you know how my hunches usually end up being correct and have steered us in the right direction before?"

"Yeah." Steph's face was somber, but she also looked curious.

"Well, I think the stories about it are probably true, or partially true, about how the book possesses people and takes control of their personalities. The writings about it, the anecdotes, the urban legends, and even the most credulous newspaper stories about the more recent owners are surprisingly consistent. In other words, I have a hunch that the grimoire is dangerous enough that it would be irresponsible to let someone buy it, open it, and potentially get their body hijacked by whatever spirit inhabits the damn thing."

Slowly, Stephanie nodded. "That sounds bad. So, I'm guessing the plan is to steal it in transit."

"Bingo." Kera plopped down in the easy chair across from the couch. "That creates a bunch of complications of its own. We'll have to come up with a cover story and maybe use a little magical persuasion to keep our reputation clean and blame the theft on 'unidentified parties.' The problems of pulling off something like that bother me less than the notion of an innocent person getting their soul stolen."

"Makes sense." Steph frowned. "What if the book possesses someone who's... dangerous by themselves? Powerful, or important."

From her place across the room, Lia called, "Yes, that occurred to us also. The buyer is probably wealthy, which is a bad sign. At the very least, the spirit would have access to a lot of resources."

Chris interjected, "I mean, if I was going to live in an old, dusty magical book, I would probably want to possess a rich person too. Ideally, someone who is a star performer in the adult film industry."

"I heard that," Kera snapped. "But you make a valid point, probably by accident. The book seems to *choose* its targets. It's never possessed anyone who just did a menial job, went home to their family every day, and that's it. All the supposed cases were of rich or powerful people or crazies who were willing to do extreme stuff or both."

Steph rubbed her chin and brushed her braids back over her shoulder. "I wonder if it's a *person's* spirit or like a demon?"

Kera shrugged. "We'll find out soon enough."

She and Steph wandered over to the gym and began sparring, both in martial arts and in magical combat. There was an underlying tension and awkwardness between them, but each perceived the other wanted to patch things up and move beyond their spat the other day. Therefore, each offered the other respect, and they gave one another the benefit of the doubt.

As the afternoon wore on, Lia surprised them all by shouting, "I've got it!"

Everyone stopped what they were doing and turned to her.

Lia cleared her throat. "I was pretty sure I had it ten minutes ago, but I've been double-checking and cross-referencing things. And, um, now that I think about it, this is potentially quite bad. The buyer's name is John Brimes, or John C. Brimes. I've seen it both ways, but it seems to refer to the same person either way. He's a wealthy recluse who lives out in Montecito."

"Wait," Stephanie interrupted, her face scrunching in confusion, "Montecito Heights, the neighborhood? Or the town of Montecito way up by Santa Barbara along the coast?"

"The latter." Lia straightened her hair with a quick whisk of her fingers. "He does not leave home much these days, but when he does, he goes to the Bay Area and Silicon Valley almost as often as he comes to LA., so I suppose that's part of it. Anyway, he also happens to be a tech genius. He wrote a lot of software that's seen extensive use by the government as well as at least a dozen Fortune 500 corporations."

Kera scratched her chin and began pacing, about six steps in each direction and back. "Okay, so? I mean, I can see potential problems but is there anything specific you're getting at, or you've heard, that affects us or relates to the book?"

"Yes," said Lia. "He has security clearance with the Department of Defense and the National Security Agency. Apparently he runs diagnostics on their systems or does 'hacking wargames' sporadically. He's semi-retired from his main business, but he's still considered a government asset. This is a man who hacks into weapons and intelligence databases for a living and could probably walk into a military research base without any significant trouble."

Silence set in as the implications dawned upon all of them. Kera felt an unpleasant sinking sensation.

"So," Chris offered, speaking for all of them, "if the rumors are true and this book body-snatches its owners, whatever scary entity lives in its pages now has access to a big-league hacker the government trusts with nuclear codes and shit. Is that what you're saying?"

It was, Kera knew, largely a formality for Lia to answer. They had all figured it out by now.

"Yes," she stated.

Kera rubbed her eyes. "Welp, we're screwed *once again*, out of a clean, easy, non-dangerous case. And possibly screwed out of continued existence on a habitable planet."

Stephanie stared at her. "Are you saying there's no point in trying? Because that's not like you at all."

"No." Kera rubbed her eyes. "I was secretly hoping for something a little easier, to be honest. But it's on us to deal with it, and we will. Let's start the planning phase immediately. Lia, you can keep looking up info, but try to keep one ear on what we're discussing. Chris, I want you to shift over to logistics and update things as we decide on the details."

He coughed. "Yes, ma'am."

Kera, smirking, asked, "Hey, did anyone see that movie *Ocean's Eleven*? It came out, like, twenty years ago, so maybe not. My dad was a pretty big fan of it, though. This shit seriously reminds me of the plot of that film, only, like, with a book heist in Montecito instead of a cash heist in Vegas. And four people instead of, y'know, eleven."

Chris raised his hand. "I did. Pretty good flick. I think it's a remake of an even older film from the 1960s or thereabouts, and all the Rat Pack guys were in it."

Stephanie shrugged. "You would know, I guess. I've heard of it and never seen it."

"Me neither," Lia added. "Odd as it may sound, screenwriters sometimes come up with surprisingly clever ideas when it comes to criminal schemes or black-ops-type missions, so reviewing the details of the story might give us a few ideas on how to go about all this."

Kera gestured at her. "Right. Oh, and I'd be Danny Ocean, obviously. Steph, I think you'd be Rusty Ryan since you were my friend before I started dating Chris and Lia came onboard. Lia, you'd be Livingston Dell, the surveillance expert, kinda combined with Saul Bloom, due to having the most criminal experience of the group. No offense."

"None taken," Lia replied in a flat tone.

"And," Kera went on, "Chris would be Linus Calwell since he was played by Matt Damon, and he's hot. You don't look much like Matt Damon, but take it as a compliment."

Chris smoothed his hair. "But of course." He stood up and stretched his arms; Kera recognized the mischievous look that crept across his face. "So, um, yeah. Since we're going to be doing some serious cloak and dagger shit, now would be a good time to bust out the trench coat to make sure I'm doing the job right."

Stephanie groaned, and Kera pinched the bridge of her nose.

"Hey, come on," he protested. "It's getting cooler out, sort of. If we're out past dark, it might even get chilly by Southern California standards. I have perfectly good practical reasons for wearing it."

Kera shrugged. "Yeah, fine. It'll help you conceal your gun if nothing else, though cops know to look for stuff like that, so be careful. The last thing we need to deal with is bailing you out of jail for illegally carrying a weapon while we're trying to pull off an even-more-illegal heist."

Lia squirmed in place. Given her criminal background, talk of cops and illegality made her uncomfortable. "Yes," she offered, "let's try to avoid any and all complications or run-ins with the law. The agency's reputation would plunge into the abyss if we were found to be criminals on par with the sorts of people we're supposed to be against."

Stephanie gave a vigorous nod. "Right. Better not to have to deal with that crap than have to fix it later, with magic or otherwise."

"I guess." Chris sighed.

Half an hour later, he and Lia had found how and when the book would be transported. An armored car company would be moving it in a safe to Montecito tomorrow in the late afternoon or early evening.

Kera considered the information. "I'm wondering if we should try a traditional frontal assault type of heist or do something clever like infiltrate the transport company."

Chris suggested, "Why not both?"

CHAPTER EIGHT

Anezka raised a hand. Everyone standing before her in the open lot, the bulk of her troops in America, snapped to attention, ready to obey. In Russian, she commanded them.

"You all have your marching orders and your assigned vehicles. Remember our communications rendezvous at 13:00 hours. If you do not receive further instructions, assume we will meet at the designated location in the city of Baton Rouge. Move out!"

The dozens of witches and warlocks vanished into their fleet of black SUVs. A moment later, engines revved, and the vehicles pulled onto the streets of Jackson, fanning out clockwise from southeast to due north. Due east and northeast were excluded since the coven was certain their targets did not lay in those directions.

Anezka sat in the backseat of one of the SUVs headed south toward New Orleans. She had little doubt that the bayou city, which was ancient by American standards, was their ultimate goal.

But in the absence of certainty, she had no choice but to widen the net before she tightened it. There was a slim chance the council knew they were coming and might try to flee elsewhere at the eleventh hour.

They would not slip away again.

Anezka glanced at the SUV behind hers as the driver took off. That one contained their recent recruits, Mindy and Dan from West Virginia. They had thus far been relatively pliant to their new masters' demands, requiring only a small amount of magical coercion to ensure their obedience.

The driver glanced over her shoulder. "Grandmistress, shall we stay within the speed limit?" The unasked portion of the question was whether they wished to avoid entanglements with the American authorities or risk dealing with the police for the sake of speed. In that case, spells could be used to dismiss the problem without much difficulty.

Anezka looked straight ahead once more. "Yes. Haste is unnecessary, provided we do not waste time. We are not far from them now. There is no way they can escape the noose we have drawn about them. Performing all duties correctly at this stage of the operation is more important than performing them quickly."

"Yes, Grandmistress," the driver responded and turned her attention to driving. Reposing in the passenger's seat, meanwhile, was none other than Hana. The woman was quiet and sullen, but continued her duty of scanning the areas they drove through for any sign of magical activity.

It was fortunate, Anezka reflected, that one of their scouts in Louisiana had stumbled across that man from Africa who had joined the council. He was not, as far as the Orthodoxy was aware, a full member of their organization, but he *was* their ally or apprentice. The man had driven the scout off before a further investigation could be conducted.

But it had been enough to confirm the grandmistress' suspicion that the council had fled to New Orleans.

By reporting this partial success, she diverted the troops' attention from how badly they had been weakened by the loss of

Milena. In essence, she was able to say, "See, we found them despite the minor setback of one of our most important members dying and taking her support magic with her. There is nothing to worry about."

Though from what Alexei had said, the coven's membership was well aware that they were experiencing major problems. They knew that what had happened in California had been more severe than their leader had publicly admitted. A large-scale success was necessary to convince them that overall victory was still within their grasp.

Hence, the importance of snuffing out the council *now*. Then she could redirect her forces toward the next targets—Kera and Pavla.

Halfway to Baton Rouge, the driver asked, "Madam, if I may, once we have overcome the council, will we be flying to California to deal with the girl Kera? The airports might be back in operation by then."

The grandmistress frowned. "It will depend. We will fly if we are able, as per the US aviation authorities. Until then, we have many other options."

Once again, Anezka brooded, her people were having to cut themselves off from certain possibilities because of the weakness and incompetence of most humans. The US authorities were wary of allowing planes to operate, so flights were still grounded. The volcanic eruption in Iceland continued to cause problems, even though the skies looked clear.

Liability, she thought. Americans sue one another any time something goes wrong, so if there is the slightest risk or danger, they take the safest possible option to protect themselves from lawsuits. How did these people become the dominant country on the planet? Luck surely played a part.

Anezka's SUV was the second to arrive in Baton Rouge since she and the one housing their two conscripts had taken the most direct route. The other vehicles were checking the cities of Gulfport, Mississippi to the east, and Lafayette, Louisiana to the west. Forward scouts of the Orthodoxy had set up basic but workable safehouses in all three towns. Another pair of scouts was monitoring the harbors in New Orleans.

The trap was set. There was no direction in which the council could flee that would allow them to escape.

The driver pulled into a large parking lot attached to a vacant corporate compound, which Anezka had rented from the lienholder after using various persuasive tactics.

"Hana," Anezka began as they rolled to a stop, "report on the state of magic in this town, as well as what you noticed along the way."

The somber Russian-Japanese witch replied in her usual monotone, "There have been no great concentrations but many small traces. It is unfamiliar; as you told us before, the magic which people use in this region is strange and unlike anything in Europe or Asia. From what I have read, some of it is indigenous, and much of it is derived from the traditions of Africa and the Caribbean. There is almost certainly a small coven operating here in Baton Rouge, but I sense greater power ahead. New Orleans is clearly the epicenter of witchcraft along the Gulf Coast."

Anezka nodded; that was what she had expected.

"Good. Once the other units update us on the situation, we might be able to make use of the locals here." She cast a brief, contemptuous glance at Dan and Mindy, who were being pulled out of the other car by the burly young warlock she had assigned as their chaperone.

13:00 hours arrived soon. Using tablets, the various SUV units joined a voice-and-video call to report their findings.

Anezka was disappointed that they had little to share. There was no trace of the council anywhere in the lower Mississippi River Delta region so far. The local covens were lying low and keeping silent, fearful of reprisals by their continent's new rulers.

The grandmistress saw no point in wasting time. "So be it. The scouts manning the forward bases shall remain where they are in case the council tries to slip away. Everyone who is part of the main assault force, convene here. Do not delay."

It took an hour and a half for the SUVs to arrive from Lafayette and a little over two hours for those heading in from Gulfport.

Vassily commanded the former. When he emerged from his vehicle to greet Anezka, he seemed cantankerous and impatient, likely due to the hot, humid weather. Anezka had found that summers in Ukraine were little better than what the American South dealt with, although they were shorter back home.

Vassily, however, was from Arkhangelsk on the Arctic Ocean, where even July was seldom more than warm and six months of bitterly cold winter was normal. He wiped his pale brow with a thin cloth. "I do hope we need not linger in this place long."

Smiling, Anezka shot back, "We shall remain as long as it takes, but I expect a swift victory. Once we rule the continent, it will be easier for you to pick and choose the theaters of your oversight duties."

He made a low grumbling sound in his throat, then insisted on asking the one question Anezka had no desire to hear from anyone, whether her right-hand man or the lowliest acolyte.

"Are we certain," he inquired, "the entire group is in the same place? Our enemies, I mean. I recall that there was a brief mention of the possibility that *some* of them might have remained at their hiding spot in New Orleans while others fled to a distant locale, perhaps to get help from unrevealed friends of theirs. I have not had a chance to review our intelligence. Have the scouts confirmed that the council chose not to divide their force?"

Anezka's nails dug into the palms of her hands. He should have known better than to ask a delicate question like that where many of the lower-ranking members could hear him and at a time when the troops' morale was tenuous.

"We are all but certain," she replied. It was technically true. "We have not been able to scry their location well enough to confirm the presence of all eleven of them, but we have not discovered any evidence of them fleeing or of council members in any other locations. The odds favor the possibility that as we speak, all of them huddle in their house in the swamp, praying we do not find them. If one, two, or three of them is elsewhere, they will be far less of a problem once we have crushed all the others."

She had confidence in the statement. It would hold true even if stragglers from the council were able to link up with Pavla and Kera.

Alexei, who had ridden with Vassily's posse, approached. "Grandmistress, if you'll pardon my saying. Some of the scouts have seen so little activity that they fear they might have missed something. Insofar as most of them are highly skilled and reliable, that suggests the council has not removed from New Orleans. Barring the one instance in which the African man was sighted, in any event."

Anezka could feel confidence returning to her followers. She considered that Alexei might deserve a promotion soon.

"Indeed," she stated. "What is that American expression about deer, something to do with those who stand stupidly awaiting their doom? Like deer in the headlights of a car. Yes. Like that."

Samantha flipped her hair and adjusted her blouse. "You know, I never thought I would be the one doing these sorts of things. I like to think I *can* fight when I have to, but it isn't my specialty. I'm primarily interested in people, especially men, and my main area of focus is brewing potions."

Ezeudo squinted. "Did you not brew the potions you used against the Orthodoxy when they attacked James' mansion? I did not see that part of the battle, but I recall you making them beforehand, and Mary mentioned it later."

"Oh," Samantha quipped, "yes, right. Good point. But potion-brewing is a fine art that takes many years of practice to come to fruition. It's generally applied to benefit someone or influence them rather than for purposes of attack or other combat applications. We'll need to drill you on things that are simpler and more direct."

The tall Nigerian had no complaints. He had learned a fair amount of battle magic, but owing to his relative inexperience, he was still several orders of magnitude below his new comrades in terms of ability.

Samantha then instructed him on how to create a throwable fireball.

"Generally," she explained, "when you wish to incinerate something, the easiest way is to conjure intense heat at the point you are targeting. While a projectile is easier to dodge, it has its advantages, primarily as a distraction. A feint, you might say. Like someone throwing a light, quick punch toward an opponent's face to get them to flinch so they leave themselves open for a devastating blow to the body."

From the side of the yard near the tree line where the plantation's half-maintained property gave way to undeveloped swamp, James Lovecraft called, "Samantha, since when are you an enthusiast of boxing? I had no idea!"

She glanced at him with a smile that looked like it might crack into laughter. "I know a thing or two about it. Two of my ex-boyfriends were fans, and one was a boxer himself."

James shrugged. "Fighting is fighting, I suppose. The analogy makes sense."

Ezeudo added, "I do not have training in boxing or the martial arts, but I understand what you mean. Show me, then."

She demonstrated by summoning a concentrated ball of matter—trace minerals, plants, and gases collected from the surrounding environment—and using a heat-conjuration spell to ignite it, creating a small, blazing meteor that, after a second's hesitation, she hurled at James.

He raised a hand and caught it against a wall of shielding gravitational force, then enveloped it with the shield combined with a wave of icy water. The flames winked out and the small amount of material she'd used as the core of the fireball dropped to the ground, now harmless.

Ezeudo said, "Impressive, both of you. And I am happy to see, James, that you are well enough to use magic again."

"Thanks," he remarked. "I still feel iffy, but I'm a lot better."

Drawing her student's attention back to the procedure, Samantha elaborated further. "As you saw, I performed each step one after the other so you could see how to do it. Of course, in the thick of battle, it must all be done in one fast, continuous motion, without a meaningful gap between the forming of the core, the ignition, and the throw. That means you must be able to cast three spells in such quick succession that they effectively become a single thaumaturgic act. From what Lauren told me, you have basic experience in things like this."

"Yes," said Ezeudo. "Let me first practice it one step at a time, as you did, then I shall increase my speed and smoothness."

Samantha gave him a nod and a flourish of her hand. "Excellent, yes."

Looking behind him at the bayou, James quipped, "Well, if we accidentally set anything on fire, at least we're in a place that's so damp that I'm pretty sure it would go out on its own after a couple seconds without us having to extinguish it. Although," he frowned, "heating up all this moisture creates even more humidity."

Laughing at his complaint as Ezeudo set to work on gathering matter in a ball, Samantha pointed out, "Nothing wrong with a little steam, James."

"Eh. Touché, I guess."

He watched the session, having volunteered to act as Samantha's second in keeping an eye on things in case Ezeudo did something wrong and swift action was needed to keep everyone safe.

Partly, he did this out of obligation to her. She had spent weeks watching over him while he was wounded and healing him to the best of her ability. Partly, he did it because it would prove to everyone that he was well enough again to fight and to be considered a functional member of the team.

After the first half-hour, though, he had to lean against a tree. Standing upright for extended periods of time still made him tired, and his chest ached. He could have used magic to select a tree branch and form it into a cane, but he decided against it. It would make him look weak. Besides, canes were Josiah's schtick, not his.

James was impressed with the progress his pupil had made since the battle in New York. Midway into the sparring, though, Ezeudo began to have problems.

When he tried to summon and throw his fireball as fast as Samantha had, the projectile exploded fifteen feet from his face. He narrowly avoided burning himself as the fiery detritus scattered about the lawn.

Samantha and James stepped in, checking on him and extinguishing the guttering fires that had formed amidst the grass.

"Careful," James warned him. "You might be pushing yourself too hard too soon on the speed thing. When the battle comes, you probably won't be on the front lines, so if you're in back launching crap at the Orthodoxy to distract them, it will be okay if you're not super-quick about it."

Ezeudo frowned. His hands were shaking.

Samantha suggested, "Or it could be an emotional issue. You seem agitated, and that can lead to failures of control. What is bothering you, Ezeudo? You can tell us."

The tall Nigerian's gaze drifted to the ground, and he made himself take two deep breaths before he answered them.

"Anger," he confessed. "Focusing on magical combat like this brings me back in my mind to what happened at James' house and all that has occurred since then. The Orthodoxy has done things that are unforgivable. It is not in my nature to hate and rage against people, but I am struggling, not only because of what they have done to us but because I can see what they mean to do to everyone else once they have power."

James looked away, surprised by the rush of emotion he felt. Since he had, at long last, recovered from his ordeal, he had been avoiding the subject. Now seemed like a poor time to deal with it.

"Yeah," he murmured loud enough for both his friends to hear. "I feel that. Like I said before, I blamed myself for a lot of what has happened, and I *expected* to die in that fight. But I didn't, and now I get to live in a world where two of my best friends are dead, the home that's been in my family for generations is nothing but a pile of ash, and I'm on the run with you guys like a goddamn fugitive. We're all hoping we can win next time so the whole country doesn't turn into a foreign criminal dictatorship with the general populace being magically compelled to pay protection money and random citizens being harvested as fuel for empowerment spells. We might not be perfect, but we never did stuff like *that*."

Samantha moved over to Ezeudo and urged him closer to James. She laid a hand on each of the men's arms.

"We are all worried," she observed. "But we have the Chalice, and if LeBlanc believes in it, then so do I. Despite them having more numbers, we fought the Orthodoxy almost to a standstill before they broke through and overwhelmed us. We know how they fight and are better prepared this time. All is not lost."

They spent a moment in silence, standing close to one another and remembering how far they had come together.

Someone approached across the lawn. It was Lauren Jones.

"Hello," she greeted them. "We're all busy, but I have a spare hour. How are things coming? I'm happy to help if Ezeudo is having any difficulties."

In unison, the trio turned to her.

Ezeudo said, "Yes, your help would be welcome. Samantha and James are good teachers, but it never hurts to have another opinion."

CHAPTER NINE

Someone had answered his call. Viator Psellus awoke.

He often slept. After centuries upon centuries of his consciousness continuing to exist, it spent much of its time in repose, waiting. There was too much information in the world for his mind to expand and take in all of it. Yet, at the same time, he was so old that he could not attach total importance to half of what happened.

Long ago, he had known old men who dismissed the concerns of children. They had passed through that phase of life and regarded its problems and concerns as silly. They had no desire to revisit them, no matter how stridently the young protested that their preoccupations were all-important and deserving of attention.

So it was with him now. Nearly all of humanity were like children when contrasted with his timeless lifespan.

And yet, there *were* some people and things that interested him and reawakened his hunger to exist in the world. To interact with it and feel it and live amidst it.

Someone had heard when he had cried out for people of importance, people experienced in the strange new magic of technology, to notice him and bring him to them in the form of the book. The details were unclear to him. He would have to be patient to discover the means by which the book would be passed on.

More importantly, to whom.

He had dreamed of the opportunity to once again live a human life with flesh and bones and hair and muscles. To feel his heart pumping blood through his veins, even if the blood had originally belonged to someone else.

He felt certain that this time, the individual who had purchased the book was a man. His last life as a visceral being had involved him seizing the body of a woman. It had been interesting, and he had been female before, but he found them more complicated. Since he had been a man in his first life, he preferred to possess male bodies.

Besides, often, though not always, women were stronger in the gift, which made it easier for them to resist Psellus' infiltration of their minds and bodies. Some men were powerful magicians, like he himself had been and still was, but not many. Usually, they had fewer defenses against him.

From what little he had seen, the new sorcery—the magic of electronics and digitized information—was a field in which men seemed more prevalent, though there were many women involved in it as well.

He would take what he could get. The important thing was to possess a host who could get him close to the centers of power, information, and influence.

Then, his immortal consciousness would have access to all the knowledge stored within the brain of his new body. Combined with his vast reserves of wisdom and magical aptitude, he would be more formidable than ever.

He scanned his surroundings and followed the astral connections that led from him to the rest of the world.

People were talking about the grimoire. *Several* people. Any of them, whatever their intentions, could probably be overtaken by Psellus' indomitable will.

He waited. His many years of hiding in the dark would come to an end, and the world would tremble again. Soon.

Lia gently tapped the microphone by the side of her mouth. "Hi, it's Livingston," she said. "How are you doing, Danny? Are you headed to Vegas yet?"

Kera's voice replied, "Hi, Livingston. Nope, still in California, but I'll be heading off soon. Waiting till I feel like my luck is a little better. Hoping to score big, what with the, uh, fight coming up."

In Lia's opinion, their code sounded phony enough that, on the off chance that anyone was listening in, they might well guess that something shady or scandalous was afoot. But they hadn't had time to come up with anything better, especially since Kera and Stephanie had set off early to scope out the armored transport company and get Kera inserted into her "new job."

"Okay, great." Lia kept her tone jovial and tried to disguise her voice, speaking in a higher pitch than usual. "Were you able to drop Rusty off at the dry cleaner's earlier?"

"Yeah." Kera sounded like she was trying to keep her voice down while walking through an enclosed space somewhere. "She needs her work clothes for that interview coming up at that casino down the street from the one I'm going to, assuming she ends up moving to Vegas after all."

Lia nodded. So far, everything was going to plan. Kera had successfully slipped into the armored car company's Southern California location undetected, or at least without attracting undue suspicion. Stephanie was in place outside the building, half a block down from them to the west. They were in North Hollywood, so when the car departed, they assumed it would take the most direct route toward Santa Barbara.

Then something popped into Lia's head, a saying she had heard as a young girl from a military guy her father had been friends with. *Assumption is the mother of all fuck-ups.* She had never forgotten that.

They did not yet have verifiable, actionable intelligence on exactly which vehicle the grimoire would be stored in or which route the car would take. It was up to Kera to figure that out before departure time.

Chris sat next to Lia in the Jeep with his laptop open and his headset active and adjusted. He said into the microphone, "Hey, guys, it's Linus. Anybody want anything to eat? I'm heading to Subway."

Lia, to her irritation, could not remember what that meant, so she glanced at the cheat sheet she'd brought just to be safe. If they were caught by law enforcement, there was a possibility of them being able to decipher the code and guess that nefarious activity was occurring.

But since Kera had cloaked their vehicle before departing, the chances of mission failure via garbled communication was much greater.

While Lia browsed the sheet, Kera replied, "Thanks but no thanks, I'm hitting the road already. We'll get something fancy when I get back from Vegas, okay?"

"Deal," stated Chris.

According to the sheet, Lia saw, Chris asking if anyone was hungry meant he wanted to double-check if they were planning to jump the gun and just sweep-search the whole facility or if they were going to stick to the original plan and wait for Kera to slowly figure things out.

Kera's response was a relief. She was still doing things the careful way.

Lia covered her microphone and motioned for Chris to do

the same, which he did. "There's one thing I'm still unclear on," she confessed. "I did not have the same amount of time to go over the steps of the operation the rest of you did since I was busy looking up info while you were hashing it out. If anything goes wrong, Stephanie is supposed to cast the necessary spells to hide our actions, delay the car, and befuddle law enforcement while Kera deals with things inside the building, right?"

Chris nodded. "I'd say you *are* pretty clear on it."

"That isn't the question I wanted to ask," Lia clarified. "It was only confirming the, um, preamble. What I need to know is, can Stephanie *do* all that? Her magical abilities aren't as advanced as Kera's, as I understand it."

Drumming his fingers as he ruminated, Chris looked out the window. "I think so. She and Kera drilled in those spells before we got started, and she did pretty well. Kera underestimates her sometimes, and that might have rubbed off on you. If Kera can't handle everything from within, Steph is our backup. She's waiting on Kera's word, so it kinda hinges on my lovely girlfriend's judgment."

"I see." Lia wasn't sure what to think about that. "Well, Kera's judgment is good. Usually."

Phil struggled not to zone out as he pushed the safe down the hall on the wheeled dolly. He had been sleeping poorly lately, and the job was boring him to the point that it was growing ever more difficult not to make mistakes.

Why, he wondered, couldn't he have applied for one of the driver positions? Then at least he would have been able to go to different places every day, or some days, anyway. Getting fresh air, seeing the sights. As it was, he was stuck in the processing center, doing the same shit over and over in a dull and stuffy indoor environment.

"No," he told himself. "Focus, man. This safe is important. What's inside it, whatever the hell it is, is important to someone. Umm," he glanced at the manifest sheet, "to Mr. Brimes. Isn't he a software guy? Probably brilliant computer stuff."

But the manifest said the safe contained a *book*. Seemed weird.

Shaking his head, Phil kept moving toward the bay with the three trucks. Right before he entered the bay, something stopped him dead in his tracks.

Someone was speaking to him, but not from anywhere he could see, and not with sounds. It was like an irresistible voice in his mind, asking him a dozen things at once, demanding answers before the questions were even spoken.

"What?" he gasped. "Why am I thinking all this stuff? What the hell?"

He knew it was his mind playing tricks on him. It *felt* like a presence or an intelligent entity outside him—in the safe. In the book. Peering into his brain, examining his soul.

And then it was gone, sliding smoothly away and leaving him in peace.

Phil blinked. "Fuck," he muttered. "I need to start getting more sleep. And maybe see a goddamn psychiatrist. This place is driving me crazy."

The wheels of the dolly squeaked as he pushed the safe onward.

As he reached the loading bay, someone came up behind him. "Hey," a voice called, "did you leave a copy of the shipping manifest on the desk? I need to double-check something."

Phil glanced over his shoulder. The voice and the figure it belonged to seemed female at first, but after the initial impression, no. He'd been wrong; it was a man, someone he didn't recognize. Skinny guy with black hair. Must be new. He was wearing the company uniform, in any event.

"Uh, yeah," he affirmed. In fact, he couldn't remember, but he was pretty sure he had. "Go ahead and check, man. I got to load this thing."

The new guy said, "Okay, I will," and left.

Phil tried to ignore the creeping sense of unreality. He'd been *certain* it was a chick, if only for a split second. Granted, you couldn't always tell. "They say not everyone is male or female, right? Maybe he's one of those folks who's somewhere in between. Whatever. Either way, I got to get my act together."

He spent a minute opening the back of the truck and pushing the safe into its usual place, then shutting the doors and making sure everything was secure. Since he wanted to get to a bathroom and splash cold water on his face, he hurried.

By the time he was done, one of their drivers, Muriel, strolled up, jangling her keys. "Hi, Phil. Is that 078?"

"Uh, yeah." He was wheeling the dolly away. "Good luck out there."

After returning the dolly to its place, he rushed into the restroom, doused his face, and stared at the mirror for a full minute. "Okay," he said. "Feeling more alert. I can do this. Only three hours to go."

As he strolled out, someone rushed up. "Hey!" they barked, clearly angry. At first, Phil thought it was the mysterious new person, but he was wrong. It was Odir, the dispatcher. "You forgot to put a copy of the manifest on the desk, Phil! Did Muriel leave with 087 yet?"

Phil stopped, staring blankly at his co-worker. "087, yeah, I think." Or was it 078? He couldn't remember. Getting two loads in the same day with similar numbers was par for the course, though. Just his luck.

Odir cursed and rushed toward the bay as an engine started and one of the trucks pulled out.

Feeling sheepish, Phil started to move on to the next shipment, at which point Odir rushed back. "Goddammit, she went off with 078. She was *supposed* to be taking 087, which we would have known if the manifest was on the desk. Why the hell did they give us two shipments at the same time with numbers like that?"

"Sorry," Phil muttered, looking at the floor.

Odir rubbed his forehead. "Whatever, man. I'll call Muriel and have her switch course. That one was supposed to go up to Santa Clarita so she can turn west and still hit Montecito in time. I'll have John do 087 next. But try to remember this stuff next time, okay? We're not pizza delivery. We handle *expensive* shit."

"Yeah," Phil agreed. "After a good night's sleep, I'll do better. Promise."

He had to admit he was happy to be rid of the safe with the book. He didn't want it talking to him again.

Kera ran up to a pleasant-looking overweight man who strolled down the hall. "Hi, are you John?" she asked. The fear of what might have happened was getting to her. She made no effort to disguise the urgency in her voice.

The man's posture stiffened, and his jolly face fell. "Yes. What's wrong? Also, no offense, but I haven't seen you around here before."

Kera knew the glamour spell was still working. No one had recognized her as the intruder she was. She had not had time to mimic a specific employee, so her "new guy" cover story would have to do.

The drivers carried sidearms and tasers. She could deal with that if she had to, but it was important not to alarm them. "Are you transporting a safe with a book? Odir just said there might be a problem."

John relaxed. "Oh, okay. Yeah, there was a mix-up; he told me about it. I'm taking a couple of other things to Santa Clarita. Muriel's got the book."

He ambled off. Kera followed him, her gut in knots. "Wait! Stop, okay? We need to, uh, examine the safe. We think it might be defective, and someone, um, called in a threat to steal it."

John did stop, and his hand drifted toward his hip. His demeanor had changed; he almost looked dangerous. "Hey, who the hell *are* you? I can't let you interfere with our timeline and poke around in secure materials without authorization, okay? Show some ID, at least, or else come back with the boss. You got a minute before I leave."

Kera ran down the hall.

Fuck, shit, ass, hell, her brain screamed. *This is not going well, is it?*

Once she was around the corner, she stopped. She could keep John from leaving with a sleep spell. Or she could let him go, focus on contacting Lia and Steph, and have Steph start after the other armored car that contained the book. It sounded like the driver had left only a couple of minutes ago.

But that would mean Stephanie would be on her own. Everything would depend on her.

Kera hesitated. She didn't know what to do. There was no spell in her inventory to bestow perfect judgment upon her.

She cast a luck spell on herself, followed by relaxation and speed augmentation charms. It took a toll on her stamina, but not much; she would still have enough energy left to get the job done.

"No," she said to herself, jogging toward the door. "I screwed this up, so I'm going to be the one who fixes it. Only fair. I just need to get outside in time..."

She passed the office. Odir, the dispatcher, yelled "Hey!" and tried to stop her, but she struck him with a quick disorientation spell that took the wind out of his sails.

When she sprinted to the exit, the security guard was on alert and started to draw his pistol. "Hold on," she called. "Someone screwed up my credentials. Let me just..."

When the man hesitated, she cast a moderately strong sleep

spell on him. His eyes rolled back, and he slumped to the floor, unconscious.

I hope the security cameras didn't pick that up, she thought, and a couple seconds later, she was out the door, running across the street and down the block. Stephanie waited next to her car, as well as Kera's motorcycle.

Even with the speed boost she'd cast, getting down the street took longer than it should have.

Stephanie saw her as she approached. "What happened? Lia buzzed me a minute ago to say the place's communications are all screwed up and someone shipped the wrong—"

Kera waved at the bike. "We need to head west." The guy, John, had said he was going to Santa Clarita. If the other one was the truck with the book, it must be headed to Montecito.

Steph held up a hand and tapped her earbud. Kera had chosen not to wear one into the building to avoid the risk of someone seeing or hearing it despite the glamour spell or its frequencies being picked up by scanners.

To Kera's surprise, Steph said, "Hold on, say that all again in about three seconds." She removed the earbud and held it up so Kera could listen in.

Lia's voice was thick with the sinking sensation of disappointment that went along with her calm recognition of undeniable fact. "They went north. They're probably a mile away by now. I have no idea if they're taking an obscure shortcut, dropping something else off along the way, or heading straight for the 118 instead of the 101 as we had guessed. The wrong truck took the right route for the *other* safe, probably, and now they might be switching course."

Kera stood frozen statue-like on the sidewalk, and ignored the weird stares from a couple of passersby across the street.

"*What?*" she exclaimed, her jaw dropping after the word was blurted out. Both eyes bulged, but the lower lid of her right one twitched. "How could that happen? How could we suck this much? If it went the other way five minutes ago, we won't be able to catch up. Fuck!"

Stephanie took a step closer to her friend and laid a hand on her upper arm. "Hey, it's not the end of the world. We know where the guy lives, right? We can go get it from his place. I'm sure that's easier said than done, but it's not like the book is gonna cease to exist just because we couldn't intercept it in transit."

Blinking and shaking her head, Kera tried to banish her useless feelings of rage and frustration and focus on what to do next. "Yes," she murmured, "you're right. Thanks, Steph."

"Don't mention it." Her friend shrugged.

Kera turned toward the nearest wall to be less conspicuous and covered her mouth with her hand as she spoke into the mouthpiece. "All right, change of plans. Lia, we're going to *try* to head them off at the pass or whatever, but that probably won't work. Our likely Plan C is to go to Brimes' house to get it from him. Yes, I know it will be more dangerous. Get me the fastest route there and any information on the place *now*."

"Kera," Lia replied, her voice thin with partly controlled concern and alarm, "we haven't scoped out his house. We know his address, and that's it. We have no idea what the layout of the place is or what kind of security he might have there."

Kera was already motioning for Stephanie to follow her back to Zee. She swung her leg over the seat, and her friend did likewise.

Not trying to be a bitch here, she told herself, *but I don't have time to argue, so Lia needs to knock it off.*

"Well," she said into the mouthpiece just before the roar of the bike's engine made conversation all but impossible, "get on it."

Stephanie had been looking up a route on her phone, and she held the screen out.

Before Lia could say anything else, Kera added, "According to Google Maps, you've got twenty-eight minutes to figure it out while we're en route. Brief me when I ping you back. If anyone can do it, it's you, right?"

She revved the motorcycle to life, and as Steph put away her phone and wrapped her hands around Kera's waist, they sped off, headed for the highway along the coast toward Montecito.

Once her mind was able to back off from the urgent necessity of the task at hand, her consciousness expanded and took in subtle cues and vibes around her.

Stephanie was *pissed.*

Kera tried to ignore it. *Yeah, the message isn't lost on me,* she chided herself. *I goddamn fucking well should have let her handle the cloaking and glamour operation outside and start the pursuit herself. She might have caught up in time. I didn't trust her abilities, and we paid for it.*

Asphalt whizzed beneath the bike's wheels as she wove between cars and ran yellow lights, heedless of cops and people honking at them in anger.

Another conclusion popped into her head. *It sucks being in charge. Sometimes I wish I still worked alone, or me and Steph were just blundering into this together with no backup. Sure, we might have failed even more easily or gotten killed, but it would have made things...simpler.*

Because now, as the boss, I'm responsible for every single thing we screw up.

CHAPTER TEN

John C. Brimes smiled, his hands clasped around the parcel, as he watched the delivery truck rumble down the private drive that led up the hill to his house. The afternoon was fading, and the warmth of the day hovered on the brink of receding before the coolness of night. He paused to enjoy the air, the view, and the anticipation of reading his new book.

But there was no hurry. He left it in its cardboard packaging for now, flipping it between his hands as he strolled back inside and shut the door behind him. Once the door closed, a light beep signified that his security systems were still functional.

"Hmm." He looked the item over. "This packing looks rather cheap and basic for something that came from a high-end auction house. But at least they sent it in a safe within a security truck. Are you okay?"

He asked the question of the book, curious if it would answer. So far, it did not. That was a shame, since what he'd heard about the grimoire suggested that it was alive and possessed its own intelligence. Such rumors were pure nonsense, of course, but they *interested* him all the same.

Brimes had plenty of time these days to pursue whatever

happened to interest him. And plenty of money. Both helped a great deal.

He moved slowly through the lower floor of his sprawling house, trudging up the ultra-modern staircase. His white bathrobe trailed along on the steps behind him, being a size or two too big.

He sighed. "Perhaps I should get out more. See what other people are doing and speak to human beings. I don't do enough of that these days. Virtual business functions don't really count."

He stopped halfway up the stairs, clutching his unopened parcel.

If he left the house, many projects would be delayed and left without proper attention. He had time for his interests now that he was semi-retired, but to indulge them, he had little time for anything else.

There were two carpentry projects in stasis in the extra bedroom on the second floor. One was a bookshelf he was building. That one probably deserved priority since he had taken to collecting rare books, not only on the occult, but on history, automotive repair, carpentry, and psychology. Fascinating subjects.

The other woodworking project was a nightstand. It might hold extra books, as well.

"Yes," he told himself, continuing his climb, "the bookshelf first. That way, after I've read all the books in the stack, I'll have a place to put them. It makes perfect sense."

When he got to his study at the top, there was a message waiting for him. Much to his annoyance, it was from the NSA. They were frustrated with the slow progress on their new security system—deployed as a direct result of Brimes' most recent hacking endeavor—and wanted him to assist.

He scratched his ear. "They have so much power, yet only the vaguest idea of how to wield it most of the time, don't they?

Disturbing thought. They might be better off hiring me full-time again."

But if they did that, his *other* projects would be neglected.

In the garage on the ground floor, he had begun repairing a motorcycle, an old Harley. Technology was his specialty, but he mainly dealt with software, so transitioning to hardware in a different type of machine was an interesting change of pace. He'd found it necessary to keep checking his automotive manuals.

"Hence," he reminded himself, "the bookshelf."

He glanced at the cardboard parcel. "Speaking of which, I'll need to have a look at you soon, won't I? But first," he tapped his lips, "how far along am I on the nightstand? It might be quicker to complete that first, and *then* the bookshelf."

As he thought it over, he had the sudden impression, strange though it seemed, that the book didn't care. It only wanted to be read. Opened.

Brimes chuckled. "I suppose if books could think, that *would* be their primary concern, wouldn't it?"

But before he enjoyed his newest possession, he glanced at the screens showing his various security cameras. He had never had a serious threat at home, but checking for them, just to be safe, was a good habit.

Besides, security was his business.

The growl of Zee's engine quieted to a purr as Kera slowed, leaning over to place her foot on the pavement to compensate for the loss of momentum. The mansion of John Brimes lay at the top of a fairly steep hill and overlooked the town and the ocean beyond.

Stephanie was checking her phone. "Yup, this is the place. Matches the screenshot on Maps. Man, he has a weird-ass house, doesn't he? I guess rich people are eccentric." She paused. "Rich people in California, anyway. I hear wealthy folks back east are a little more traditional."

Kera was tempted to make a joke about her parents, but there wasn't time. Her focus was on getting the book before it acquired a new host.

"What we need to know is how much security he has and how it works. We don't have time to plan everything out again; we're going to have to wing it."

Steph put away her phone. "Yeah, no shit. And when you say we, is that what you really mean? Because you can't afford to leave me out babysitting our ride this time."

Kera scowled. "I know. I'm sorry. We can talk about all that later. For now, we need to get in there."

The house was extremely modern, even avant-garde. Much of it was constructed of glass or transparent polymer as well as stainless steel and blocks of glistening stone that looked like gypsum. It was not so much ostentatious as eccentric; it was less a vulgar display of wealth than a reflection of a quirky mind that sought novelty and amusement.

With so much of it consisting of endless windows in place of walls, concealment would be a problem.

"Fuck it," Kera muttered. "I say we both go with full cloaking. Invisible, with total sound-blockers around us, and we blunder right in. If we set off an alarm, who cares? He'll check and see no one. We'll snatch the book out of his hands before he can read it."

Stephanie examined the mansion. "We're close to the wall. How do we know we're not on camera already? I don't see anything, but he might have some hidden in the bushes."

Both women dismounted. Kera walked the bike down the street past the entrance to Brimes' private drive before she stashed it behind some shrubs, then turned back toward their target.

Kera tried to recall the details of the times she'd infiltrated El Peluquero's operation. Both the first and the second man to claim the title of the Barber had presided over a tight operation security-wise, complete with cameras, alarms, patrolling guards, tripwires, and even snipers, and yet she had managed to sneak into the cartel's bases on multiple occasions.

Brimes did not appear to have a private army. On the other hand, he was a wealthy tech genius. He could afford the best security systems and might have improvised a few things of his own.

Kera shook her head. "We don't have time to stall. Like I said, just the usual stuff to avoid detection. Otherwise, we'll have to wing it."

"Okay." Stephanie shrugged. "I'm coming in too, then?"

Hesitantly, Kera said, "Yes, but I might need you to stay behind at some point, depending on what happens. If so, it's because your skills would be put to their best use somewhere other than right next to me, okay? It's not because I don't trust you or anything like that."

A faint vibe of hostility emanated from her friend, but Steph didn't say anything. They both knew (or Kera hoped Steph knew) that getting the book was more important than their personal issues.

Kera cast spells of visual and aural cloaking around them and they marched toward the estate, finding a thin spot in the bushes where they could climb the wall without disturbing the foliage much. Then each woman cast a physical augmentation spell on herself.

First, Kera jumped to the top of the wall, floating magically into place and scanning the area behind. The sloped yard was landscaped into terraces, and nothing was conspicuous. It was a semi-dark expanse of grassy ridges, trees, stones, and shrubs, beyond which lay the bright transparent walls of the house.

She motioned to her friend, and Steph jumped up as she jumped down. Once they were both on the ground, they hastened toward the side of the mansion. A figure was moving within.

Kera picked up her pace. Brimes, or anyone else who might be there, would be unable to see or hear her, but she wasn't sure about his security systems. They might be capable of picking up her heat signature or something like that.

As they came closer, the witches saw that the person wandering around inside was an average-looking middle-aged man in a long bathrobe. He was making himself a pot of tea. Kera couldn't recall what John Brimes looked like, but the person obviously lived there.

"Hey," Steph whispered. "Kera, look." She pointed at a section of the garden wall they had just passed.

Kera stared, seeing nothing at first, then noticed a tiny blinking light mostly hidden under the leaves of a creeper vine. "Oh, fuck," she growled. "That's either a silent alarm tripwire or a scanner. I can't tell if we set it off, or if it always does that to show it's on and working."

Glancing back at the big window of the kitchen, she saw that the man she presumed to be Brimes had stopped, stiffened, and seemed to be listening for something. Then he abruptly strode out of the room, passing out of her sight.

Kera ran toward the house. "Shit. Pretty sure it was an alarm. We need to get in and out ASAP."

Steph jogged right behind her. When they came to the house's side porch, Steph said, "There's something buzzing weirdly behind us."

Kera did not want to pause, but she didn't have a choice. A small object, little more than a silhouette in the near-darkness, had risen out of the bushes and was moving toward them.

"Drone," said Kera. "Steph, stay here and deal with that damn thing. Do whatever you have to. I'm going in."

She struck the side door with a tiny but concentrated blast of electricity, and it sparked and fell open.

Steph cursed under her breath. "Dammit, Kera! Don't leave me behind again. How do we know—"

The door slammed shut, and Kera was in the house.

For such a big, open place, it had a curiously labyrinthine and oppressive quality from what little she could see. The side door opened into a foyer that was little more than a hallway. To the right was a door that probably led to a garage. The kitchen lay to her left, and she could see the beginnings of a staircase. Brimes might have headed upstairs, perhaps to a panic room.

Did he have the book with him, or was it lying around somewhere? Sucking in her breath, she dashed to the left.

A metal door, seeming to appear out of nowhere, slammed over the opening and a little red light near its top started flashing.

Kera gritted her teeth and looked back. Clicking sounds emanated from the entrance and garage doors, suggesting that they too had been locked by an automatic system.

She headed toward the other end of the hall. Before she was halfway to the garage door, a voice, soft and friendly, spoke to her from a hidden intercom.

"Hello, there!" it announced. "I can see you on the infrared camera, though the regular one seems to be malfunctioning. You won't get into my living quarters before the security company arrives, closely followed by the police, unless you happen to have a pound of C4 with you. If I were you, I'd try to break down one of the other doors, though you might have trouble with that, too. And if you get caught, the property damage will be added to your charges. Sorry!"

Kera thought about trying to burn through the heavy security door, but that might take too long and created a risk of setting the whole house on fire. She might be able to put it out by summoning freezing rain, but it would take far too long.

Instead, she charged the garage door, conjuring a localized dome of kinetic force around her hand, and drove her fist into its center, shouting at the top of her lungs. The door sprang off its hinges and fell with a crash on the concrete floor beyond.

Kera burst into the garage. It was big enough for three cars, though it contained only one: a Prius. The extra space was taken up by a profusion of junk and parts and tools, including a half-completed motorcycle.

There was no time to indulge her curiosity about how skilled Brimes was in the ways of motorbikes. She searched for another door or window leading into the house but saw none.

"Dammit," she rasped. Using magic again, she knocked down the door leading out of the garage to the other side of the mansion, then looked at the nearest window.

Less of the house consisted of open glass on the rear side. Still, there was a big opening not far from her, though she would have to jump a good ten feet to reach it. As she was about to spring toward it, a hidden device in the flowers near her feet sprayed a cloud of gas in her face.

Choking and spitting, she fell back, overcome by dizziness and a coughing fit that gave way to nausea.

Good Lord, this guy's house is like a Bond villain's secret lair or something. Struggling not to collapse or puke or faint, she cast a healing spell of low-moderate strength, though that was still enough to sap half of her remaining magical stamina. She had barely enough for one or two more spells.

As her condition stabilized, she could hear sirens in the distance.

Stephanie ran around the corner. "Are you okay? The whole place is going nuts. He's got this house rigged with shit I've never even heard of. We've got to get out of here."

There was something else. From an indeterminate point within the mansion, Kera could feel magic rising like a dark miasma from an ancient pit. The dead Byzantine wizard was seizing a physical life.

Covering her eyes and trying not to fall to her knees in frustration and despair, Kera let her friend lead her off the property toward where they'd stashed Zee.

They were too late.

John C. Brimes grimaced, blinked, and shook his head.

"So glad *that's* over," he muttered. There was no indication on his security systems that the intruders were still on his property. Things were quiet, just the way he liked them.

As he was about to sit down, his phone rang. It was the security company.

"Mr. Brimes," the man on the other end began, speaking with obvious urgency, "is everything all right? We haven't spotted anyone suspicious nearby, and we're almost there. Hang tight."

John coughed. "Yes, I'm fine. They ran off. I don't think they expected my system to have as many layers as it did, so kudos to your tech people. I made a few improvements of my own, too. Anyway, I don't think it's necessary for you to come into the house. Do a couple of drive-arounds near the property and keep an eye on the cameras and such on your end, and I think all will be well."

Exhaling with relief and speaking more slowly, the security guy said, "That's great to hear, sir. We'll do as you request and update you if we find anything. Call us if you need to. I'd also suggest filing a police report to establish that people have been prowling around your house. It helps in legal cases if there are further problems and they make an arrest."

"Yes, of course. I believe the scanner by the window harvested their phone data and perhaps their IP address, so that should help as well. Thanks." Brimes hung up and put his phone away.

He stretched and the sleeves of his bathrobe fell down to his biceps, then glanced around his study, trying to decide what to do with the remainder of the evening. His eyes settled on the *Grimoire of Viator Psellus*.

"Ah, yes." He smiled, stepped over to it, and opened the cover.

His first impression was of how brittle and grimy the pages seemed, though he only touched them gently and did not notice any negative effects.

His second impression was that the temperature of the book had changed. When he had handled it earlier, it had seemed unusually cold, as though it had been stored in a refrigerator before being shipped to him and the ambient heat of the day had been unable to penetrate the shipping company's safe.

Suddenly, it seemed warm, and he had the brief impression that the book had a pulse like a living thing.

"Brimes," he told himself, "snap out of it. You've been spending too much time home alone. The isolation is getting to you." He closed his eyes, breathed, counted to ten, and then looked at the book again. "It was my own pulse. Still, tomorrow or the next day, I think I'll go out to eat at a nice, crowded restaurant. It will be good to be around people again."

The book's Table of Contents—or what he assumed was a Contents page—intrigued him. It was written in an old-fashioned elaborate script and was not in English. Feeling a bit foolish, he struggled to remember which language the Byzantine Empire had used. Greek?

"I'll figure it out later. Surely there must be someone around I can hire to translate it. Now, let's have a look at the illustrations and diagrams."

He flipped through the pages. Aside from the elaborate calligraphy adorning the first letter of each chapter or section, pictures were few, though he did encounter two depicting types of magical circles to be drawn on the floor of a ritual chamber, replete with occult symbols he did not recognize and paraphernalia that...that...

That looked familiar.

He glanced at the page opposite the second diagram and with no difficulty, read the text. It described a procedure for summoning a spirit who could help a sorcerer locate forgotten sources of wealth. His eyes skimmed it, barely pausing to read the individual words.

It seemed strange that he had been unable to comprehend what he was looking at a moment ago. Now, it was as though he had written it himself. Long ago. It was like seeing something from his childhood his conscious mind had forgotten but which sprang easily back to memory when properly stimulated.

"Ha, yes," he said, and his voice sounded a bit odd; the pitch had deepened half an octave. "I remember this. That cache of gold in...what was that town's name? It was half an age ago, it seems. Odd. So very odd..."

He reflected on his rise to wealth and power. Once the nostalgia trip was over, he found himself curious about and interested in matters of the present. Technology, the field he had mastered—the magic of the modern age.

Brimes sat down at his computer, woke it up, and pulled up a website associated with the company that bore his name. He'd sold it two years ago. He still received briefings and dividends, and he held a nominal position on the Board of Directors, but its day-to-day operations were now the problems of others.

Blankly, his eyes stared at the screen. It all seemed *wondrous* to him. The interplay of lights and patterns. So much information condensed into such a sleek, compact package. Things that would have been impossible a thousand years ago.

His gaze focused on his name, printed in the side margin of the website. John C. Brimes. He blinked. It *was* his name, and he would have to remember that. Important information.

For a moment, he could have sworn his name was Viator Psellus.

CHAPTER ELEVEN

To Chris' surprise, Lia was flipping out.

"Fuck!" she shouted, banging her fist on the dashboard, her hair flying in all directions. "Goddammit. We don't need this. I do *not* need this to be happening right now. We've got to get the hell out of here."

Then she stiffened, fell silent, and glanced around. Her nostrils flared. "Sorry. You didn't see that. Please don't tell anyone. It's...unusual for me to lose control of myself like that."

"Yeah," Chris observed. "I've noticed. Don't worry, I have no idea what you're talking about since I was out taking a piss when it happened."

She managed a smile. "Okay. But we *do* need to leave."

His mouth pursed in anxiety and concern; he still wasn't certain Kera had gotten away safely. "We'll relocate," he decided, "then make contact with them. They'll understand if we need to rendezvous somewhere else, but I don't want to be too far away in case they need help."

Lia agreed. They had been parked in the little community of Summerland, just east of Montecito down the highway. It was far enough away for them to avoid suspicion associated with anything Kera and Steph did but close enough to come to their rescue if necessary.

Chris took them a short way down the road toward LA, intending to stop in the town of Carpinteria. As he drove, he asked, "All right, what happened?" He hadn't been monitoring the computer systems when the shit hit the fan. All he knew was that Kera and Steph had failed to get into the house and had had to abort the mission.

Lia explained the gist of it while he found a couple of parking spaces alongside a line of Carpinteria shops that were closed for the evening on a side street that wasn't seeing much activity. He pulled the Jeep into the nearest one.

"Here." Lia passed him her tablet and pointed at the screen. "Brimes had some kind of scanner that tagged Kera's or Stephanie's phone. If it's hooked into his security system, including links to his cameras and the local police band, it could send the authorities straight fucking to us. We do *not* need that in our lives, Chris. I...I don't want to get caught *now*, not when I'm trying to go straight and be a good person."

Chris was stunned. He grabbed the tablet. "I'll cut off Internet on this thing unless you did that already. No? Okay, well, it couldn't hurt. Um, is there a way we can cover our asses? Like, with an alibi or something?"

Lia was staring straight ahead and taking strong, deep breaths to calm herself. "I'm sure there is, but I can't...wait, we can report a hack. We can talk to someone and say our device was tampered with, so there's a record establishing that we were not responsible for the device when the incident happened. I think. It might not work."

Chris nodded. "And report Kera's phone stolen, maybe? If both those reports conveniently go in right after Brimes reports the incident, it will look pretty damn suspicious." He put a hand over his eyes. "Ugh, this sucks. It might end up being one of those things the girls have to solve with magic. That's the bright side.

We have the means for getting our asses out of this that most people can only dream of."

"True." Lia's hands were clasping and unclasping in her lap. "Chris, thank you for trying to keep a clear head and taking action. Could I have a moment alone, though? Could you pull over somewhere?"

He frowned. "Yeah, okay, just a sec. I wouldn't mind some fresh air myself."

He slipped the tablet into his pocket and nodded at his partner as he unbuckled his seatbelt.

Chris climbed out of the vehicle once it was clear outside: no other cars, pedestrians, or loiterers. Trying to look casual, he wandered toward a bench and took out the tablet.

Too bad I don't have a pack of cigarettes, he lamented. *Not that I smoke, but it would complete the image.*

Then again, there was nothing strange about a man pausing to look at his tablet. The issue was the trench coat. Wearing it, he *should* have been smoking, lungs be damned.

He shifted his hips and felt the weight of the .357 Magnum within its hidden holster. It wasn't enormous as handguns went, with a three-inch barrel and medium-frame construction. But since it was made of steel rather than polymer, it was on the heavier side and bulky enough that it would have been hard to conceal while wearing nothing but a t-shirt and slacks.

Thank God for the barely cooler weather. Clearing his thoughts, he set to work on disabling the device's Internet. Later, he could fuck with the code to make it look like a proper hack. Next, he took out his phone and checked his text messages.

There was one from Kera. He hadn't noticed the buzz while driving. She planned to meet them at her place ASAP and didn't want them to wait for her.

He wrote back, **Okay. Did you find your phone? I thought you said you lost it this morning.** If that confused her, he could explain it after they got home.

Sighing, he returned to the driver's seat, hoping he had given Lia enough time.

She seemed okay, though her eyes were pink around the rims. "All good?" he inquired.

"Yes. Thank you. Where are we meeting Kera and Steph?" She was back in full control of herself.

Chris fired up the engine. "The office. Warehouse. That place. And I laid some groundwork for our sorry attempt at an alibi. Let's hope someone knows a spell that will smooth out the rough parts."

The drive to Kera's place seemed to take an agonizing amount of time. Chris had occasionally joked with people from out of town that the distance from downtown LA to anywhere along the Pacific Coast was *always* longer than one expected it to be, but tonight was the first time he'd felt the effects so acutely.

He and Lia didn't talk much. There wasn't much to discuss until they reunited with their partners and heard the other half of the story.

When they finally arrived at Kera's warehouse, it was getting late. Lia commented, "Kera gave me a spare key. Did she give you one also?"

"What?" Chris marveled. "I'm her *boyfriend*. In other words, no. I'll have to mention that to her. Then again, she might have been planning to give it to me, but you ended up holding onto it while we were on the other side of the country."

He parked in his usual space and they unbuckled themselves, secretly grateful they wouldn't have to wait in the vehicle until Kera returned.

Lia said, "That could be. But yes, it would be more efficient for both of us to have one."

Once they were inside, Chris checked his phone again. There was nothing from his girlfriend, so he sent her a message saying he and Lia were back.

To his pleased surprise, the distinctive growl of Zee's engine approached the building less than ten minutes later. "Nice. Granted, they weren't much farther west than we were."

Lia had gone into the kitchen to make some tea. Though it would not be obvious to someone who didn't know her, she was still fighting anxiety and stress.

Chris peeked out the window to confirm that the approaching motorcycle was Kera. A moment after she dismounted, Stephanie's car pulled up behind her. He opened the door to greet them.

"Hi," he said. "Okay, let's hear the damage report."

Kera took off her helmet, revealing a tight-jawed, sullen scowl. "In a minute. What the hell was that about losing my phone?"

He waved a hand. "Lia and I will explain in a minute. It's an alibi thing. Your phone got scanned, and it's possible our info got beamed to the cops, so we're trying to put together a phony story about our stuff being hacked or stolen."

Kera shook her head. She looked even less happy with the situation than he could have guessed. "I cannot *believe* we fucked up to this extent."

She accompanied him into the warehouse as Stephanie hurried over to join them. "Brimes opened the book. I felt *something* happen, but there wasn't time to determine what. Maybe all that happened was he experienced a wave of spookiness or déjà vu or whatever. Maybe he's now possessed by an insane ancient sorcerer. We'll have to find out later."

Steph, having caught up to them, added, "We might have been able to get the book if both of us had gone into the house from different directions." There was an edge to her voice, and Chris grasped that part of Kera's shitty mood pertained to a disagreement between them.

Lia brought out tea for everyone. "That's worth considering for the future. Right now, we need to deal with throwing the law off our tail. Chris and I did what we could, but our alibi probably won't hold up. You two will need to do something with magic to help us along."

Kera accepted a steaming mug. "Thanks. And yeah, I'm sure I can figure it out. But give me a minute here."

"You mean," Steph interjected, "*we* can figure it out. Isn't that what you mean? Isn't that what we agreed on?" She was trying not to be confrontational, but her eyes blazed with subdued fury. "I want us to find a way out of this, but how the hell can we if you keep trying to do everything yourself and not trusting me…us… to help?"

Chris coughed and looked away. Uh-oh. Kera was reverting to her original style, and that could be extremely bad news in this case.

His girlfriend impressed him by keeping her cool.

"Fine," she declared. "You're right, and I was wrong. What are your ideas on how we deal with this? We need to keep ourselves from getting arrested, *and* we need to find out what happened to Brimes. If it's as bad as we feared, we have to finish what we started and get that goddamn book away from him."

She and Steph were looking into each other's eyes, ignoring the others.

Stephanie inhaled through her nose. "All right, since you're willing to listen to reason again, I have an idea or two."

Doug Lopez and Mia Angel sat on opposite sides of a small table in the corner of the restaurant. They had split a footlong meatball sub, and each had a mug of coffee.

"Not bad." Doug mopped his mouth with a napkin. "Sauce could be a little tangier."

Mia ignored him. Out of boredom, she was using her earbuds to listen to the local police scanner. They hadn't had an independent scoop in far too long. All the stories they had covered in recent weeks were run-of-the-mill stuff handed down by the boss.

Last week, they had been obliged to do a report on a rise in graffiti at a local skate park. It had taken a lot of effort on Doug's part to pretend to be interested, but a paycheck was a paycheck.

It was admirable that Mia continued to monitor the radio for any sign of a scoop. Her official reason was that one never knew when something would come up, and that was true.

But both of them, deep down, were *longing* for a certain black-helmeted vigilante to resurface. That story had been almost overwhelming. They had each devoted a whole chunk of their lives to it, only for it to cruelly blue-ball them and vanish into the oblivion of half-assed, unsubstantiated Internet rumors. MM himself was nowhere to be seen.

His partner yawned and gave him a terse report. "Not much going on tonight so far. A few minor traffic incidents, domestic disturbances, and petty larcenies—that sort of thing. If anything happens close to us, we might as well check it out, but there's nothing that demands our attention."

Doug looked into the distance. "Don't you miss the good old days when bullets were flying all over Los Angeles every night? Wait, don't answer that question."

Mia suddenly tensed. "Hold on," she said, her breaths coming short and sharp. "We've got something. Don't know what yet, but my Spidey sense is tingling. This *has* to be big."

Raising an eyebrow, Doug waited patiently for his friend and co-worker to fill him in on the details. He could barely hear electronic chatter from the earbuds, but it was impossible to make out the details. Instead of trying to listen, he finished his sandwich.

"Mmff. Yeah, the sauce is a touch bland, but the meatballs are fantastic. Next time I'll ask them to use extra Italian seasoning or crushed red pepper if they have it. Good bread, too. Just the right balance between fluffiness and—"

Mia held up a hand. "Quiet. Okay. Yeah…"

When she didn't say anything for a full minute, Doug added, "And firmness. Speaking of marinara sauce, we need to go back to that one bar, the Mermaid, and get their mozzarella sticks again. God, those were amazing."

"Agreed." Mia took out her earbuds. "But, um, yeah. Here's the deal. You paying attention?"

Doug wiped his mouth again and nodded.

"Good. So, there was an incident, apparently a home invasion, up in Montecito. The unincorporated community up the coast, that is, not Montecito Heights."

Squinting in a quizzical way, Doug asked, "Um, so why is the LAPD talking about it? Wouldn't Montecito be, like, um, the Santa Barbara Police?"

Mia smiled. "That's just it. They mentioned a 'Mr. Brimes' and said something about how he's scheduled to be in LA a couple days from now for a conference. They're considering the possibility that it might be a stalking, harassment, or extortion case, and they think whoever's responsible could turn up here."

Doug experienced a faint fluttering in his stomach, a feeling he could only describe as excitement. A hunger that for once had nothing to do with food.

"Well, well. Isn't *that* interesting. Who the hell is Mr. Brimes, though?"

Their waitress reappeared to ask if they wanted refills on their coffee. Both accepted, realizing they might have work to do before the night was out.

Once they were alone again, Mia explained. "Technically, it could be someone else, but I'm guessing it's John C. Brimes, the tech security whiz. He's a millionaire now and semi-retired, but he used to work with the NSA on making all their databases hacker-proof. That type of guy could attract fascinating stalkers. Don't you think?"

"I do," Doug stated. He pointed at Mia's half of the giant sub, which she had devoured only sixty percent of. "Are you going to eat that? If not, either give it to me to polish off quick or ask for a box since I think we ought to get going."

Mia picked up the sandwich and took a single bite, then flagged down their server for a box and their checks. "I'll eat the rest of it later. Sorry."

Doug frowned but accepted his fate.

"Anyway," Mia added, "where do we go first? Montecito to talk to the cops? Or do we sit down at a computer and learn whatever the hell we can about any conferences coming up soon at which Mr. Brimes is one of the honored guests? That would be boring but probably productive."

Her partner scratched his temple. "We could split up and cover more territory. If you want to go up to Montecito tonight, go for it. I'll do the boring computer stuff. I'm kinda...full. Feeling sluggish."

Mia stood up. "You've got yourself a deal. We'll switch duties tomorrow and compare notes." She paused. "What happened to Motorcycle Man? We never got the chance to unmask him."

"Eh," Doug grumbled, "who knows? I think that ship has sailed. Kind of sad, isn't it?"

CHAPTER TWELVE

Mother LeBlanc mopped the sweat from her forehead with the sleeve of her billowing multicolored dress. Though she had spent much of her life in the region, the balmy weather required adjustment after one had lived in a temperate clime. And not everyone was able to adjust equally well.

Behind her, James called, "Hey! Crystal! Is she around? My air conditioning is wearing off, I think."

LeBlanc looked over her shoulder. "She's on the other side of the property, but I suppose she heard you. You will notice, James, that the sun is sinking behind the tree line. The worst should be over by this point."

His face was red and his shirt was drenched at the armpits. "Are you sure about that? Humidity holds in heat, doesn't it? Christ. It's not like the desert, where the temperature plummets thirty degrees after dark."

LeBlanc shrugged. "It might not go down *that* much, but nights are always easier. Keep drinking water."

"I'm out," he said. "That's the *other* thing I could use. Crystal! Can you hear me? Yes, I know I could cast a spell on myself, but I'm still not back at peak functionality, y'know?"

Trying not to chuckle, LeBlanc returned to her work.

The council was transforming the grounds around the old plantation, as well as adjacent sections of the bayou and most of the private drive leading from the road, into a no-man's-land. The newly hostile stretch of territory would, they were quite certain, soon be a battlefield.

No one disagreed about what was coming. No one disagreed about the necessity of making preparations for the hell that awaited them.

Where dissent *had* reared its head was in how to fortify their new base of operations. LeBlanc had stood aloof as two factions formed. One wanted to use a similar approach to the one they had used at James' house in New York, and the other felt that, since the previous tactics had failed, they should try something different.

LeBlanc had waited until everyone had said their piece. Then she had reminded them that the landscape here was different, the Orthodoxy's personnel composition and numbers might be different, and that, most importantly, the Chalice changed everything.

Mary Mitchell, once again presiding over the discussion as the unofficial master of ceremonies, had responded, "Very well, but we have yet to see the Chalice in action. We must have confirmation of its functionality if our plans are to revolve around it. We all sense its power, of course, and we trust you, Mother. But let us do a test run before the eleventh hour."

Everyone had agreed with her, and LeBlanc had vaguely promised to see what she could do that coming evening. They'd all been annoyed by her stalling, but they had moved on to deciding on a defensive strategy that was a compromise between the two factions.

As LeBlanc busied herself using magic to dig pits and trenches and then covering them by hand with woven-grass nets, she paused to glance at the artifact. She had brought it out with her, and it rested on a chair, looking incongruous in the middle of the lawn.

Then she looked at James. It was tempting to make fun of him, but his complaints were legitimate. He was still recovering from the last of his injuries and illness, and the day's long labors were taking a serious toll on him.

Old Jack, she mused, *it would be better if you, in the form of your chosen human guardians, were still here or if you could manifest in your true form to explain the secrets of your gift. I think I know enough. Were it all but impossible to use the Chalice, you would not have given it to us. Getting it was hard enough, was it not?*

The sacred cup collected the residues of magic; the wasted energy, the bleed-off, the by-products. LeBlanc had brought it out on the lawn in the hope and understanding that it would have an easier time scooping up extra magic if it was physically close to a dozen thaumaturges engaged in intense labor and prolonged spellcasting.

She could sense it brimming with power. It was on the verge of overflowing. A smidgen of its reserves could be spared.

Time for a demonstration.

A moment later, Crystal Green appeared around the corner of the house, along with Mary Mitchell and Ezeudo. The Nigerian was carrying a gallon jug of water, which was covered with frost despite the heat, thanks to Crystal's efforts.

"I heard you, James," she called. "This is the fourth time today, but I suppose you need it more than the rest of us do."

James coughed. "Yeah, I'm special. Thanks, though."

LeBlanc wondered why Mary and Ezeudo had accompanied the Duchess. Probably, they were tired or bored and taking a break, helping Crystal for the sake of something different to do. She cleared her throat, catching the attention of all four.

"Excuse me. Crystal, you may commence your cooling spell, but if it's all right, I would like to try a little something."

Mary asked, "Oh? What?" She was not being skeptical or hostile; she appeared to be legitimately curious.

By way of response, LeBlanc waved her hands and turned to the out-of-place chair on the grass thirty feet away on which the brazen cup rested.

Old Jack. Guide me in this. Show me the way and prove how much you care for us to have given us such a mighty gift.

A soft white glow appeared in the mouth of the Chalice, accompanied by a gentle, high-pitched humming. The light grew brighter.

"Whoa!" James exclaimed. "LeBlanc, you're doing that, right? It's not an accident?"

She smiled as a jolt of vitality entered her being. "You are correct."

A faint misty radiance flowed from the blazing cup, looking like the shadow or the ghost of the central light. It coalesced around LeBlanc, and she felt its power submitting to her will as though it were a spell she had cast a thousand times before. It was shockingly easy.

She directed it toward James. He stood still, mouth agape, as the glowing vapor surrounded and enveloped him before sinking into his body. He *absorbed* it.

Mary gasped, "My goodness. It's true, then."

James remained unmoving, slack-jawed and wide-eyed. Then he trembled, and a grin rose on his face. "Hey! I feel great. Damn. Like I just spent a weekend at the health spa." He stretched himself, flexed his arms, and looked as though he might start skipping through the grass. LeBlanc bit her tongue to keep from laughing at such a ridiculous mental image.

Smirking, Crystal asked, "So, I came across the property for nothing?"

"Well," James replied, pretending to be serious, "I *could* still use a little air conditioning boost and a drink of water. Where the hell is my cup? Oh, there it is. But I don't feel...haggard anymore.

Since I stopped spending all my time in bed, it's like every day is one of those mornings where you have to go to work on too little sleep. Now it's just...*gone.* I feel normal again."

Ezeudo nodded. "It is incredible. Is it a relic of healing, then?" He stared at the Chalice, whose white glow was dying down to a faint shimmer.

LeBlanc interposed herself. "Not exactly. To be honest, I do not know all the ins and outs myself, only that it stores our magical waste and returns it to us when we need it."

"Nice," said James. "Like, how the government generously refunds us a lump sum of our own money in the form of tax returns."

Chuckling, LeBlanc elaborated, "A bit like that, perhaps. But I do not believe that the Chalice is meant to be understood the way we comprehend our usual magic. Thaumaturgy is a *scientific* form of magic. Old Jack came from an older intuitive tradition. We are all miracle workers, used to specifying the nature of our miracles. With the Chalice, I think that we must trust our benefactor to provide whatever miracle we require most at that particular moment."

As Ezeudo and Crystal saw to James, Mary went over to LeBlanc. "Mother. I am convinced, and I'll tell the others we have proof of the Chalice's efficacy. This is wonderful news. Do you know how much of its power you drew upon just now? How much is left?"

LeBlanc furrowed her brow. "Though I cannot say for certain, I sensed the Chalice was nearly overflowing when I called upon it, and I requested only a small amount. Its full strength is likely far beyond the minor rejuvenation effect it had on James."

For a second, Mary's face showed superstitious awe bordering on dread. She, like all of them, was a master of the arts of magic. Yet they had been forced to confront the fact that there were things in the world they could barely understand.

"Astounding. It could well turn the tide of battle for us." Mary took a step closer. "Might each of us call on it in turn, or is that your exclusive privilege?"

LeBlanc shrugged. "When we are finished with our preparations for the day, we'll have everyone give it a try, though we don't want to use up too much of its stores. Old Jack allowed me to have it on the grounds that I am the last link to the relic's original line of caretakers. Since you are my friends and allies whose cause I serve, I see no reason it should be forbidden to you."

Mary nodded, and they turned to their other three companions.

Crystal had, at last, perfected a spell that continually circulated air around a person in a sphere about six feet in diameter. The slight breeze passed through fixed points of coldness above the individual's head, which kept it at a nice, brisk temperature. She completed the renewal of the enchantment around James.

He sighed as it took effect. "Much better. Thanks a bunch, Crystal." He raised his cup, allowed Ezeudo to fill it with water, and drank.

The Nigerian turned his eyes toward LeBlanc. "Mother. You say this Chalice will give us the miracle we need. Does that mean..." he hesitated as though embarrassed by what he was going to ask, "we could call upon it *now* to simply defeat the Orthodoxy before they reach us?"

James blinked. "Now, *that* is a good question. What say you, LeBlanc?"

LeBlanc raised a slim dark hand to her lips, and her eyes went vacant. "I do not know. But somehow, I suspect we cannot use it in that way. Though our cause is just, given that we are certain of the Orthodoxy's malevolent intentions, I doubt the Chalice could be used in such an aggressive fashion. It is meant to be used for defense rather than attack, the last resort of the virtuous when evil possesses the upper hand."

"Well," Mary commented in a low voice, "we would never have contemplated destructive action against another coven *except* in circumstances like the present. In my opinion, such an aggressive spell is a last resort. Perhaps we can discover that when we experiment with it tonight."

LeBlanc hesitated while the others watched her and awaited her input. "I will study it and see if I can uncover its will on the matter, but it's too powerful for us to risk anything drastic when our need is not immediate. The higher powers in the universe are greater than we are in most regards, but they can also be simple-minded by human standards. Obliterating an adversary in advance, even one we *know* will slaughter us if they can, might be beyond the Chalice's understanding."

"Damn," James said.

One other thing popped into LeBlanc's head as the others were about to return to the day's last round of fortifications work. "Wait. I just remembered. Though I cannot put my finger on it, I perceived not long ago that the Orthodoxy had been weakened. Possibly, it is wishful thinking or a faulty reading of complex data, but if they are not as strong as they were the last time we met, the Chalice will be that much *less* likely to allow us to use it as an offensive weapon. It exists to restore balance, not to provide unfair advantages."

Ezeudo closed his eyes. "I believe I understand. And this council exists to maintain a balance in the world of magic, does it not? Yes."

"So be it," said Mary. "All you have said thus far about the Chalice has proven true and valuable. We trust you, and we will have faith in it."

James pouted but did not object. "Agreed. I was hoping we could pull off some sweet Ark of the Covenant melting action against those fuckheads, but that would make us only slightly better than them. Still, if this nice old house ends up even *half* as damaged as *my* house did," he cocked an eyebrow at LeBlanc, "your friend will have to settle accounts with Old Jack, won't they?"

"I'm sure we can cross that bridge when we come to it. Now, since you troubled Crystal for a cooling spell, you'd best get back to work. I'll do the same."

James sighed and turned back to the compression traps he had been laying, the spellcraft for which could be prepared in advance before the final charm activated them at the appropriate moment. "Fine. Seriously, though, I feel like I could work all night. Maybe we can get the Chalice to rebuild my mansion?"

LeBlanc laughed. "That might be worth a try. I cannot promise anything, though."

Niah and Calvin sat together on the porch, watching the mixed light of dawn transform gradually into the full blaze of day. The thick mists of the bayou began to dissipate under the sun's increased intensity.

Sipping her coffee, Niah stated, "It's gonna be a hot one again. Summer's lasting a long time this year."

Her husband nodded. "I do believe you're right. Folks in other countries always say that when it's a bad year, it's like *winter* never ended." He chuckled at the thought.

Slowly, stretching his limbs and hearing his joints creak and crack, he got to his feet. "Think I'll head into town and pick up..."

Niah heard his voice trail off. She looked up and saw Calvin's gaze wander across the boggy fields toward the haze of humid heat that obscured the horizon. Toward the highway, which wasn't far away.

He said, "Something's wrong. Can you feel it?"

Niah stood and moved to his side. "I believe I can. What is it? Just a feeling of...*wrongness*, ain't it? Like a storm coming, but worse."

It was often said that women were stronger in the gift than men, but the two of them were among the rare exceptions.

Though Niah had abilities of her own, her man was a step or two ahead of her when it came to perceiving things. Obscure things most folks would have called *magic*.

Calvin's face was grave. "Yeah, like a storm. One that's headed toward the Old House. Or maybe not."

Niah took his hand. "Want me to come with you? Into town." It was less that she feared for herself than that she knew he would worry if he left her alone.

"I believe that would be best," he agreed. "Don't take too long getting ready."

She scoffed as she gathered their empty cups to take to the kitchen. "Don't go getting me confused with my younger self. I ain't need much makeup these days."

Three minutes later, the old couple stood beside their truck, about to climb in, but they paused at the sound of approaching footsteps. They looked at the dirt road which led to their home.

A youngish white couple appeared at the bend in the path and strode casually down it, holding hands and moving in near-perfect unison. Nothing seemed to be amiss, but there was a faint uncanniness to it, as though the two did not belong there.

And not only because they were trespassing.

Calvin glanced into the bed of the truck, where his loaded shotgun lay under a tarp within arm's reach. Then he looked at their unexpected visitors. "Excuse me. Can I help you? Me and my wife own this land."

The two newcomers stopped. The woman raised a hand, waving slowly. "Oh, hello. We were taking a walk and got a bit lost. We didn't realize this was private property. We were just looking for something."

She spoke in a dreamy way, as though not cognizant of what was happening around her. The accent was Southern but not Louisianan. Maybe somewhere in Appalachia.

Her partner added, "We heard about an old plantation. A lot of folk tales about it. We like to see stuff like that all over the country. Paranormal things. Have you heard of a place like that nearby?"

He had the same accent as the woman and spoke in the same odd fashion, though there was an underlying tension in his delivery as though he was in a bad mood but was trying to be polite. Or trying to say more than his words implied.

Niah stepped closer to Calvin. "Well," she called, "I'm afraid we don't know nothing about that. There's a lot of old stories about this whole region, you see. We wish you luck. Maybe go look it up on the Internet so you can get an exact location for whatever place you want?"

The couple didn't reply. After two or three heartbeats, they continued their slow, steady approach.

Calvin frowned at them. "Hey, now. This is private property. You folks seem nice enough, but we was just about to head into town. No offense, but you don't have no reason to be here."

Both strangers paused, then kept walking. Their movements were perfectly synchronized.

The woman said, "We're sorry, but we can't leave until we find out more about that house. We heard about it in town."

Calvin reached under the tarp and pulled out his shotgun, a double-barrel that had belonged to his father. It was ancient but it still worked, and the buckshot-filled shells were new and high-quality. "You can leave." He kept the barrels aimed at the ground but cocked both hammers.

The white couple didn't stop. Niah looked from them to her husband. "Calvin, do something. Not with the gun. Something *else*. Those two *have got it*. Can't you sense it?"

Without warning, the young man twisted away from his partner, grabbed her by the sleeve and threw her to the ground, and barked, "Run! We're being forced. They're going to—"

The air split and there came a terrible cracking noise and a flash of light. Niah feared her husband had opened fire, but the initial shock dispelled that notion as quickly as it had come.

A bolt of lightning had fallen from the clear sky and struck the young man dead-on. His smoking corpse tumbled to the earth and lay still. The woman, his wife or girlfriend, stood frozen and staring at him, twitching as though she wanted to fling herself beside his body but was being held back by an invisible force.

Calvin gasped, "Niah, get in the truck. *Now.*"

Neither of them was as fast as they'd been thirty years ago, but Niah surprised herself with her speed in leaping into the passenger's seat. Calvin waited till she was behind the truck's closed door, holding his shotgun at half-ready, before he climbed into the driver's seat.

As he turned the keys in the ignition, figures coalesced at the fringes of their property as though emerging from fog, though by now, the morning mists had evaporated.

The engine started without trouble and Calvin stomped on the gas pedal, sending the truck bouncing down the dirt road. He swerved to avoid the poor woman and the dead man. The figures encircling the property closed in.

"Earth," said Niah and closed her eyes.

Calvin nodded. "Earth."

They had learned long ago to collaborate on certain acts. The two of them being among the few who could do such things had made it easier to bond.

Sheets of mud, dirt, and rock rose from the ground beside the road, rushing outward in rippling waves toward the ring of intruders. Niah heard one of them cry out in alarm.

Then a gale-force wind knocked the earthen waves aside and struck the rusty vehicle, knocking it off the road. Calvin struggled to control it, and it came to a sudden stop two feet from a tree. He worked the gas, the gear shift, and the steering wheel to no avail. The truck was immobilized.

There were fifteen of the mysterious trespassers, and they were only ten yards away. Most were white, but one or two looked Asian. They dressed in a semi-formal but unremarkable way that seemed inappropriate to the muggy swelter of rural Louisiana.

The exception was a woman Niah instantly identified as the group's leader. She was extremely pale, with black hair and long black fingernails, and her dress, tight around the torso but loose and billowing below the waist, looked like something out of a play or a historical movie.

None of them carried weapons but all had intense, powerful, and hostile auras.

Niah's heart was having trouble beating regularly. She clutched her husband's arm. Calvin, for his part, was looking at the floor of the truck and breathing in and out through his nose. "Okay," he said in a tone of deep resignation, "guess I'll talk to them."

He opened the door and slid off the seat, drawing himself up to his full height and tossing back his shoulders. "I'm Calvin Grandis. This is my home. Who are you people, and what do you want?"

The pale woman smiled in a way that made Niah's skin crawl. "Hello, Calvin Grandis. My name is Anezka. We want what Dan and Mindy said they wanted. To know the location of this house in the swamp, which people in the city say has such a long and interesting history. It would have been easier if you had answered *their* question. Now you must answer to *us*."

Her accent was Eastern European, though she was fluent in English. Behind her, another witch was forcing the captive woman, the one who'd been used as a decoy, forward. Tears streamed down her face.

Calvin hesitated.

Anezka took a step closer, not to him but to the truck. She looked at Niah. "And this must be your wife. Do not pretend you know nothing about the house. According to the people we interviewed, it belongs to your family. So sad that none of them knew its location. If they had, we might not have needed to come here. We *will* have the information we seek. You will...what is the expression...do it the easy way or the hard way. Now is your chance for the easy way."

A tall, gaunt-faced man moved closer to Niah, scowling at her and flexing his hands.

Calvin shook his head, and his wife saw the sadness on his face. "It sounds like we will end up helping you whether we choose or not, so I'll tell you this. It is God's honest truth that I have never been to that house. I know only the general neighborhood."

"Hah!" The gaunt man scoffed. "You will pay for every lie."

Anezka held up a hand to keep him from doing anything. "No, I believe he is telling us the truth. Tell us, then, where is the general neighborhood?"

Niah allowed herself a moment of relief. What her husband had said was no lie; he had inherited the house, but had no use for a large place far from the city and in need of expensive repairs. He occasionally rented it to his friends, such as that strange but charming woman who always wore the colorful dress. Niah could never remember her name.

Calvin exhaled before looking up. "I will tell you willingly, but only because it won't matter. You won't win at what you're trying to do. Probably, all of you people are going to end up at the bottom of the swamp."

Anezka's eyes flashed, and Niah flinched.

"You and your wife will be spared in exchange for your cooperation. But after we have won, I will *remember* you said that."

CHAPTER THIRTEEN

Mr. Kim's mouth was full, so he waved his hand, still holding a fork, at his son, indicating that he could go.

Sam nodded. "Thanks, Dad." He pushed his chair back and stood up from the dinner table, taking his empty plate, teacup, and utensils to the sink. Then he left the dining room and headed to his bedroom to gather his things before leaving for the evening.

Mr. Kim swallowed the last of his food and said to his wife, "I am too indulgent with him, don't you think? I should have checked to make sure his homework was done before letting him run off like that. He might have only completed eighty-five percent of the assignment and figured he could skid by with a B instead of trying for an A."

Ye-Jin gave a dry chuckle and sipped her tea. "He is usually good about taking care of his duties before he goes off with his friends. Besides, even if he is not done, if he gets back early enough, he will finish the last of it before class."

Her husband shrugged. He started to get up, but Mrs. Kim put a hand on his forearm to keep him in place, then gathered their dishes and took them to the sink.

"Well," Mr. Kim remarked, "I am glad you're feeling well today, but you don't have to do everything. Unless you plan to tell me that you *enjoy* washing dishes. How could anyone enjoy that? Cooking is one thing. Dishes are another."

"Be quiet. Dishes are not so bad. They go by quickly once I begin as long as everything has time to soak first."

Mr. Kim grunted, then stared at the wall. He found himself wondering how Kera was doing, but it would be pointless to ask out loud since Ye-Jin knew no more than he did.

He wondered what kind of trouble she was getting into *this* week. It was always something.

Mrs. Kim seemed to sense his thoughts. "I felt something strange last night. It was faint and distant, but it seemed as though it was connected to us. Connected through someone else. It did not seem good, but signs and echoes can be deceiving. We never know what they mean until their effects unfold before our eyes."

Ceramic clanked and water sloshed. Mr. Kim kept his eyes on the wall.

"I believe I noticed it too. It's probably something to do with Kera. She is all over every weird thing that happens in Southern California like flies on shit."

Mrs. Kim made a wordless sound of disapproval. "That is not generous of you to say."

"Bah," he replied. "It's not an insult. *Someone* has to deal with that stuff, don't they? I hope she's okay. I also hope that whatever problems she is stirring up do not find their way back to us. She is like our second child, but I look forward to the day when things in LA are nice and peaceful again, even if it means that she has to suffer boredom. Ha-ha."

His wife rinsed her hands. The dishes needed to spend a few minutes in the hot, soapy water before she began to scrub them. "You might be right."

Half an hour later, as the aging couple relaxed in their living room, someone knocked on the door—the *back* door that led into the stairwell that ascended to their living quarters.

Mr. Kim got to his feet. "I'll get it. Stay here."

Ye-Jin squeezed his hand. "It is someone with the gift. I can feel it. It is not Kera, though. Please be careful."

He hesitated, then went to the window and peeked through the curtain. Since it was dark out, the residual light from the street that filtered into the back alley did not allow him to see much, though he thought he could discern a slender silhouette standing below. They would almost certainly have seen the curtain on the second-floor window open.

Steeling himself, he exited the room and went down the stairs. Once he reached the bottom, he flicked on the rear porch light and saw his guest through the window in the door.

Shaking his head, he opened the door and stepped out. "Oh, it's you. I will not lie; I am not happy to see you."

Pavla's smile was rueful. "I understand. I am, as you might say, a bearer of bad tidings. There is nothing terrible to discuss yet, but I must speak to you all the same. May I come in? We will have more privacy indoors."

Mr. Kim wasn't enthusiastic about letting the European witch into his home. He thought he had seen the last of her many weeks ago when she had gone on the run after her falling-out with her former employers.

"Very well, come in. You did give us those charms, after all. They seem to be working well. Thanks for that. As for restoring our powers, well, we only did that to keep Kera happy. My wife and I did not miss them much."

Pavla followed him in, and they stayed at the bottom of the stairwell. Above them, Mrs. Kim's soft footsteps came out of the living room.

Mr. Kim looked up. "It's Pavla. Remember her? She has more bad news."

Ye-Jin leaned over the banister and nodded at the strange woman.

Pavla seemed too absorbed in her own aloof sadness to be nervous or awkward, which was a relief. Whatever troubled her, it didn't suggest immediate danger.

Mr. Kim waited for her to speak. She was a trim woman on the attractive side of average, with brown hair and an undeniable sense of style he attributed to her Europeanness. Czech, if he recalled correctly. She looked to be in her early to mid-thirties, but he perceived that she was closer to his age, perhaps even older.

"Mr. and Mrs. Kim," she began once she had collected her thoughts, "I fear that things will soon become more dangerous than ever. Is your son here?"

"No," Mr. Kim replied, and his protective instincts kicked in. "He is with his friends. If I should call him home, say so *now*."

Pavla held up a hand and shook her head. "No, the storm is not here yet, but it is coming. I wanted to warn you of that and also to ask about Kera. I think she and I must see each other again."

Mr. Kim was about to lean against the post propping up the stairs but thought better of it. "Come up into the living room. No offense, but I wanted to have this conversation down here. However, it is too uncomfortable. I'd rather hear this with a proper couch under my ass."

Pavla smiled and agreed, then followed him up to the sitting room. When they arrived, Mrs. Kim watched her attentively but without hostility. Both Koreans could sense the aura of their guest's intentions, which held no wish to do them harm.

Once they were settled in, the Czech explained, "The Orthodoxy, my former comrades in arms, have launched a war against the council that controls magic in North America. They drove them away from the East Coast, and I believe they are now in the Deep South. Whatever happens next, there are two things you must understand. One, the Orthodoxy has marked Kera for death. Two, they mean to rule *all* magic users on this continent, which includes you."

Mrs. Kim's gaze darkened, and Mr. Kim put a hand over his face. "Oh, that is lovely, isn't it? We will have to thank Kera again for turning us back into magic users. Pardon me; for some reason, I am not in a good mood."

"I understand," Pavla said. "But that leads me to bring up the other thing. If I can speak to Kera, she and I can perhaps work out a solution. But I don't think she would be happy to see me. No one is anymore."

Her voice cracked on the last sentence. Ye-Jin, seized by empathy, went over to the woman and rested a hand on her shoulder. "You will find a place for yourself," she assured her. "In time."

Pavla put a hand over Mrs. Kim's. "I hope you are right. Thank you." She had managed to keep herself from crying, though her eyes shimmered. "I have been...away. I wandered across much of this country, looking for a place where I could settle if the Orthodoxy is defeated and there is a chance for peace. Or I might return to Europe; I don't know."

She paused, touching her nose as she sniffled, then added, "But my problems are not yours. I am able to speak to Kera via magic if I must, and I know where she lives and can find the place easily. But I hesitate to do so."

Mr. Kim surmised, "You want us to play middlemen and contact her on your behalf because you feel weird about it. Yes, got it. I suppose we can do that, but only if she is willing to talk to you. I draw the line at passing fifty messages back and forth between you. It's unfair to put me in the middle of an argument."

Pavla shook her head again. "You are right. Please ask her if she will see me."

Mrs. Kim nodded.

Her husband agreed. "I'll call her in the morning. *Late* morning. Her sleep schedule is ridiculous, even though she doesn't work for a bar anymore. In return, promise you will let us know if there is any danger. You seem like a nice lady, and I would not want you to come to harm. Or Kera, of course. But Sam has to come first."

"Of course." Pavla, for all her knowledge, vast powers, and classy demeanor, was as bashful as a young girl in her gratitude. "I appreciate this so much. Do not worry about how to contact me. I will come to you if I have anything important to share. And if Kera agrees to speak to me, tell her she knows how to contact me."

Mr. Kim shrugged. "Okay. Is there anything else?"

The Czech hesitated. Now that she was regaining control of her emotions, her poker face was back, but Mr. Kim saw through her. There *was* something else, and she was debating whether or not to divulge it.

"Yes," she finally admitted. "There is another development. I am still not certain what it is, but a force of magic has been unleashed here or somewhere nearby in California. Ancient, powerful, and perhaps extremely dangerous. I have my suspicions, but it would be useless to speculate before I have proof. It's another thing I wish to discuss with Kera. She is one of the few who can take care of it if it is what I think it is."

Grumbling, Mr. Kim replied, "You are extremely vague at times. In fact, my wife and I were just discussing that we felt something strange the other night. Difficult to say what. Could that be what you are talking about?"

Pavla stood up. "I do not know, but I mean to find out. I will fulfill my promise to warn you of any threats and help you if I can. Please, contact Kera and let her know I'm sorry and I want to help her."

The Kims exchanged glances. Ye-Jin declared, "We will."

CHAPTER FOURTEEN

At Kera's suggestion, everyone had spent the night at her place. For about ten seconds, they had seemed less than enthusiastic about the idea, but she had reminded them that going home meant they would have to drive back in the morning.

"Okay," Chris had said, "but most of us get up at, like, 'normal' time, so it's only fair for you to get up a little earlier than usual so we're not all waiting around at 10 a.m. Besides, the sooner you're up, the sooner we can have breakfast."

Grudgingly, Kera had agreed and gone to bed early, setting her alarm for 9:30.

At present, it was 10:17, and she was halfway into her second cup of coffee.

"Okay," she began, "the first part was easier than expected, so *that's* good. But that still leaves the problem of Brimes and the grimoire. Maybe, just maybe, that will turn out to be a big nothingburger, but if it isn't, it could be incredibly bad."

Lia guzzled coffee. She still seemed nervous about the prospect of cops, lawyers, judges, and other such representatives of the law coming after her. If she was arrested, her criminal past might come to light, adding years or decades to any prison sentence she might garner.

"Are we *certain*," Lia queried, "your enchantment will work? Neither of you has ever done anything like that."

Stephanie piped up. "Ain't no guarantees in life, Lia. But Kera and I have been doing this for long enough that I'm pretty confident about it. What about you?" She looked at her friend and new boss.

Kera had crossed her arms. "Well, the spell clung to the report. It sounds odd since you don't think about magic affecting intangible things, but it's not much different from attaching a virus or a piece of malware to an email. It's just a question of how big the effect will be on the officers who read it."

"And," Steph added, "in the past, we've had good luck with influencing, you know, normal people. If we get a cop who has the gift or is into psychic stuff, *maybe* they'd have the mental strength to resist it, but probably not."

Specifically, the charm would convince the police officers who handled their hacking and stolen phone reports that there was an error, and they would then "correct" it by backdating both reports to well before Brimes had experienced the home invasion.

Lia nodded. "Okay. I hope you're right. But if the law comes after us, that is something we *must* deal with. In fact, I think we might need an employee contract that specifies," she cleared her throat, "the agency will hire a defense attorney if we are taken to court in the course of doing what the agency demands."

Kera grimaced. She didn't want to be bothered with stuff like this right now, but Lia had a point. "In other words, if I make you break the law and we get caught, it's my responsibility to bail you out of jail and see to it that you have legal representation. That's...fair, and I give you my word we'll work on something like that soon. But right now, we have to focus on the job."

Chris had stayed silent thus far. "While I agree that dealing with the Brimes situation is important, don't forget the well-being of the people who *do* the job is crucial."

Kera's hand tightened around her coffee mug.

For fuck's sake. Am I doing that much wrong? Am I that much of a bitch all of a sudden? It's like no one is on my side anymore.

She kept her thoughts to herself, though. "I couldn't do it without you guys. You mean the world to me, and that's not just glad-handing, let alone an exaggeration. Still, let's at least get a better idea of how bad this grimoire situation is before we get distracted."

They agreed, but she suspected they weren't going to let it go. She would have to deliver on her promises and soon.

The group laid out the obvious strategies. Kera and Steph would perform psychic searches, checking the astral plane for weird disturbances in the regional flow of magic. Lia and Chris would comb through reports of unusual things happening in the Santa Barbara area or any news regarding Brimes or his company.

That left the prospect of physically removing the book from his custody.

Kera had an idea, but it pained her to admit it for more than one reason. "Hey," she began, attempting not to cringe, "I know this is going to sound odd coming from me, but I think we should bring Pavla on board for this one."

Chris blinked and readjusted the position of his head as though trying to get a second look at something that had made him doubt his eyes. "*Pavla?* Is she still in America at this point? Do either of you *want* to see the other? I mean, yeah, you had that ESP conversation on the train, but that was different."

Stephanie and Lia were silent for the moment, but Steph's face showed her doubt. Lia's was neutral.

"No," Kera protested, "it *wasn't* different. She helped me, and there weren't, um, too many hard feelings. I think. She helped you guys with those emails too, right? She's still on our side. As to where the hell she is, I don't know, but it would not be hard to find out. We need someone who, to put it bluntly, is better at magic than Steph or me. We're pretty good, but Pavla is an order of magnitude beyond us. We might need someone on that level if the grimoire is as powerful as the rumors say."

Steph held up a hand. "Hold on a second. The two of us damn near beat Pavla in a duel, remember? And that was back when we knew less and had less experience than we do now. Is she *that* much better? Are we going to hold everything up to wait for her when we could just have the two of us work together?"

Kera fidgeted. This again. *She's not going to let it go until I let her resolve a situation for me and take the limelight, is she?*

"You may have a point." She glanced absentmindedly at her phone. "First, let's see if we can come up with a plan that involves the four of us, and if we think there are any weaknesses in it, we can consider adding Pavla to the equation."

Lia pointed out, "She's knowledgeable, but I agree that the logistics of waiting for her if it turns out she's in Sweden would create a lot of problems."

They spent another half-hour outlining a potential strategy for going after Brimes if they obtained evidence that Viator Psellus had indeed possessed him.

Kera had another idea. "He has a private security firm protecting him. We may have screwed up the whole thing where we infiltrated the armored car company, yeah, but it would have worked with a couple of adjustments. This time, we can pose as members of his security team. It would minimize how much we need to rely on magic, and we'd potentially get access to a shit-ton of information that could help us weave through the cracks in his system."

Chris raised his eyebrows and gave an appreciative nod.

"Hmm, yeah. Not to mention we might be able to finagle some of the data pertaining to our failed break-in in case there's any lingering stuff that might implicate us. That sounds bad, doesn't it? Oh, well."

Steph commented, "It would've been better if we didn't have to do stuff like that, but yeah. We've got to get the book. If we have to break the law, we'll unbreak whatever we can after the fact."

Kera saw that Lia was more aloof than usual. She disliked the situation but was trying not to bring her feelings into the equation.

"Right," Kera affirmed. "Let's focus on infiltrating his security, then. We'll be careful about it and have the means in place to cover our tracks and cause as little harm and disruption as possible. Furthermore—"

Her phone rang. Frowning and turning away from the group, Kera pulled it out and saw that it was Mr. Kim. She contemplated letting it go to her voicemail so she could call them back after the meeting, but...

No. She swiped the green icon and held the device to her face. "Hi there."

"Hi, Kera. I hope you are awake and I didn't disturb you. Do you have a few minutes to talk about something?"

She glanced at her friends, who had overheard, then stepped away. "I have a couple minutes. I'm doing stuff with the agency right now, but it's always nice to hear from you, and if it's important, I will make the time."

"Yes, pretty important. Last night we had a visitor. Pavla. You remember her?"

Kera's eyes widened, and her abdominal muscles clenched. "Yes. I remember her. What did she want?"

"To speak with you. In person, I think, though she said something about contacting her through magic if you were willing to do that. She is worried about all of us and said she wants to help. Something about those witches she used to work for coming after her…and you. And also how she felt a new source of power appearing nearby and was concerned about it. Ye-Jin and I felt it, too. She feels bad about what happened between you. I told her it wasn't my place to force you to do anything but I would pass on the message."

Kera hesitated. "This thing about a 'new power.' Did she say anything else about it?"

"No, not really." Mr. Kim's voice suggested he knew more than he was letting on, but he would not keep important information from her if it might lead to her getting hurt or in trouble. He must be waiting for more information before he leaped to conclusions.

Grimacing, Kera replied, "Okay. I'll agree to meet her again soon. We're kind of busy, but maybe she can be of help. I'm sure it will be," she sighed, "awkward, but I'm starting to trust her again. I think. Thanks for calling. Are you guys doing okay?"

Mr. Kim reassured her that he, Mrs. Kim, and Sam were all fine. He also mentioned that he would take everyone to Sacramento if things got dicey.

"I understand," Kera informed him. "The last thing I would ever want is for you or your family to get hurt as a result of something I'm involved with. Again, thank you. I'll come see you when I can, and I'll get in touch with Pavla."

They said their goodbyes and hung up. Kera chewed on a fingernail before she spun back toward her friends and co-workers.

Lia stated, "We overhead much of that. Is it something to do with Pavla? That's the impression I got, but I didn't hear enough to be certain."

Kera nodded. "It sure is. And since we had considered asking for her help anyway, I guess I'd better get in touch with her. Let me get that out of the way first, then we'll go back to the plan."

Everyone agreed, and while the rest of them continued to hash out ideas for how to slip Kera and Steph into Brimes' security detail, Kera sat on her bed facing the wall, cleared her mind, and prepared herself emotionally to speak to an old friend.

Or whatever Pavla was at this point.

CHAPTER FIFTEEN

"My name," said the man who looked like John C. Brimes, "is...what is it again? No, it's *not* Viator Psellus. Not supposed to be, in any event. Heh, heh. We all know who I really am, but it's supposed to be...Brimes. John Brimes. Yes, that's me."

A smile spread slowly across his face, and he bowed his head before his image in the mirror.

His new body was not impressive, but in the past, he had done excellent work with mediocre-looking people. Brimes was an unassuming middle-aged man, not so different from Psellus many hundreds of years ago when he had "died" for the first time.

A person's knowledge, wisdom, resources, and power had nothing to do with their appearance. The man whose body was now his, Brimes, possessed all of those things in tremendous quantity.

By now, Psellus had had time to review the contents of his host's brain. Much of it was only half-comprehensible to him. The advances in magic—technology—that had taken place over the last century were incredible. The pace of social and scientific change had accelerated almost beyond the capacity of humans to keep up with it.

Still, he had gained a good working knowledge of who Brimes was and the role he played in the present American society.

He was considered a genius, a great weaver of technological spells, a creator of useful and highly advanced devices. He had grown rich running a mercantile operation that sold his inventions, and he was also a friend of the country's leadership, including its secret police and military establishment.

He had money of his own—a great deal of it—and he had access to the most advanced weaponry and security systems in the United States. If Psellus was not mistaken, he had claimed the mortal form of an individual who did not need permission to examine the government's most potent secrets.

Soon, Viator Psellus would teach John Brimes to read his grimoire and practice the magic contained within it as well as the sorcerer had in his original time. Brimes would teach Psellus the ways of computers.

They sat down at Brimes' desktop PC and stared at the glowing screen.

Viator Psellus had long prided himself on his ability to make informed and reasonable decisions. He did not, generally speaking, leap into doing anything stupid, but there had been exceptions. Some of the schemes he had pursued over the centuries had also carried a certain amount of risk.

To ascertain how much risk, the first thing he did was go to whatever option seemed the most foolish, the most overwrought —the one that was the height of madness.

Occasionally, madness ended up being the best way to accomplish his goals.

A faint tingle of excitement formed in the pit of his belly. It was a familiar feeling that had accompanied him during his most momentous discoveries in the ancient arts of sorcery, not to mention when he had done risky things like encourage that man,

Gavrilo Princip, to go through with his assassination plot against Archduke Ferdinand. A mistake, perhaps, but the results had been so *interesting*.

Psellus receded and loosened his hold on John Brimes. The Byzantine wizard was still in control, but he left the specifics to his host, giving him general directions and hovering in the background while Brimes did as he was told.

His fingers moved across the keyboard, and the words and numbers and backlit images on the flat screen changed. As per Psellus' instruction, Brimes had entered the Pentagon's computer systems in search of access to the US military's most powerful and fearsome weapons.

The consciousness of Psellus watched, analyzing the information processed by his host-servant to the best of his ability. He took note of the emotional echoes that came from what little remained of Brimes' will and personality. The man had a particularly interesting reaction to the phrase "nuclear launch codes."

Fear and awe.

That, Psellus commanded. *I wish to know more about that. Show me what it is, what it means. Tell me what you can do with it, and what I could achieve with its power.*

Psellus felt his new body going cold and sweat breaking out across his brow. Nonetheless, the typing fingers and intellectual intelligence of Brimes did as instructed.

He left behind the Pentagon website and went to another site that displayed videos. Captured images of real things in motion, or in some cases, false images that had been fabricated by sorcerous or technological means. The vid Brimes pulled up was clearly real.

It depicted a bare horizon. Then there was a flash of brilliant light like the rising of the sun but brighter and a shockwave rippled across the land, destroying all before it as an enormous cloud of smoke and fire rose from the point where the flash had originated. It formed into a shape like a mushroom.

Incredible. What are its effects?

Brimes' hands were shaking. His will had largely been crushed by Psellus', but a little bit of him tried to resist his new master. Psellus focused, tightened the reins on his host, and repeated his question.

Within the man's brain, the two voices conversed. Brimes told Psellus that nuclear weapons such as the hydrogen bomb were the most powerful implements of destruction ever devised by humanity. A single one could wipe out an entire city and render the land uninhabitable by living things for years.

And the US government possessed *thousands* of them.

Two reactions took place in Brimes' body simultaneously. One, inspired by Psellus, was to drool with anticipation. The other, Brimes', was to shudder in horror.

Within the software mogul's mind, his weak little voice shouted, *Wait!*

Though he was annoyed, Psellus listened. Brimes explained that other countries, particularly Russia, also had nukes, and if the United States deployed any, they would retaliate in kind. Nuclear weapons were intended to be deterrents. To *use* them would potentially destroy the entire planet, killing nearly all life on Earth.

Viator Psellus hesitated. Within the embattled mind of John C. Brimes, there was a long, agonizing moment of total silence.

So be it, Psellus concluded. *I shall not seize control of these weapons unless it becomes necessary. I wish to rule, to have influence over events and achieve great things. Ruling over a world of dead and barren rock would be pointless.*

He felt the body of Brimes relax.

But, Psellus went on, *I am certain that there are other things you have access to that are just as mighty in their way while being less dangerous. Yes?*

Brimes was forced to answer in the affirmative. He was hesitant and disturbed by his new master's intense interest, but when

Psellus tightened his grip, there was nothing he could do to resist.

Brimes explained and explained, and when he tried not to say too much or forgot or grew afraid, the ancient wizard probed his mind for the information and found it himself. He discovered all that Brimes knew about the National Security Agency, the Pentagon, FEMA, and other vaunted and feared organs of the US government.

Psellus learned about the DEFCON system, about airspace and cruise missiles. He became an expert on secret protocols and cyber warfare initiatives. Most interestingly, he learned that Brimes had the ability to shut down large portions of the country's infrastructure or to launch attacks against other countries that would achieve the same result.

With that much power, he could hold the world hostage. Blackmail the planet's governments into giving him what he wanted.

Yes, Psellus' disembodied consciousness crooned from within Brimes' skull, *that is better. That is what I want.*

Kera saw through the window of her warehouse that Chris, standing outside the front door, was carrying a large, flat, rectangular box. Her stomach growled as her face split into a grin. She opened the door.

"Good news!" he announced before anyone could greet him or ask what was up. "Not only did I bring two dozen donuts, but there was also an interesting development in the tech situation."

Kera almost bounced with excitement; both halves of her boyfriend's statement were the kind of thing she liked to hear. "Good, good, good. Set the donuts over there. The coffee is, um, thirty or forty minutes old but should still be okay."

Stephanie was present. Lia was not; she would be meeting

them on-site later. She had a personal errand or two to attend to before she joined the mission. Knowing Lia, she would time everything well enough to avoid conflicts.

Stephanie had been sitting on the couch, checking things on her laptop during a break. "Nice," she said. "Me and Kera sparred all morning with martial arts and spells both, so we could use a recharge."

Nodding, Chris set the box on the kitchen table as Kera had requested. "I got the most sugary and fattening ones I could find. Dig in, ladies. I'll take what's left."

Unfortunately for him, there wasn't much after the girls had their pick. He made do with what was available, an apple fritter and a glazed sponge-cake donut.

While munching on the fritter and washing it down with coffee, Chris extrapolated on the second half of his announcements.

"Mkay, I intercepted a couple of communications that Brimes sent out. That's the, um, good news." He hesitated as the mood in the room darkened. "It means we got to hear about it in advance. We wouldn't be happy if we only found out after the fact."

Kera steeled herself. "All right. Give it to us, and don't bother to sugarcoat."

Chris sighed. "The bad news is the message. He's been speaking to the National Security Agency and the Pentagon. He canceled his appearance at that conference in LA, so we won't be able to deal with him there. Instead, he wants to tour a facility out in the desert that has control over emergency broadcast facilities, mass shutdown protocols, fleets of drones, and stuff like that."

Stephanie's jaw dropped. "What the hell? And this happens right *after* he opens the book? Whoa, man!"

It took a moment for Kera to reply to either of them. Her brain had gone into overdrive, putting the new information into place alongside what she already knew, making connections, and exploring all options and possibilities.

One thing was abundantly clear; they had zero time to waste. Brimes, or rather, Psellus, had to be stopped.

Steph turned to her. "Kera, you're quiet all of a sudden. You know something we don't?"

"No," she replied. Her nostrils flared, her jaw clenched, and she made fists with her hands. "But we need to move our timetable forward, like *now*. We're jumping the gun. I want all three of us on the road to Montecito in fifteen minutes. We're going to take over Brimes' security detail as soon as we can, regardless of risks or changes to our original plans."

Her friends frowned. She knew them well enough to guess the problems they were anticipating, but neither of them protested. An ancient, power-hungry sorcerer in control of the US security grid's tech was not something to be taken lightly.

"Okay," said Chris, "but Lia might not make it to us in time. We're going to have to wing it."

Stephanie caught Kera's eye. "You'll need me even more than you already did, you realize. We might have to use more magic if we're gonna just bull our way in and take over. You'll need me to do some of that since otherwise, you'll spend too much energy and might not have enough for an emergency. And that's not me talking myself up, it's common sense."

Kera closed her eyes, nodded, and took Stephanie's hand. "You're right. We do this together." She glanced at her boyfriend. "Tell Lia I'm sorry, but I'm sure she'll understand. She is to join us as quickly as she can. As for us...hey, at least we have our previous failure to teach us how *not* to do it this time around."

CHAPTER SIXTEEN

Kera put a hand on Chris' shoulder. Droplets of sweat stood out on his brow and rolled down his face. His muscles were tight with nervous energy and exertion. She could feel his half-desperate effort and the fear that he might not be able to succeed combined with the knowledge that he had what it took.

"You okay?" she asked.

He had barely managed to hack into the mainframe of Assured, the security company employed by John C. Brimes. Kera had offered auxiliary assistance using both magic and her not-inconsiderable computer skills, but the bulk of it had fallen on her boyfriend.

The difficulty was creating something that looked like an error and would cause a brief false alarm, immediately after which Chris would send out an alert that "the guys in tech" had experienced a slight screwup and minor flubs in functionality should be expected and largely ignored for the next half-hour.

The company's personnel had bought into the scheme, or they had seemed to.

Chris swallowed acrid saliva. "Yeah," he blurted after a second.

"I'm on the upside. I got this. It's about showtime for you two, right?"

Kera and Stephanie nodded.

They had taken Chris' Jeep and Kera's motorcycle to the eastern reaches of Montecito and stashed the bike in a ditch with a protective cloaking spell over it before all three of them piled into the larger vehicle and got down to business.

Steph confirmed, "Right. I hope Lia gets here soon, but we'll be okay. We've done worse stuff than this in the past."

Kera couldn't object. "Okay. We'll be in touch. Don't get worried if we don't answer right away, though." She tapped the bud in her ear to make sure it was working, then accepted a blank CD-R from Chris, slipping it into her pocket.

Without further ado, they opened the doors, and the two young women hopped out. Their boots hit the pavement and sent them into a smooth stride toward the headquarters of Assured Security Solutions.

Both wore dark clothes that would offer them cover in shade without looking suspicious or obvious. Also, each had cast a glamour spell on herself to make her outfit resemble the uniforms issued by the company. They'd been able to duplicate the jackets, hats, and badges based on photos from Assured's website. As for pants and footwear, they'd had to guess and had ended up going with slacks the same dark blue as the jackets, along with nondescript black combat boots.

They were halfway across the parking lot. The building was protected by a fence and a gate, and a guard waited for them in a booth.

"Remember," Kera whispered, "we use the minimum amount of force or magic, but we don't stop. We do not let them slow us down or take us aside to answer a bunch of questions. The fate of the world might be at stake here."

Steph responded with a sharp nod. "Got it."

When they reached the gate and the booth, the guard stepped

out. "Hi. I don't recognize you two. Can I see your ID? I may need to call it in, and—"

While Kera held his attention, Steph hit him with a combination charm and persuasion spell. His demeanor softened at once.

Kera smiled and flashed her driver's license. "Yep, no problem. We were at that seminar a month or so ago. Maybe you forgot?"

Stephanie came around and showed him her license for a half-second.

Nodding vacantly, the man returned to his booth and buzzed them through the gate. The pair made a beeline for the main building.

Kera leaned toward her friend. "When we're in, you handle the diplomatic spells, and I'll reinforce our cloaking enchantment so we don't show up on their cameras."

Steph said nothing. They were both clear on the plan.

The front door was a simple glass affair. Assured must have felt an additional layer of security was unnecessary when they had a gate out front and many of their employees were armed and well-trained. Kera opened it, her eyes flicking toward the walls and ceiling for surveillance equipment.

Meanwhile, Stephanie came through behind her and went to the front desk, where a skeptical woman guard was eyeing them. "Hello," Steph began. "We're new transfers."

Kera could feel her partner marshaling the energy to "persuade" the guard. She would have to trust Steph to handle her side of the equation.

If she can just buy me thirty or forty seconds...

Having pinpointed the locations of the security cameras, Kera sent a subtle current of electricity into their circuits, overloading them. She would have to hope the enchantments she and Steph had employed, combined with Chris' earlier hacking endeavors, would cover their asses and keep a general alarm from being sounded.

She glanced at Steph. The desk guard was sitting slack-jawed in peace and contentment, nodding vacantly every two or three seconds.

"Sounds good," Stephanie concluded. "We'll pick up the car and be on our way, then."

Moving in unison, they proceeded down the hall, trying to figure out the quickest route to the company's vehicle bay. From what they had seen outside, it was in the far rear of the building or perhaps in an outbuilding beyond it.

Halfway down the hall, a door opened, and a man, wide-eyed, bristling with tension, and resting his hand on a holstered pistol burst out.

"Hey! Who the hell *are* you two? We just had a security cam malfunction *after* a hacking attempt, and you expect me to believe two newbies are just going to walk right in and—"

There was no time. Kera struck him with a relaxation spell of moderately high power. To have seen through their bullshit, the man was strong-willed, and he paused for a second on the tipping point between resistance and succumbing. Then he slumped, snoozing peacefully against the doorframe.

Steph blew out her breath. "Good work. I was afraid we were busted." She had slowed but not stopped, and Kera picked up the pace to keep up.

Kera did a rapid assessment of her magical stamina. She had used more than she would have liked but still had substantial reserves. If they could get clear of Assured's building and make their way to Brimes' house without further incident, she would have a little time to recharge.

"They won't be fooled forever," she pointed out. "But so far, so good."

At the end of the hall, there was a wall rack from which keyrings hung. Kera selected a ring at random, figuring that if the fobs were present, the vehicles must be, too. Beyond the rack, they entered a large garage where five cars were parked.

Steph offered, "I'll drive." Kera tossed the ring to her, and she matched the number—3—to a roomy late-model sedan on the far right of the line of vehicles.

After opening the doors, they did a quick inspection for gear. There were no guns in it; Kera figured those were kept in an armory. She had her Glock tucked into her waistband, and there was pepper spray, a taser, a gas mask, a pair of walkie-talkies, and a well-stocked first-aid kit.

"Good," Kera commented. "Okay, let's roll. The quicker we get out of here, the better."

Stephanie started the engine, then tapped the button on the remote device for opening the garage door. As they rolled out onto the pavement beyond, red lights flashed, and an alarm started to blare.

Kera slapped her hand across her eyes. "Shit! There must be a code we were supposed to punch to disable the alarm on the garage entrance. Keep driving. We'll deal with this later."

"My thoughts exactly," Steph agreed and hit the gas.

She wheeled the sedan around the corner of the main building and another guard ran out, waving one hand while drawing his gun with the other, though he kept it aimed at the ground.

As Kera prepared to knock him out with another spell, the alarm ceased. A familiar male voice came over the compound's loudspeakers.

"Sorry about that," said Chris, "it's me again. We were checking the system to see if it's still vulnerable after that attack earlier. Looks like we've got some work to do. Disregard any irregularities for another ten minutes while we patch things up."

The car sped past the guard, whose face was contorted with confusion, but he let them go.

"Hah!" Kera chortled as they left Assured's facility behind them and hit the road. "Chris came through. He's better at that than I thought. Better than I am with computers, but then again, I'm out of practice."

Steph nodded. "Mmhmm. You've been directing all your energy toward magic, fighting, and investigation. Not that there's anything wrong with that."

"Right." Kera leaned back. "Now we just have to hope we bought enough time to deal with Brimes and the grimoire before Assured calls in guys from their other locations and brings the SWAT team along for the ride while they're at it."

Stephanie drove quickly and efficiently but without hurrying to the point where they risked getting pulled over or having an accident. After a minute of silence, she snapped her fingers. "Oh. You were gonna call Brimes with our cover story?"

Kera blinked. "Yes, right. Do they have a…" She found a company cellphone in the central console area and plucked it from its cradle, then dialed Brimes' number. She could have called him from her phone, but that would be risky. He would have a record of her number, and he might not answer an unfamiliar number anyway.

She waited for nearly a minute before someone picked up. "Hello, it's Brimes." She recognized the voice from the announcement he'd made over the speaker when she had broken into his house.

Kera cleared her throat. "Hi, Mr. Brimes, it's Felicity with Assured Security. We recently had a breach of our system, though we think it's just a technical error. More importantly, we found something we think will be of interest to you. I was instructed not to talk about it over the phone, so if it's all right, we would prefer to show you in person."

The man sighed. "Is that really necessary? I don't feel like being disturbed right now. I have things to do. It would be easier to explain it in an email. I'm well-encrypted, you know."

It sounded like he was about to hang up. Kera wove a quick persuasion spell and tied it to the sound of her voice so it was transmitted through the phone line. "Sir, I'm sorry, but based on what I've seen and what the higher-ups have told me, this is really important. It will only require about five minutes of your time. We'll be there shortly, so we can get this out of the way, and you can go back to whatever you were doing."

There was a pause, during which Kera's stomach rolled up in knots.

"Okay, fine," Brimes' voice said. "Buzz me when you get to the gate, and I'll let you in. Of course, I'll be checking your vehicle ID."

Kera frowned but agreed. "Okay, thank you, sir."

"Bye." Brimes hung up.

Stephanie looked at her. "Vehicle code? Is that another scanning thing, or does he expect *us* to give him the number? Also, what the hell is up with 'Felicity?'"

Kera snorted. "What's wrong with Felicity? It's a nice name. And I have no idea on the code. We'll have to figure it out as—"

Chris interrupted, speaking into her earpiece. "Kera, hey. Two important updates. Lia just got here, which we expected. I just got an email from Pavla, also. She's in the area and wants to help if you'll let her."

Cursing about having so many new developments to consider at once—and they were almost to Brimes' house—Kera risked pulling out her phone to call Chris. "Hey, it's me. We don't have time to brief Pavla on our plan, so if she barges in, there's a chance she'll do more harm than good. But, um, tell her where we'll be, and maybe she can stand by and offer emergency aid if need be. Steph and I can handle the main stuff. Okay? Over and out."

Chris agreed. After she hung up, Kera noticed Stephanie smiling. "Thank you," her friend said. "We *can* handle it, and we're going to prove it today."

Kera grinned. "I believe it. And we're practically there. Let's go."

They ascended the hill and drove up to the gate. The drive was covered with lengthening shadows as the afternoon waned toward evening. Steph, as the driver, hit the buzzer, at which point Kera leaned over her so Brimes would recognize her voice.

"Hello, Mr. Brimes, it's Felicity from Assured. We're in Car Number Three. I haven't worked your house before. Do you have a scanner for the vehicle code?"

The man's voice responded, "Of course. Stay where you are; it's working right now...and you're clear. Come on through. The doors will be unlocked."

The gate opened. Steph piloted the car toward the side of the house, stopping on the pavement halfway between the garage and the front door. Kera saw the gate close behind them.

Before they stepped out, Kera remembered something. "If Psellus has possessed Brimes, then it's possible that he will, um, have the same abilities Psellus does. That could be bad."

"Goddamn," Stephanie remarked. "That's an understatement. Wasn't he supposed to be one of the most powerful wizards ever? Don't answer that. We don't need anything undermining our confidence. Let's just get this done."

They approached the front door, and Kera reflected that her friend was right. Psellus might be able to channel all of his old powers through Brimes, which would make him incredibly dangerous. They would have to hope Brimes had no touch of the gift, in which case he might act as an obstruction to Psellus' magic.

As the software genius had promised, the door was unlocked. They stepped into the front foyer. It was odd to see the place they had spied upon last time and be able to walk right in.

Kera called, "Mr. Brimes? We're here from Assured."

There was no answer.

Shrugging, they moved past the foyer into a broad living room that lay hidden within the house's interior, away from all the windows.

Both women stopped. Their mouths fell open and their eyes widened as they took in the scene.

"Wow," Steph whispered. "Kera, is this the kind of setup your parents have?"

Kera shook her head, still staring at the decor. "They're the old-fashioned type of rich people."

What she and Stephanie had seen of the Brimes estate before had been misleading. The sections of it that faced the broad open window-walls, looking south down the hills toward the ocean, were ultra-modern and classy but spartan. Deeper within the mansion was where Brimes had exercised his unique approach to staggering opulence.

Kera's parents had friends who collected rare and unusual art, as well as some who always had to have the latest technology or made weird aesthetic improvements to their domiciles with an eye to showing off in front of their social circle. Given that Brimes was well-known to be a recluse, she had to conclude that the stuff he had spent so much money on was only for his quirky enjoyment.

Embedded in the ceiling was a fish tank, or rather, the entire ceiling was a fish tank, a long flat one about three feet high. It was filled with bright cerulean water that caught the light from the surrounding lamps and bathed the room in shifting soft blue light.

The effect was striking, given that the room was brimming with custom furniture. No two pieces were alike. There was a loveseat whose frame resembled an incomplete globe of latticed lines, the front half cut away like a broken eggshell to reveal the two cushions within.

Next to it was an end table carved of twisted wood that was an astounding bright reddish-orange hue; Kera intuited that it was the wood's natural color, probably coming from some obscure and exotic locale. There was also a desk made mostly of glass or hard transparent plastic, with a gypsum panel on the top. Next to it was a chair of glossy blued steel with black velvet cushions.

"Well," remarked Stephanie, "all this stuff is sure eye-catching, but he doesn't seem to care much about things clashing with each other, does he? I'd imagine a feng shui person would see all this and have a nervous breakdown."

Kera bit her tongue to keep from laughing out loud. "Sounds about right. It seems like the home you'd expect from a guy who collects dusty old grimoires as a hobby when not hacking into fucking NORAD. Speaking of which, let's find the book."

They were two-thirds of the way across the floor when a figure appeared in an empty doorway at the other end.

"Hello," Brimes greeted them. He was wearing a dark red bathrobe over what looked like a tank top, as well as thick white socks. The robe was belted at the waist. Up close, he was the unremarkable middle-aged man he had appeared to be from a distance. He could have been anyone—a random manager at one of Kera's father's companies, perhaps.

The one thing about him that was *wrong* and set off sirens in Kera's mind was his aura. He—or Psellus—had cloaked it previously, but now that they were in the same room, it was impossible to hide.

Kera's spine went cold. The impression she got of Viator Psellus' astral signature, the shape and scent of his consciousness and power, reminded her of the awful sensation that had surrounded Milena's sacrificial altar. It was clear she was dealing with something terribly powerful that was older than human memory could conceive.

Psellus did not radiate the absolute evil the aura had, but there was a suggestion of extreme danger—a ruthlessness and sense of imbalance. His power was far greater than the altar's to boot.

Kera glanced at Stephanie. She was silent, staring at the man with big round eyes.

Maybe Steph is almost at my level. She feels what I feel. It's obvious to her.

Kera gave her head a quick shake. "Mr. Brimes, hi. I'm Felicity, and this is my partner Andrea. We believe the previous home invasion you suffered, as well as the malfunctions of our system earlier today, are related. There are some pretty bad people who, if we're not mistaken, want to steal something from you."

Brimes blinked. "Well, that's no great surprise. I'm pretty rich. Didn't you say there was something you wanted to show me in person?"

Kera slipped the blank CD-R out of her pocket. "Yes. We recovered this in an abandoned vehicle near your property this morning. We believe the would-be thieves left evidence on it, but we were reluctant to run it on any of our computers, what with the earlier issues."

"Oh," Brimes drawled, and his face took on an expression of wry amusement. "You want me to do the hard work of quarantining any nasty things they might have left on the disc. Well, I can do that. I haven't worked with a CD in quite some time. Might be fun."

He turned and motioned for them to follow him. As they left the living room behind, Stephanie added, "And they weren't just after any old knick-knacks or cash. They seem to want a valuable object that you purchased recently. An antique or something like that."

Beyond the bizarre living room was a curved hallway with a gently spiraling staircase that led to the second floor. Brimes was five steps up it when he stopped. "What?" He turned around.

Kera added, "It's been known to happen, sir. Some professional burglars watch the expensive auctions and then move on their targets after the item is with its new owner. The logic is that things are easier to steal in transit, so people will be less vigilant if it's a home robbery." Her dad had told her something like that once.

Brimes stared at them. "What object?" His voice had changed. "And who are you people in truth?"

The sirens in Kera's head went off again. Though the aura of

Psellus had remained constant, she had figured that the sorcerer was dormant within Brimes' persona. But now...

Stephanie said, "We're with Assured, but we only transferred to this branch last—"

"*No,*" Brimes interrupted her, and his voice had grown deeper and raspier, like that of an old man who rarely spoke aloud. "You are not who you say you are. You are people of *power.* Especially you." He looked at Kera.

Oh, fuck, she thought, and scanned her mind for every backup and contingency plan she could think of.

Psellus went on, "I thought I would claim Brimes and use his skills during my return to life, but he has given me enough. I crave true magic again. Technology is only worth so much. Come here, young lady, and our skills will become one."

Kera fell into a fighting stance, conjuring a shield in front of her and her partner as she shouted, "Steph! Find the book! And be careful with it."

Then all hell broke loose.

CHAPTER SEVENTEEN

Anezka raised her pale, slim hand and extended a black fingernail. "Here?"

Calvin Grandis was grim-faced, speaking no more than necessary and making it abundantly clear that he had no fondness for the work they had forced him to do. No loyalty whatsoever to the cause they espoused.

Behind him, at the rear of the posse, a pair of witches guarded his wife Niah. It had been unnecessary for them to elaborate on what would happen if he failed to obey their orders or give them what they wanted.

Calvin nodded. "Yes, ma'am. Like I said, I honestly don't know the exact location, but it's in this here swamp, somewhere between here and the old highway. It's a private sort of residence. You won't find it right next to a bunch of other houses. That's all I can tell you."

He looked across the flat, empty, waterlogged land. It teemed with greenery and buzzed with insect life while birds circled overhead. Beyond the marshy plain, the trees grew higher and denser. That was where the serious bayou began. Not many people tried crossing it on foot.

Anezka gave a soft yet cold laugh. "You led us to the edge of this swamp, which is crossed by no roads, yet you say we could have approached the neighborhood from the highway on the other side. How clever of you to hope that we would become lost in the marshes before we could find the house."

Calvin clenched his fists, forcing himself not to betray the sharp pang of fear stabbing him in the gut. If the Orthodoxy's grandmistress suspected he was trying to sabotage her, she might retaliate against him. Or worse, against Niah.

"This," he explained, "is the most direct route from where I live. You probably have a better chance to sneak up on them if you don't come from the highway."

Anezka tittered, and laughs went around the group. The grandmistress retorted, "Now you wish for us to succeed? Very well, then. You and your woman may stay here and watch."

She twisted her hand and Calvin felt his muscles go rigid, combined with the bizarre sensation of being swathed in a sheet. He could see no visible disturbance around him, but he felt the witch's power.

Alexei and another witch brought Niah up to the front of the group, planting her next to her husband. "What did you do to him?" she demanded.

"Very little," said Anezka. "You will see." She repeated the spell, and the old couple stood like statues in the damp, knee-high grass, forced to stare across the marsh, unable to move a single bone or muscle.

Alexei said, "They will not be able to see from so far away."

His leader gave him a scowl of contempt. "That is obvious. I will *help* them watch the battle." She tapped her finger upon each prisoner's forehead, linking their mind's eyes to herself. Then she leaned back, smiling again.

"You will see what I see until the hour of midnight. You will be my audience; both of you shall watch your friends die. After we have won, we shall discuss what is to be done with you. Of course, I will not harm you since we agreed upon your safety. The question becomes how to make good use of you. How to win your...loyalty."

Calvin and Niah said nothing. They could not move their mouths. All they could do was blink.

After allowing them to stew in their fear for another moment, Anezka turned to the bayou. In Russian, she commanded, "Come, let us begin the search. Everyone is to use all available stealth measures and remain within proper distance for quick response to one another's calls. When we have found the house, we will encircle it and move in. But first, detection. Go!"

An invisible cloud of magical steam rose from the war party as everyone enchanted themselves with cloaking charms, shields to muffle sound, shields to keep water and mud solid beneath their feet, and auras of confusion to dispel any attempt by the council or its members to trace their activity.

Then the army of witches invaded the swamp, fanning out through the vegetation, walking over water when necessary. With them was Mindy, the woman they had used as a human shield when first approaching Calvin's and Niah's home, compelled by magic to fight with them. They dwindled toward the horizon as the Grandises watched with captive eyes and minds.

Calvin had a last thought as they passed out of sight.

You're going to end up at the bottom of that swamp. You're not as good as you think you are, my friends.

Ezeudo held up his hands, palms outward, and shook his head. "No, no," he clarified to them. "I am volunteering because I *want* to go. Someone has to, and since all of you are more powerful than I am, you are needed here to finish our preparations. I am...what is the word for one who can be lost without great consequences?"

While the others balked, James answered him. "The word is 'expendable,' but the problem is you *aren't* expendable. You saved my life, remember? And you're at least as powerful as the Orthodoxy's frontline grunts, maybe more so. Give yourself some credit, man."

Mary Mitchell glanced at James, nodded, and looked at the Nigerian. "Ezeudo, none of us want you to come to harm. Please be careful on your patrol. If you see, hear, or notice *anything* unusual or dangerous, turn back at once. You will do yourself a favor in addition to being able to warn us sooner."

Ezeudo shrugged. "That is logical. I will go now. LeBlanc, is there anything I should know about the swamp?"

Mother LeBlanc was seated at the dining room table, studying the Chalice. She did not move her eyes from it but replied, "Only that if you see a dead tree in a pool of clear, shallow water, you must turn back immediately. And that the bayou is treacherous, of course. Take a long stick or pole with you to test your footing. There is a pair of tall boots in the cellar that ought to fit you. No need to get muddied up to your knees."

Ten minutes later, Ezeudo advanced across the lawn toward the tree line that separated their temporary home, rented from the Grandis couple, from the waterlogged wilderness. In his home country, there were places that were similarly difficult, though he had lived in the savannah region that separated tropical southern and central Nigeria from the desert to the north.

Since then, he had traversed almost every type of terrain known to man on his charitable missions, in addition to all the time he'd spent amidst the cities of Europe. Particularly Geneva. He liked it there, and for all intents and purposes, it had become his home.

Yet these people, the North American Council, had become his friends. They were growing into a new family.

I will not let them be destroyed, he vowed and stepped into the swamp.

To his surprise, he did not sink into the mud or the water. The land was *mostly* solid, though between the weeds and branches and brambles, he could see spans of glistening water that were undoubtedly deeper. And there might be areas of sedge floating atop boggy pools that looked solid but would betray him if he stepped on them.

He carried a long wooden pole, retrieved from the tool shed, originally part of a tree-trimming device. He used it to test the ground ahead of him as he moved.

And of course, he wrapped himself in cloaking and muffling spells and sent out his expanded consciousness, probing the surrounding area for any signs that their enemies might have arrived at last.

It is my fault that they know we are in Louisiana, he lamented. *I was careless and unbalanced by anger. I must not make that mistake again. Caution and compassion must be my guides this time.*

He slowly advanced into the wilderness for about ten minutes, leaving the house behind and out of sight. Then he sensed danger.

But it was an unusual signal, unlike any he had encountered before. He couldn't tell if it was a threat directed at him, a call for help, or a generalized miasma of hostility and anger.

Ezeudo stopped where he was. He was next to a droopy tree and mostly surrounded by tall grass and weeds with other trees nearby, so he had good natural cover in addition to the magical precautions he had taken. Taking a deep breath, he focused his mind.

There were subtle signs of terrible power nearby, either dormant or heavily cloaked; he could not be sure which. It might mean the Orthodoxy was coming, or it could have been related to Mother LeBlanc's vague warning about the dead tree in the clear pool that should be avoided.

Ezeudo moved a few meters toward the largest concentration of power he could identify, which was tied to what sounded in his mind like someone crying out but being forcibly muffled.

He didn't want to let down his defenses in case a threat emerged from some other direction, but he had to know if someone was in trouble. He directed all of his consciousness toward the strange signal.

Then his astral signature broke through the shroud, and he realized what it was.

A person nearby was trying to sound an alarm that only those with the gift could hear. For obscure reasons, Ezeudo felt sure that it was an older man, someone who had lived here all his life and knew the land well. Certainly not someone from the Orthodoxy.

But what, Ezeudo wondered, was he trying to say? Was he begging for aid on his own behalf, or was he trying to warn others to stay away?

Ezeudo closed his eyes and moved toward the signal. It did not waver or change in intensity, so if the man was in trouble, there was no rush to reach him. The tall Nigerian could afford to move slowly and scan in front of him and to the sides for any sign that he might be walking into a trap.

Water sloshed; he was now up to his knees in the sludge of the bayou, and the trees were thicker. He parted the hanging moss and thin branches and stepped onto a higher area, and the water receded to his ankles.

The obscure voice issuing its alarm saw him, focused on him, and for a fraction of a second, linked to him and shouted into his mind.

They are coming. Don't worry about me. Run!

Ezeudo's heart jumped into his throat. He turned and pushed back through the swamp. The trees and foliage to the left of him parted, and a figure turned to look at him—a slim fortyish white woman, stern-faced with hooded dark eyes. He had never seen her before.

And she was surrounded by an invisible field that pushed the water away from her legs and feet, creating an egg-shaped depression that allowed her to walk through the swamp as easily as if she were strolling down a sidewalk. She raised a hand, pointed, and shouted something in what sounded like Russian while looking over her shoulder.

Ezeudo raised his hands and conjured a concentrated blast of percussive force formed into a spearpoint. It struck the transparent shield around the woman, cracking it and driving her backward. She tumbled against a tree, and brown water seeped into her artificial sanctuary.

The Nigerian fled. He cast another spell on himself to augment his speed and strength and left the woman far behind him, traversing the bayou at three times the rate he had previously crept through it. His thoughts and heartbeat raced together.

I gave us away. It was a trap, and I walked into it once again. How could I have been so stupid? I must lose her. There might be others prowling about, too. Dammit...

As he neared a familiar-looking area not far from the plantation, he slowed and forced himself to relax as rational thought returned.

The Orthodoxy was combing the entire landscape looking for them. They had found the correct area, so it was only a matter of time until they reached the house, no matter what.

The council had no plans to flee. They intended to make a stand here no matter what. By blundering into one of the witches, Ezeudo had done nothing except bring the situation closer to its inevitable climax.

Further, the Orthodoxy was likely to attack from the direction he had come. Knowing this, his friends could make their preparations accordingly. And they now knew the time had come. There would be no more waiting around, anxiously wondering when the hammer would fall.

There is no reason to curse myself. We knew this would come.

As he sighted the trees that surrounded the plantation's grounds, he thought he could hear voices calling to each other behind him. He also felt malevolent forces gathering, turning their collective eye toward him and his friends.

Ezeudo wondered who the old man was—if he was a poor soul the Orthodoxy had taken prisoner or an astral illusion they had crafted to lure him out. It didn't matter for the council's purpose, but if he was a real person, they would have to rescue him.

If they survived.

Ezeudo looked at the sky. It was getting dark.

CHAPTER EIGHTEEN

Stephanie bolted in the opposite direction from where Kera stood. Her heart ached at the thought of leaving her friend to face the wizard alone, but she was pretty sure Kera could handle herself.

She looked over her shoulder. Brimes, or rather Viator Psellus in the mortal guise of Brimes, had raised his hands and unleashed what looked like a net of curling green lightning. The sizzling tentacles raised smoke and sparks from the walls, ceilings, and fixtures as they wrapped around Kera.

Kera had shielded herself and was buffeting Brimes with a succession of fast telekinetic blows from multiple directions, knocking him around so he alternatively stumbled up the broad spiral staircase or crashed into the walls. His spell faltered and Kera moved ahead, fists raised.

Sweet Jesus, Stephanie thought. *This is gonna get real ugly. Kera girl, I hope you know what the fuck you're doing. Now, where is that book?*

She ran toward the door leading into the eccentric living room, but hesitated next to the opening. There had been no bookshelf within it, nor had she seen anything like a book in any of the other rooms they'd been in since entering the mansion. The grimoire had to be somewhere else.

Beyond the door, in the opposite direction from the staircase where Kera's battle with Brimes raged and crackled, the hallway continued until it reached a T-intersection with another corridor beyond. Steph ran to it and looked both ways fast.

The passage to the right led to the kitchen, which was visible through the windows out front. It seemed an unlikely spot for someone to leave a valuable book.

She turned left, moving at a trot, toward a door and another juncture with a passage leading to the left. At the intersection, a glance revealed another staircase, though this one was narrower and more conventional, rising in short flights to multiple landings on its way to the second floor.

Before bothering with that, she opened the door ahead of her. It led into the garage.

"Nope," she panted and heaved herself onto the stairs, jogging up as fast as she could without tiring herself too quickly. She gave thanks that she and Kera had been sparring and that she'd managed to keep herself in good shape, despite her transition from waitressing to detective work meaning that she sat on her ass these days more than she used to.

Deep within the house, on the other side of two or three walls, she could hear giant whooshes of air or perhaps fire, combined with crashes that shook the foundations and voices shouting. Kera grunted and cursed, and Brimes, speaking in the voice that was not his own, issued half-comprehensible threats and demands for surrender.

It sounded like their struggle was working its way up, so Stephanie picked up her pace. If she could find the grimoire before Brimes got to the second floor, she might be able to end the fight and save Kera from getting flattened or possessed.

Steph cleared the final landing and found herself face to face with a wooden door. She opened it and emerged into a small bathroom coated with seafoam green tile and a marble sink and shower.

"Who the hell puts a bathroom right next to a staircase?" she blurted. The house made no sense, and she had lost her orientation. She had no idea where Kera and Brimes might emerge onto the second story or how close to or far from her current position it would be.

Ignoring questions of architecture, she dashed across the tiles and flung open the door on the opposite side of the lavatory. Past it was a master bedroom, which was surprisingly humble and normal when contrasted with the rest of the house.

Steph checked the nightstand, the bed, and under the covers. There was a book on motorcycle repair—briefly and crazily, she wondered if Kera might be interested in it—but nothing that resembled an ancient grimoire.

"Shit," she grumbled and vaulted over the bed toward the next door.

The room beyond was a study. Shelves lined the walls in the back half of the massive chamber. The front half was empty aside from a computer desk.

The shelves were *filled* with books. Hundreds of them.

Struggling not to panic or to break down in tears of desperation at the impossibility of the task before her, Stephanie forced herself to stop and think for a second. She blotted out the increasingly violent sounds of magical combat, which drew closer by the second.

There was a simple wooden desk and chair in the near left corner of the study and a pile of books atop the surface. If Brimes had only recently acquired Psellus' tome, he might well have it out to look at it and read it. She leaped toward the stack.

The book on top was about cybersecurity. Stephanie tossed it aside. Her eyes fixed on the one beneath, which was bound in dark leather and inscribed with Greek letters in faded gold script.

And it had an aura. Like a person with the gift, it gave off the undeniable scent of magic.

Stephanie hesitated, worried that she risked being possessed if she touched it. However, Psellus' spirit already inhabited Brimes. His soul, essence, ghost, or whatever it was probably couldn't be in two places at once.

Or so she hoped.

She reached down and the grimoire was in her grasp, then held tightly to her chest. "Kera!" she shouted as loud as she could. "I got it! What, uh…fuck! What do I do with it?"

The voice that responded was that of the strange man, the hybrid of two beings. *"What?* Put it down. Wait, no. No. I have changed my mind…"

The spells ceased their thunder, and footsteps pounded up the stairs.

Kera cried, "Steph! He's coming for you."

Brimes appeared beyond the end of the bookcases, where the broad spiral stair presumably ended. His eyes blazed with unnatural light, and a dark cloud hovered around him. "Your friend," he declared, "is too powerful and stubborn, but you possess significant talent as well and are less practiced. You will make a better host, I think. Come, I will teach you things you can learn no place else. The two of us shall achieve incredible greatness."

Thinking fast, Stephanie condensed the atmospheric moisture in the room, as well as some from the bathroom behind her, into a half-sphere of water that coalesced around the book in her hand.

"No," she stated. "I don't think so, and if you try anything, your book is gonna suffer serious flood damage. Is it insured for that?"

Brimes hesitated, then stopped.

Behind him, Kera threw herself into the air and struck him in a full-body tackle. The two rolled across the carpet.

Stephanie let the water fall to the floor and ran toward the scuffle. Kera, being fitter than Brimes, regained her feet first. "Give me the book!" she said.

Steph tossed it to her. No sooner had it left her grasp than Brimes sat bolt upright and flung out his hands, channeling the will and the power of Viator Psellus.

A field of static electricity closed around Stephanie, sparking on the residual moisture around her hands and shoulders. Her muscles seized, and the field drew terrible pain from the nerves of her skin. She screamed and fell.

Kera kicked Brimes in the head, and he crashed into his desk. Then she turned to the book. "There has to be some way of trapping him in this goddamn thing," she muttered.

Steph recovered at the same time Brimes did. The pain of the static shock had taken her breath away and made her want to weep, but she did not. It didn't seem to have done her any serious injury. She thought of something.

When Brimes got to his feet and slowly advanced toward her, the floor beneath him exploded. Dozens of gallons of blue water with confused exotic fish still swimming through it surged upward and engulfed him. He struggled to swim through the current as Steph directed it toward the far wall in a massive splashing wave, but disorientation and the liquid interfered with his magic.

Kera blurted, "I think I have it! The entire text is basically just one spell. I can't read Greek, but the writing is infused with magic. I'm reverse-engineering it right now. Keep him busy for a minute."

"A minute?" Steph protested. "We're both going to be dead or possessed by then!"

Brimes had frozen most of the water she'd summoned and he shattered it with a localized sonic boom, killing the poor fish trapped within. He advanced toward her, but halfway there, he stopped, glancing from her to Kera and back.

Recalling Kera's lesson that manipulating fire was surprisingly similar to water, Steph cast a heat evocation that caused the hem of Brimes' tattered bathrobe to burst into flames. He put it out with a blast of frost.

Kera glanced at him. "Possessing Brimes handicapped your ass, didn't it? He has no magic, so you're trying to cast spells with one hand tied behind your back. No wonder you want *us* so bad. Well, as it happens, you don't belong in the world of the living. By rights, we should destroy this book and banish your spirit, shouldn't we?"

Brimes lunged toward her. "No!"

Kera kicked him in the chest, knocking him back, and Steph cast an inverted shield around him to obstruct his movement.

Kera said, "Steph, help me. I'm going to lock minds with you. Focus on the idea of Psellus as someone who doesn't exist anymore except in the form of the book. He belongs inside its pages, not in our world. If we destroy the book, he might escape, but we can lock him away again."

As Brimes began tearing through the transparent barrier, Stephanie exhaled. "Okay."

She felt Kera's thoughts and personality, her aura and astral signature, reaching out for her. They moved together even as their sight of one another in the material world faded. In its place, their inner eyes opened.

Steph pictured a swirling purplish void around them. She perceived herself as an orb of watery blue and Kera as a blazing golden star. Across the expanse was what looked like a churning thunderhead of charcoal-hued vapor and smoke, crackling with multicolored lightning.

She intuited that Psellus was not so much willfully evil as batshit insane. His unnaturally long life had created a mixture of megalomania and extreme boredom, so he had a desire to push people's buttons and stir up trouble. He wanted to participate in it and see what happened, and aggrandize himself for doing so. She saw his plethora of bizarre schemes and his hunger for excitement, experience, and recognition, which had not been sated even after more than a thousand years.

Stephanie, Kera's inner voice pleaded, *focus on me, not on him. You have to trust me. I'm sorry I didn't trust you before, but I should have. You've saved my ass more than anyone. We've been through things together most people can't imagine. He doesn't belong in this world anymore, but we do. Concentrate!*

Stephanie felt her heart thumping against her ribcage, its throbbing pulse resonating like a bass drum as her body grew totally still and her mind focused. She opened herself completely to Kera. There were no barriers between the two of them, only an unobstructed flow of mutual energy. They were in this together. They functioned as one.

The storm cloud of Viator Psellus' aura, unable to hold up before their combined strength, shuddered and shrank, retreating from the liminal realm between astral and physical into the safe haven that had sheltered it for centuries—the grimoire.

Stephanie remained focused on the spirit of the ancient sorcerer as her mind's eye closed. The vision of the astral realm faded, and her mundane eyes began to see again. A shadow, lighted from within like a dark cloud flashing with lightning, was coalescing around the opened book and sinking into it. Her and Kera's mutual power continued to push it, forcing it back.

The shadow collapsed inward, falling into the old pages, and the book slammed shut.

The room fell silent, the storm of magic having abated. Both young women stood panting and staring at the grimoire, daring themselves to believe they had won, at least for now.

"Steph," Kera breathed, wiping her brow with her forearm, "are you okay?"

Stephanie nodded. "Yeah. Mostly. How about you?"

"I'm fine." Kera took a step closer to the desk and gazed at the cover of the aged tome that served as Psellus' home, prison, and coffin. "Looks like we pulled it off. He's still in there, but he's not coming out again anytime soon. He won't dare try to possess anyone else as long as we're around."

Steph wasn't sure if she wanted to weep or laugh or a little of both. She grabbed Kera and hugged her. "We did it. Girl, we got it done *together*. Who would have thought?"

Kera let out a shaky sigh that transformed into a gentle chuckle. She smelled of sweat and ozone. "Yeah, we did. Thanks so much, Steph. I'm glad I brought you along. Couldn't have done it without you. But, um, let's check on Brimes. Looks like he passed out. We don't want him dead. None of this is his fault. Then we need to figure out how much damage Psellus did to the fucking US cybersecurity infrastructure before we scared him off."

Taking a moment to catch her breath, Steph closed her eyes and nodded. "Yeah. You're the computer science student, so you handle the second part. I'll have a look at Brimes. Pretty sure we didn't kill him. I hope not."

Kera went to Brimes' computer desk, where his PC was running in idle mode, and sat down to check things. Stephanie went past her and knelt beside the body of the software mogul.

Brimes wasn't in good shape. He was covered with bruises, burns, and lacerations. His clothes were torn, and his hair was mussed. It looked like his ankle had taken a fracture in the course of his tumbles. His chest was rising and falling, which reassured Stephanie that he was alive, but he needed medical attention.

She just hoped he didn't need it immediately. They couldn't afford to have the authorities burst in while they still had work to do, but allowing the poor bastard to die would be wrong and would only complicate their lives.

"Dammit," she cursed, "wish I'd become a nurse like Mom said." She couldn't detect any injury that looked life-threatening. He wasn't bleeding too much and didn't have any major head wounds, nor was he going into spasms or turning strange colors.

The one thing that worried her was the possibility of internal bleeding; she imagined if that was the case, he'd pale, but so far, it didn't appear to be the case.

Stephanie stood up. "Okay, I'm no paramedic, but I don't think Brimes is going to die if we let him rest for half an hour while we deal with all that stuff there. He'll need to go to the hospital, but unless I'm wrong, he's not in critical condition."

Kera, absorbed with the screen in front of her face as her fingers clicked keys, took a couple of seconds to respond. "Okay, that's good. *This*, on the other hand, isn't. We could be in serious trouble."

Frowning, her friend jogged over to the desk. *Just what we need right now. Don't we ever get a damn break?*

Kera leaned a few inches to the side and flourished her hand at the screen. "Check it out. Brimes, under Psellus' direction, was using modern technology to learn more about what was going on in the world of magic. In one window, he was doing research on the council and the Orthodoxy. Sound familiar?"

Stephanie's skin crawled. The sensation of danger she'd experienced when they had first come to the house was back, even if the threat was no longer physically close. "Yeah," she conceded. "It does."

"And," Kera went on, "he was also trying to hack into a FEMA alert system, including a fleet of drones operating out of New Orleans. I think that either the council or the Orthodoxy is in NOLA right now, and maybe they're fighting there as we speak. I'm looking into it. The sum total of all this crap doesn't look good. Fuck, I'm hungry. That fight took a lot out of me."

Steph laughed. "I'll raid Brimes' kitchen while you keep up with the technical stuff. I worry that with his taste in decorating, he might only have, I don't know, weird shit that's barely edible. Maybe we'll get lucky and he'll have a leftover pizza in the fridge."

"Worth a look," Kera agreed and turned back to the screen.

Steph trotted toward the stairs. Her course brought her close to the window, where something caught her eye. She stopped. It was difficult to see, thanks to the reflection and glare, but a human figure was standing on the lawn out front.

Though her first instinct was to duck for cover, something told her it was unnecessary. Stephanie leaned closer to the glass and peered through it.

"Hey, Kera," she called. "Pavla's here."

CHAPTER NINETEEN

Mia Angel stared at her partner, mouth agape. "Are you fucking *kidding* me?"

Doug Lopez pouted as though hurt by her words. "That's a rhetorical question, isn't it? If not, then no, I'm not kidding. It would appear that things just got a whole lot more interesting. Here, have a look."

He wheeled his chair aside, and Mia sprang out of her chair and crossed the office they shared to read the report and confirm that she had heard him correctly.

She half-muttered the words while skimming them and then going over them again. There was a new development in the burgeoning case involving John C. Brimes. He had, very unexpectedly, canceled his appearance at the tech conference in Los Angeles. Then, better yet, Assured Security Systems, which protected the homes of a lot of rich people in the coastal area from Ventura to San Luis Obispo, had experienced a strange breach in their security.

A supposed technical difficulty was being investigated as a hacking attempt, and their office in eastern Santa Barbara had been infiltrated by two unidentified subjects who had stolen a car. One was a slim figure wearing a black biker's outfit, including a helmet.

According to internal phone records, the thieves had made a call to the residence of John C. Brimes.

Mia examined the fine print on the document. "Where did you get this? Is the source reliable? How recent is it?"

Doug coughed. "A guy I know. He trolls the juicy government leaks, compares them to Internet gossip, and sends them my way. I haven't heard from him in months, so I was kinda afraid he might have gotten arrested or something. That made me not want to contact him, you know? In case the Powers That Be were considering any of his acquaintances to be a person of interest or whatever. But it looks like he was just busy and distracted. I hope."

Mia flapped her hand, shaking with excitement. "Message him back, dumbass! If this is for real, we *have* to be the first ones on the scene. It would be big enough without the mysterious black-clad biker person. I mean, come on. But if Motorcycle Man is back..."

Way ahead of her, Doug typed and pressed Send. Both waited, breathless but not expecting a prompt response.

"So," Doug said, "since the convention that Brimes was supposed to show for would have been in our great and glorious city, I'd say that's enough of a justification for us to gallivant up to Montecito. Right?"

"Of course," agreed Mia. "And...holy crap, he responded already."

She tried to keep her hands to herself as Doug took almost a full second to click open the new message. Far too slow for her taste.

He laughed. "Oh, ho, this is rich. The fucking *feds* are on their way since they think it might be terrorists trying to access the national security mainframe. It sounds like Assured was trying to keep the thing under wraps and handle it internally so the FBI,

NSA, DHS, FEMA, and whoever else wouldn't put the smackdown on their asses—do the kids still say that these days?—but it got leaked right away regardless. The government must have an inside line or something, given their close relationship with the client in question."

Mia rubbed her eyes and reread the message to confirm.

Doug added, "Their delay means that our perpetrators have had a good hour alone with Mr. Brimes."

Mia grabbed her jacket from the back of her chair. "By the time we get to Montecito, the action will probably be over. Why the hell didn't one of us think to go back up there today?"

Doug hoisted himself to his feet. "Good question, but better late than never. Since you're in such a hurry, I'll let you drive, provided you don't get us ticketed or go through a barrier and into the Pacific or anything. One thing I have to ask, though."

Mia opened the door leading out of their office. "What?" Her impatience was as palpable as a cloud of steam.

Her partner smiled. "When we see Motorcycle Man again, do you think he'll recognize us? I mean, it's been a while."

Stephanie had let Pavla in when she went downstairs to look for food. Now, the three women sat around Brimes' computer desk, finishing a platter of sandwiches and trying to ignore the miasma of awkwardness that had arisen between them.

Brimes, meanwhile, lay sleeping on his bed. Kera had hauled him into his room, casting a light healing spell to help stabilize his condition. Then Steph had joined in, keeping the man asleep with a moderate relaxation charm.

"All right," Kera said, breaking the silence, "I got in touch with Chris and had him contact the feds anonymously. Which is still...scary since they'll probably be after *us* soon, but the important thing for now is that they're going to clamp down the stuff

Psellus was trying to interfere with. Before we get the hell out of here, there are one or two more things I want to do."

Pavla sat quietly, observing her. She had barely spoken since Stephanie had let her in.

Steph inquired, "What? Something to do with the Orthodoxy?" She glanced at Pavla, seeking her input.

Kera nodded. "Exactly. Brimes, Psellus, whatever, mobilized a drone to do a flyover of a particular rural area in the bayou outside New Orleans. I just managed to get a couple of the photographs it took. I'm seeing people who have weird visual distortions around them, and sometimes magic does that when it's caught on camera."

Pavla finished a square of sandwich and gently raised a hand. "May I speak?"

Kera's jaw clenched. "Why the hell are you asking permission, Pavla? We could use your help. That's why we let you meet us. Now isn't the time to get all personal. Just focus on business, okay?"

Surprisingly, the graceful Czech woman responded with a slow, bittersweet smile. "You are still the same driven, hotheaded person, Kera, even if you have grown in power and wisdom."

"Thanks," she replied. "Now, tell us what you wanted to say about the situation at hand. We don't have all goddamn night."

Stephanie frowned. "Kera, come on. Go easy on her. She's trying to help, and she's putting herself at a lot of risk by being here since the Orthodoxy wants her dead probably even more than us."

Pavla sighed. "True. But Kera is right. Let us focus on the necessities. Yes, the council and the Orthodoxy have gathered in New Orleans. I finally determined where they were, and it seems like Viator Psellus figured it out, too. They are on the cusp of an immense battle, perhaps the final one between them. I can feel the forces gathering around them. The entire balance of magic in this country will be different after tonight."

Kera locked eyes with her. "So, they're, like, sworn to fight each other to the death? You're certain it's *that* serious? I don't doubt the Orthodoxy wants to wipe out the council since I have personal experience with how ruthless they are—as you well know." Her nostrils flared, then she resumed speaking. "But I would have thought the council would attempt, like, a plea deal where they get to at least be the Orthodoxy's puppet regime or vassals or something."

Pavla shook her head. "Since you have remained a renegade and have not joined the formal world of magic users, you do not understand the way the ancient traditions work. In a war between covens, there can be no partial victory, no compromise of the sort you describe. Either the Orthodoxy will crush the council and take over North America, or the council will triumph and eliminate so much of the Orthodoxy's forces that they are unable to control anything beyond Russia—perhaps beyond Moscow—for a generation or more."

"Damn," said Stephanie. "I guess Kera and me are on the right path then if joining a coven means getting involved in that kind of shit."

Kera laughed. "I concur. Anyway, I have no reason to like the council. They've never done anything for me except make my life more difficult. They seem arrogant, old-fashioned, and not as competent as they think they are, since if they're the ones who published *How to Be a Badass Witch*, they caused themselves more problems than they solved. However..."

Pavla seemed about to interrupt, but Kera held up a hand and continued.

"However, I've accepted that the Orthodoxy is a lot worse. After I dealt with Milena, that was clear. Nobody performs human sacrifices in my country, period. I'm willing to intervene and make it an unfair fight. What I don't know, though, is how? What the hell can we do to help them from nineteen hundred miles away?"

Pavla stood, folded her hands behind her back, and began slowly pacing across the study and back.

"Kera. And Stephanie. To answer that, I'm afraid I *must* touch upon what you call 'personal' things."

Steph drew a sharp breath. "Uh-oh."

Kera said nothing. Her eyes narrowed.

The Czech continued her leisurely progress across the floor. Her eyes were bright yet distant, focused on some indeterminate point beyond the walls and windows.

"Since we last parted," she elaborated, "you both have grown by great leaps. As I said, Kera, you are incredibly powerful, and your self-control and insight have progressed at astounding speed. I did not have the chance to tell you, but I am amazed that you were able to defeat Milena. She sat at the table of the elders with Anezka, the grandmistress, making her one of the coven's most important witches. She was the newest member to ascend to that level, but still, she was a fearsome opponent."

Kera shrugged. "She was mentally unstable and distracted by trying to perform a ritual while fighting me. But thanks."

"You are welcome." Pavla glanced at Steph. "And you, Stephanie—your progress is even more impressive. You have not had the benefit of formal instruction from a traditional teacher. I taught Kera for a time, but I did not have the opportunity to teach you. You are nearly Kera's equal, which is doubly admirable since, to put it bluntly, your natural ability is weaker than hers. Kera is a true prodigy, but you have attained a level that will easily grant you access to a respectable coven through hard work, determination, and courage."

Stephanie bowed her head, embarrassed by the praise. "Well, thanks. I try my best. My mom always said, anything you end up doing, do it well and give it your all. Plus, um, I was getting a little tired of being second fiddle. But me and Kera worked all that out." She looked at her friend and smiled.

At last, Kera's demeanor began to soften. "Yeah, we did. And it's good to know Steph is doing so well with only *me* as a teacher, har har. But a lot of it is probably her own effort as much as mine. So," she sighed, "we appreciate the flattery. And I guess I'm sorry I've been standoffish, but there are a lot of wounds that still aren't healed if you know what I mean."

Pavla stopped pacing and shut her eyes. "I do."

"Right," Kera said abruptly, realizing that she was being needlessly cruel and regretting it. "Fuck. Sorry. You're the one whose whole life got turned upside down because of this, more so than mine. And we wouldn't have been able to stop Milena without your advice. You've helped us a lot. But back to the present. We don't have unlimited time. What's the big conclusion you're building up to? What's the point?"

Pavla spread her hands. "I know how we can help the council. At least, in theory. Part of what we can do is a variety of spell I am very familiar with. But I think it would be even more potent if combined with your knowledge of computers—with all of this technology that Brimes controlled and Viator Psellus was trying to claim."

Stephanie took a swig from a glass of water. "We've actually done some enchantments on tech before. Saved our asses a few times by now."

"Excellent," said Pavla. "But Kera, to do this, there must be a total connection between us—all three of us—with absolute trust and cooperation. Do you understand? I had thought of requesting we do such a thing earlier since I knew what was coming. But I thought that... that you would be resistant to the idea."

Kera leaned back in Brimes' computer chair and rubbed her eyes. "Goddammit. So basically, I have to totally forgive you and go through a big Hallmark Moment in order for this last-ditch scheme to work. Is that right? Well, I suppose I can give it a shot."

Pavla allowed herself a light chuckle. "You are not very comfortable with the tender emotions, are you? Remember what we shared in the past. Realize everything that happened since then, everything that 'ruined' it, was a mistake, and that you cannot be any more sorry than I am for the difficulties between us."

Stephanie leaned forward. "You forgave me for riding your ass about the equal partners thing, and we beat Psellus half a damn hour ago doing basically the same thing. You can do it again with Pavla involved. Can't be *that* hard."

The room was quiet as Kera stared blankly at the computer screen. It went dark, and she jiggled the mouse to reawaken it.

"Okay," she finally said. "What choice do I have? I would rather be friends. Maybe it doesn't sound genuine when I'm saying it under pressure like this, but I mean it. I would rather have our old friendship back than feel obliged to hold a grudge. And I sure as *hell* don't want the people who made you betray me rule the whole continent. Let's do this."

Pavla made a short coughing sound, and it took Kera a second to grasp that the Czech woman had come close to bursting into tears. "Thank you. Yes, let us begin."

Something caught Kera's eye on the screen. "Message from Chris. He says...uh, let's see here... Oh, *crap*."

"What?" asked Stephanie, getting to her feet.

Kera shook her arms as though preparing for a workout. "His security alert thing went through. It succeeded so well, in fact, that multiple government agencies are sending the cavalry in right now to shut down Brimes' access by force. As in, they're willing to kill him to stop a massive national security breach. We have ten minutes tops before they get here."

The other two women stood in silent shock.

Stephanie remarked, "Well, fuck."

CHAPTER TWENTY

Anezka looked around. Her face was a placid, statue-like mask of prideful satisfaction, and she stood at her full height, chin angled upward. "Is the auxiliary force in place?" she queried.

Vassily smiled, the expression drawing creases across his gaunt face. "Yes, Grandmistress. They have managed to field a solid dozen witches 'recruited' from local covens, in addition to the few we possessed. After the main force's initial attack, they will be sent in from the direction of the highway, compelled to behave as though they are coming to the council's aid. *Some* of the council members may fall for the ruse. For a short time, anyway, which is all that is needed for us to get the upper hand."

Low chortles went around the group.

"Good," Anezka stated. "And remember that they are expendable. Without Milena, sadly, we cannot harvest the full effects of a proper sacrifice, but still, enough of us are trained in the basics to claim some benefit of rejuvenation or augmentation from their lives."

The higher-ranking and more skilled members nodded.

Anezka raised her hands, savoring the moment. She had gathered the bulk of her army here in a relatively dry spot deep within the swamp, surrounded by a ring of gnarled trees and clouds of mist she had conjured herself. Of course, they were also cloaked.

The grounds of the old plantation where the council had taken refuge were about two hundred meters from their current location. The stupid Nigerian, the newcomer, had come looking for Calvin Grandis and had led them right to the estate.

"Now," Anezka intoned, not loudly but with a slight magical reverb that made her voice seem more thunderous than it was, "we end this war. Victory is expected. *Total* victory is *demanded*. There can be no excuses, no second chances. Everyone must operate at her or his full potential. Be wary of the strange magic embedded in the swamps of this land. It shall *not* be enough to save them, but beware the mistake of underestimating our foes. The council has proven to be a worthy opponent. So much more glorious shall it be when we *destroy them once and for all!*"

The witches and warlocks pumped fists in the air and barked harsh battle cheers. In mere minutes, they would have the opportunity to vent all the frustration they had felt these last weeks upon the people responsible.

And once LeBlanc and her foolish cohorts had been reduced to carbon residue, the Orthodoxy would be the mightiest coven in history. Anezka would consolidate power over two vast continents. The other inhabited lands would fall that much more easily thereafter. In another fifteen or twenty years, she might well, for all intents and purposes, be the ruler of the world.

"Remember the plan," she urged. "And fight to the *death*. Go! March forth!"

Dozens of the coven's best troops streamed out from the circle of trees, walking over water and mud, charging through the swamp in a carefully articulated formation disguised as a baying mob of berserkers. The council's terror was almost palpable.

And yet, there was something that troubled the grandmistress. Staying near the middle of the horde where she could observe everything and intervene as needed, she tried to focus on the moment and put her lingering doubts to rest.

There was *something* nearby. Something strange and powerful, a form of magic she could not identify or comprehend. She strongly suspected the other elders had sensed it as well, but they had kept their mouths shut.

Was it, Anezka wondered, the sum total of the Cajun swamplands' folk-magic traditions, which LeBlanc was attempting to weaponize? Or was it something more potent—a secret armament, an "ace in the hole" as the Americans would say?

She dismissed her concerns. The time of their final conflict with the council was nigh. She would think of nothing else but victory until LeBlanc and all who stood beside her lay dead.

"Old Jack," LeBlanc began, "we beseech you. Give us a little of the power you have stored to help us in our struggle to come. The rest we entrust to you to keep in this holy Chalice until our hour of greatest need. Which, we can no longer deny, may soon be upon us. Let not the balance of magic in this world be tilted in favor of tyranny and disorder. Each nation, each coven, has its place in the order of things. It was not given to any of us to rule all the world. Though we have not ruled our own land with perfect wisdom, we have tried our best. Forgive us, and help us."

The others stood in a circle around her. The Chalice sat on the wooden table in the center of the mansion's musty old cellar.

Brilliant white light began to pool within its cup, overflowing the edges and streaming outward to surround the eleven thaumaturges. They shuddered and exhaled, invigorated. The worst of their fears subsided. Calm but alert, they felt ready for what was to come.

And yet, they had no illusions. Though the Orthodoxy had

seemingly lost some of its power since the terrible fight at James' former home, they were formidable adversaries. They had been lazy and overconfident after their initial victory, but the frustration of losing their chance to exterminate the council had likely whipped them into a frenzy of anger and bloodlust.

This time, LeBlanc knew, their enemies would make no stupid mistakes. They would leave them no avenue of escape. The war would end tonight.

James smoothed his hair and adjusted his glasses. "Mkay, then. I think I'm *finally*, as of that last boost from the Cup of Goodness, ninety percent back to normal. Nice timing on Old Jack's part."

"Indeed," was all LeBlanc said.

Ezeudo put a hand on James' shoulder. "The rest of us are feeling *better* than normal. Perhaps the Chalice has given us the advantage we need. We should not fear. I think that even if we all die this night, the Orthodoxy will not rule here for long. The people of this country will not accept it forever."

Lauren Jones sighed in a wistful way, the sound of it scarcely audible.

"I hope you're right, Ezeudo. You have not been here long, but Americans are a strange, paradoxical people. In some ways, they are deeply rebellious and independent; in other regards, they are prone to submissive conformity, content to suffer in silence their entire lives if they think it will prove a point. While teaching so many generations of students, I have found it useful to play on both of these tendencies, depending on which is stronger in the individual learner. The one thing I can say with confidence is that the Orthodoxy does not understand this land they mean to rule. It is the great blind spot of all would-be foreign conquerors."

No one could think of anything to add to her statement. In silence, they ascended the sturdily built yet moldering staircase to the ground floor of the mansion.

LeBlanc quipped, "I am amazed the cellar has remained dry.

Half of it is below the waterline. Much of this region precludes the use of underground structures of any kind. Of course, it might flood if the secret exit is used, but nothing lasts forever. My friend Mr. Grandis can tolerate a wet basement in a house he never uses."

They all nodded, grasping the subtle message that the cellar would be their penultimate recourse—followed, if all else failed, by a flight into the hidden tunnel which opened into the swamp.

Night had fallen while they activated the Chalice, but the yard outside, visible through the small portions of the windows that were not boarded up, shimmered under a steady and intense white light that illuminated the grounds.

James smirked. It was an ingenious plan, and he regretted that with all that had happened lately, he couldn't remember whose idea it had originally been. Probably not his.

A diffused light spell hovered over the estate, creating a silver noon. The glow was tied to a subtle double-masked illusion that obscured the many traps littering the yard and protecting the house.

If the Orthodoxy proceeded into the light, their magical senses would have to be well-attuned to catch the illusions. If they killed the spell, thinking they would be able to attack more easily under cover of darkness, their physical senses would have to be just as sharp to avoid blundering into the traps.

Hugh Buchanan, in a mildly weary tone that belied how energized they all felt, asked the question that was in all their minds. "Do we know how many personnel they have with them this time? I would guess fewer than they did during the first major battle since they've had their people roving all over the country looking for us."

Mary Mitchell chose not to treat it as a formality and gave an actual answer. "Perhaps. The weakness of our long-term strategy was that we've spent quite a long time here. They might have recalled almost all of their forces, leaving behind only a handful to maintain control of other territories in the US. I doubt we will face less than sixty. Perhaps more."

Amanda Moore puffed out her chest. "Bring them on. Twenty seem like a fair price to pay for Damian and Zacharia."

On some level, Ezeudo was disturbed by her anger, but he empathized. Whatever violence befell the Orthodoxy in the hours to come would be the direct result of the coven's own actions. They had it coming.

Amanda, Crystal, Josiah, James, and Ezeudo climbed the stairs to the second floor, where they would offer a mixture of long-range offense and behind-the-lines defense to the others, who would remain on the first floor and fight the attackers directly.

James took Ezeudo by the hand. "With the Chalice handling augmentation, I'd say you can fight alongside us as an equal this time. I know you're a peaceful person by nature, but *they* aren't. Do what you have to do, my friend."

Ezeudo nodded. "I will." Then he looked up, his sharp eyes scanning the tree line. "They are here. They wasted no time. The battle has begun."

He had returned from his scouting trip less than an hour ago. Somehow, he had thought it would take their enemies longer to marshal for an attack—three hours at a minimum. They were more organized and aggressive than anyone had anticipated.

"Good," Amanda snapped. "I'm sick of waiting."

Crystal flipped her hair away from her face. "Indeed. Let's begin by cooling them off, shall we?"

James grinned. "They probably worked up quite a sweat, trudging through the swamp to get to us."

Crystal raised her hands, and the other three felt power surge into her and then outward as she spoke the incantation, a variation of the air conditioning spell she had perfected not long ago.

Cold wind encircled the mansion's grounds, centered on the tree line, and the temperature dropped by close to a hundred degrees Fahrenheit. Water and mud froze instantly, and faint cries of pain and alarm rose from the bayou. James could barely make out obscure silhouettes struggling around the edge of the yard. The magical light had dissipated the Orthodoxy's predictable cloaking spells.

Oddly enough, they only seemed to be attacking from one direction.

Amanda's hands clenched into fists. "Yes. They're sitting ducks now. Speaking of which..." She raised her arms and sent a resounding call into the sky.

Birds, thick swarms of them, forming clouds dark enough to blot out the illumination enchantment where they gathered, descended from the firmament, from nests in distant tree roosts, or from the open waters where they hunted. All manner of species flocked together, massed into attack formations against the enemies of their friend and master.

James saw pain on Amanda's face as she commanded her avian allies to die for her. He knew what would come next.

Lights flashed, and the mass bombardment by angry birds grew even more chaotic as the creatures screamed and squawked. Flames, lightning, and ripples of sonic or concussive force shot through the air, killing birds by the dozen wherever the witches blasted.

Still, as near as James could tell, Amanda's feathered friends picked off a fair number of the Orthodoxy's frontline troops. Unable to move, they had been caught off-guard, and he estimated that three or four of them had died. Others were wounded. How badly, he couldn't say.

As Amanda released the remaining birds and they fluttered off, James and Ezeudo stepped up to the windows, which they had opened in advance. "Hey," James told his student, "don't worry about subtlety. Just keep bombarding them with fireballs or something obvious like that. They're probably shielded, but it will keep them on their toes and maybe drive them into a nice pit or one of Mary's little botanical experiments."

"As you say," Ezeudo agreed. He reared back his hand, summoning a ball of mineral detritus and igniting it as Samantha had taught him, and hurled it at the dark figures below. Some of them had begun to blast or melt their way free of the ice. The meteor crashed against a shield, dissipating into a mass of burning particles but slowing or stunning at least two witches near the point of impact.

James conjured a wave of fear and despair. He disliked negative-emotion spells since he found them insidiously creepy, but they could be effective.

Into the spell, he put his memories of every ghost story, every horror film, every nasty stereotype associated with the American rural wilderness, and especially the Deep South. It was a land relatively strange and unfamiliar to a Yankee like him, and on some level, the Russians must have been primed to believe it.

James' hair stood up as terror emanated from him. His mind's eye perceived it as an inexorable mass of solid black, all the scarier for how slowly and deliberately it moved. He could *feel* it ignoring the shields that blocked mere physical attacks and energy spells. It seeped in, undermining the charged-up bloodlust of the attackers, playing upon their uncertainties about invading a foreign land and challenging a powerful foe.

Some of the witches faltered, dropping to their knees, moaning and hugging themselves. One's shield faded, Ezeudo, barking a wordless battle cry, threw another fireball at her, which blasted her to pieces.

Others stumbled in circles. Two of them simply disappeared.

Amanda's face broke into a vicious grin. "Excellent! They are too disoriented to see the traps."

James nodded. One of their hidden pits lined with poisoned stakes had claimed one. Another had probably been eaten by a blob-like, gape-mawed moss monster Mary had created the day before, promising it sustenance before long.

But though the first wave of the assault had faltered, the Orthodoxy would not be defeated so easily.

A woman's voice echoed with unnatural force and volume. James didn't know Russian, but he suspected it was the grandmistress or another high-ranking subcommander, rallying the troops and preparing a mass counterspell. Though the Orthodoxy had fewer people to spare than they'd had the first time, he doubted Anezka would lose much sleep over the sacrifice of low-ranking recruits if it meant teasing out the council's defenses before the *real* attack began.

All at once, the brilliant white light that had bathed the estate winked out. Deep natural darkness engulfed the grounds, leaving no light except the faint glow of the stars and the single candle LeBlanc had left burning on the kitchen table below.

"Crap." James sighed. "Let's hope their night vision sucks."

Beams of green radiance like those from a flashlight emanated from half a dozen of the dark figures. Within the beams, the hidden traps were revealed. Witches swarmed forward, dodging most of the pits, leaping over tripwires, and blasting Mary's murderous plants before they could come within killing range.

James' gut clenched.

Crystal turned her head. "You were saying?"

CHAPTER TWENTY-ONE

LeBlanc watched the battle, scanning the lines of killers advancing toward her and dispassionately observing their injuries, fear, and deaths.

She did not enjoy violence, but she had seen enough of it to tune out the sensitive parts of her mind when there was no avoiding it. Knowing the threat these people represented, she wished to deal with them as swiftly as possible. But to charge out onto the yard, which was a no-man's-land, would be suicide.

She waited. The time for her to act would be soon.

Josiah Kane, gazing at the green observation beams the coven's soldiers were using, said, "They're uncovering the traps. We should hit them with *something* to throw them off-kilter and pick off a few more of them."

Samantha Martinez added, "Yes. We can't just stand here and allow them to break in. They're halfway across the yard."

LeBlanc waved a hand. "So be it, but please be careful. None of us is expendable. Survival, in this case, is preferable to glory."

Josiah and Samantha advanced toward the one window that had been left mostly unboarded. Each held not a burgeoning spell but a material object they intended to throw at their foes.

Josiah hurled his cane like a javelin. It streaked out, then veered left. Guiding it by echolocation, he jabbed it between the legs of confused witches, making one trip into a mass of strangler vines. Another he struck in the head, knocking them unconscious as their comrades swarmed past them.

Samantha pitched a small bottle through the hole. It struck a tree stump and shattered, releasing a wispy pinkish gas. Most of the Orthodoxy's minions were heavily shielded, so it did little but obscure their vision, but some had not used full-enclosure shields; they had only blocked themselves off from the front and top.

The fumes seeped through whatever openings it could find. The witches afflicted by it stopped where they were, overwhelmed by feelings of sentimental guilt and shameful regret. They thought of their families and friends and children and small animals they had played with or fawned over and contrasted those days with their current mission of extermination. They froze in place, paralyzed by emotion.

Then Anezka's voice echoed out. The hair stood up on the backs of everyone's necks. The grandmistress was using a tone of command that was further enhanced by a persuasion spell designed to induce infectious hysteria, driving her troops into a frenzy.

Hugh Buchanan furrowed his brow. He was learned about languages in general and was the only one among them with any skill in translation spells.

"She's calling them fools or dunderheads or something," he clarified, "and telling them to ignore any and all thoughts and feelings that come out of nowhere. Thus far, it seems that every trick we've thought up, she unveils within a matter of seconds. Unless I'm mistaken. Russian is a difficult language."

A current of unease passed amongst them.

Rufus Mayer stepped forward. New holes had been blasted in the wood covering the windows, and cracks appeared in the walls. He shook his hands in front of him and puffed air from his nose. "The principle of equal exchange," he stated, "is key to the advanced arts of transmutation. I would be willing to bet that for all their Old-World traditions, the Orthodoxy came here in *cars*."

He swept his hands upward and to the side, speaking the necessary charm.

In front of them, the wooden walls and barricade grew indistinct, shifting. A second passed, and they had transmuted from wood to steel. He even plugged the newly-blasted holes with chunks of slag iron.

"Hah. If any of them flee back to their vehicles, they will discover how effective axles, brakes, and catalytic converters are when they're made of wood. Which is to say, not very."

To the surprise of the rest of them, Mary Mitchell laughed. "That's an oddly comforting thought, Rufus. I'd say you've purchased us a few more moments of security. Do you think—"

Then thunder struck, causing their ears to ring, and the portion of the steel wall directly in front of Rufus screeched horribly as it detached from the house, was formed into a horizontal stalactite by sheer force, and pierced Rufus' shield. He shot back, impaled, and crashed through the wooden wall behind them to land in the kitchen or the sitting room.

"Rufus!" Mary cried.

Behind her calm veneer, LeBlanc's mind howled in anguish, but there was no time for pain. "Mary, see to him. Do what you can. The rest of us *must* hold."

Mitchell was already dashing through the wreckage of the wall toward their friend. LeBlanc supposed there was a slim chance she could save Rufus, but she had seen him for a split second before he was blasted beyond their sight. His torso had nearly been ripped in half by the steel projectile.

He was dead. To survive that would require a miracle beyond even Old Jack's abilities.

Their foes were swarming toward the breach in the wall.

Fireballs, tentacles of freezing water, and other projectiles streaked down from the second floor, and Amanda seemed to have summoned a trio or quartet of alligators to attack the Orthodoxy's rearguard, but it wasn't enough to halt their advance.

A young man with light hair, his face crazed with ambitious overconfidence, appeared in the opening, with other witches massing behind him and to the sides. In English, he bellowed, "You! Your time is over. I, Alexei of the Orthodoxy, challenge you to—"

LeBlanc pointed a finger at him and he exploded. So little of him remained intact that he appeared to have been deleted, and the force of the blast sent his nearby comrades, covered with blood and debris, tumbling into the grass.

Then she sensed something—another group of casters approaching the estate from the opposite side. Her first assumption was that the Orthodoxy had deployed a reserve force in a pincer maneuver to cut them off in case they tried to flee, but something was wrong. For all her experience, the battle had grown too chaotic for her to perceive the truth of everything at once. Some things remained clouded.

Josiah ran to the side window. Halfway there, his cane slipped through a crack in the wall and returned to his hand. "It appears to be locals," he announced. "I recognize a couple of them from our convention with the lesser covens. They finally turned up, after all. Wait...wait."

The thaumaturges of Louisiana marched down the driveway, coming from the direction of the road, in broad ranks and deep files, their faces blank of emotion. In unison, they raised their hands.

Samantha gasped. "They're under compulsion! We need to—"

The rear of the house burst into flames. The shielding they had put there blocked some of the heat, and Josiah, cursing his lack of perception, was able to retreat with no more than scorched eyebrows. On the second floor, Crystal was already putting out the fire.

But the distraction had served its purpose. Half a dozen witches advanced through the breach in the steel-transmuted wall, one of them pausing to telekinetically bend the metal aside, widening the gap for others to enter.

LeBlanc and Lauren Jones struck the intruders with a wave of pure force tinged with confusion and relaxation, and most of them rolled back or stumbled aside, reeling stupidly and shooting bolts of flame or other projectiles into thin air. But others came in behind them.

From the second floor, James reported, "We can't hold them off much longer. Too many. A bunch slipped in after the fire started. And what the hell happened to Rufus?"

LeBlanc closed her eyes as Mary, barely audible over the general racket, called, "He didn't make it."

LeBlanc turned around. "To the cellar. We cannot hold here any longer. We must make our stand there."

The Chalice awaited.

Old Jack, LeBlanc mused, *can you save us now, or is the time not yet come? Do I empty the cup of your goodwill at this critical point, or must this battle be stretched out as long as possible before you can restore the balance?*

I do not know, and if you cannot tell me, then I hope someone among us knows what they're doing.

Kera *attempted* to tell herself that she could do this. Time would tell if she could and soon.

Her right hand clasped Stephanie's, her left Pavla's. The three women formed a circle, their minds interlocked.

It had been rough at first. When she and Steph had communed during their struggle with Psellus, there had been little time to examine each other's souls. Now, under the pressure of the ten-minute timeframe Chris had warned them of, there was even less. Still, Kera has been shocked by what she saw within the minds of her friends.

She saw Stephanie's lingering resentment of her, the rich white girl who possessed a greater endowment of magical talent. And she saw her vague sense of dismissive superiority toward most people. But there was also their legitimate love and loyalty toward one another, and their mutual compassion for humanity. Their desire to do good, no matter what.

In Pavla's case, she saw more of the Czech witch's career. The evil things she had done for evil people, and the lies she had told herself all those years to justify them. But she also perceived the heartfelt truth of Pavla's desire to make amends. Nothing she had said to Kera since her departure from the Orthodoxy had been a lie.

There was no time to examine the cocktail of emotions so much sudden intimacy created. Kera clamped down on it, filed it away for later, and focused on the task at hand.

All three of them were in agreement. They would bestow magical aid and necessary insights upon the council to provide them with an edge, and they would bring the US government's substantial arsenal of automated machinery along for the ride.

That was where it got difficult.

Kera had reached out to Chris. While struggling to maintain her circuit with her friends, she had to divide her mind, sending another part of it out to her lover, conveying to him—a person who did not possess the gift—how to aid them.

But with all three witches united in their goal, the burden could be shared.

Chris, said the three voices that were one. *Chris. It's Kera and Stephanie and Pavla. You must do as we say. Don't worry about how to respond. You will probably hear this as a voice in your head. Listen to it! We can see beyond what most people are capable of. We know what we* have to do and how to do it. Go back to your computer. Don't worry about us.

We need you to hack into a particular mainframe located in New Orleans. Follow your intuition, which is our voices guiding you. Here is how to do it. Set off every alarm. Send everything they have to this place, an old house in the bayou outside the city.

Kera felt resistance at first. Chris' mind had opened to the fact of magic's existence, but he had no direct experience. He was trying to tell himself the voice in his head was his own, but his resistance weakened. On a deep level, he grasped that his life could not be explained in normal terms so long as Kera was a part of it.

The resistance gave way, and he set to work.

Kera continued to guide him. Her knowledge of computers melded with his as the magical will of the trio flowed through her and guided his actions.

The clock was ticking. Another part of Kera's mind detached from the complex task and became consumed with worry. It had been at least seven minutes since Chris' email warning them to get out of there.

There wouldn't be enough time to walk her boyfriend through the whole process. They would have to trust him to handle the rest on his own or with Lia's help while they got the hell out of Brimes' house.

We have to go.

Kera wasn't sure which of them had said it; it might have been her, or it could have been Pavla or Steph. But she agreed.

Chris! Good luck. We will see you soon. We promise.

Letting out a grunt that transformed into a near-scream, Kera broke the circuit. Her hands flew up, shaking, and she tumbled out of her chair. The sudden crashing return to reality always came as a shock.

When she peered through the broad window-walls of Brimes' strange house, black vans were advancing down the street.

Kera sprang to her feet, and the others did likewise. "Shit," she gasped. "Feds are here. We need to leave. Um, I'll leave a psychic message that influences them to suspect, uh, someone other than us. Or Brimes. The Mafia or some shit."

Stephanie added, "I'll cloak us."

Pavla pointed at the desk. "The book! We have to take it. Psellus is still trapped within. He will possess one of the police if we leave it here, though he might try the same with us..."

Kera grabbed the grimoire. It was ice-cold to the touch, and she felt the ancient wizard's hostility emanating from it like a subsonic radio signal, but nothing happened. "He's still licking his wounds. We'll have time to deal with him later."

She threw a crude, delayed-action psychic message toward Brimes' computer, leaving it there for the cavalry to find. Regardless of evidence, the responding officers would assume the recent shenanigans were the work of an obscure organized cybercrime ring.

They went out through the bedroom, passing the sleeping Brimes and the tiled bathroom before descending the stairs to the garage. As they left the house behind them, the vans pulled up out front, and men in tactical vests holding rifles burst out.

Chris, Kera thought. *Your time estimate was perfect. Don't let us down with this one last thing, though. I trust you. I love you.*

CHAPTER TWENTY-TWO

Chris gulped, forgetting that spit was pooling in his mouth.

Lia leaned over and touched his arm. "Are you okay?" She was as nervous as he'd ever seen her. Between their increasing risk of running afoul of the law and his weird behavior, she was out of her element and losing her cool.

"Yes," he stated. "But I need you to not bother me for a few minutes unless I ask you for something. Can you please do that? This is a Kera thing. It's important."

His fingers were madly striking the keys of his laptop. Bizarre pieces of information were being fed into his head, and things he could not possibly have known were simply appearing in his brain. The voice in his mind telling him to act on that info sounded an awful lot like his girlfriend's.

Lia bit her lip. "Okay, but please explain this to me later. I'm scared. I'm sorry, but I can't help it. We're going to have the FBI, NSA, and everyone else after us if we screw this up. Please tell me Kera has a plan for how to deal with that."

"She does." He knew for a fact it was true, and his tone must have been convincing since Lia breathed deep and got hold of herself. They were parked on a dark side street, and so far, there were no signs of trouble around them.

What was strange was how important Chris' hacking adventure had become to him. In the back of his mind, he was aware of an ancient and hidden struggle, an important event involving the world of magic. He knew nothing about it. He only knew he wanted one side to win and had to help them in any way he could.

Kera was feeding him emotions as well as knowledge. It was the closest thing he had to a rational explanation.

A video feed appeared on his screen. It was a camera of moderate quality, attached to the front of a drone. The device was taking flight, along with others buzzing alongside it. The fleet was departing from a military base or governmental facility in Louisiana and heading into the swampy countryside.

"Ha-*ha!* Fuck, yes. This is going to work. Whatever *this* is."

Lia grimaced. "I think Kera owes us *both* a highly detailed explanation."

"No!" Samantha cried.

In trying to determine what was happening upstairs, on the ground floor, she had sought out the minds of the magically-enslaved members of the local minor covens since they were less well-guarded than the minds of the Orthodoxy.

Ezeudo listened closely. He could hear the witches barking orders at each other in Russian and someone wailing in fear and pain, then a wet sound and the gurgle of a dying voice. A cold, loathsome sense of malevolence oppressed the expanded portion of his consciousness, as though the fabric of magic itself had been somehow polluted.

Samantha burst into tears and leaned against the damp, moldy wall. James went to her side and held her.

"Ah," LeBlanc said, and her voice was sad. "They sacrificed one of their pawns to empower themselves, and they did a rather inefficient job of it. That poor soul had little power to go around. They threw her life away for the sake of a one-percent boost in effectiveness distributed across their forces."

The unnaturally reverberating voice of the grandmistress issued another command.

Hugh frowned. "She said she wants two more."

Amanda stepped forward. "We *cannot* allow this, LeBlanc! These are our people, whom we pledged to protect. Letting them die to save us is—"

To everyone's shock, LeBlanc raised a hand and struck Amanda full in the face with a relaxation spell. She slumped, and Josiah caught her and kept her on her feet. Amanda's face was contorted in amazement, but the charm did its work. She lolled, complacent and half-conscious for the next minute or so.

"Hold," LeBlanc ordered. "I will suggest something."

She sent out her mind, not toward the compelled locals but toward her archnemesis.

You are wasting your time by sacrificing ones so weak. It is among the stupidest things you could do right now.

She didn't have to wait long for a response; a cold, hard voice spoke directly into her mind.

I heard that, said Anezka. *You are trapped like rats, however. We can take our time. If we must kill every one of your serfs, we shall.*

LeBlanc's blood went cold, but she made herself act flippant. *A waste of time. You would derive more benefit from sacrificing one of your own lower-middle troops.*

There was silence, then the voice shouted again in Russian.

"Hmm," Hugh translated. "She changed her mind and is asking for...a volunteer?"

Voices argued and protested, and again they heard the disgusting gurgle of a human dying. The repulsive aura of black magic grew stronger.

LeBlanc raised a hand. "We will have to flee into the swamp, but not yet. Please trust me."

James left Samantha, who had stopped crying but was still distraught, and came to her side. "Mother. We want to trust you, but what the hell are you talking about? What do you know that we don't?"

"I *know* nothing," she retorted. "We treat thaumaturgy as though it were a science, but in truth, all of our powers come from higher and greater beings. Was it not originally an outgrowth of religion? In this, our darkest moment, what I have is not knowledge but faith."

Crystal Green asked, "In the Chalice?"

LeBlanc shrugged. "That and something else. Somehow I sense we still have friends in this world. Do not ask me to explain. But whatever faith you are capable of, now is the time for it."

They knew that the Orthodoxy would break into the cellar in a matter of minutes. Lauren Jones had been struck by a falling beam of burning wood as they retreated underground; she was still alive, but her shoulder had been crushed, and she had serious burns across a third of her body. Crystal and Mary Mitchell had healed her enough to save her life, but she might not be able to rejoin the fight.

And Rufus had joined Damian and Zacharia in the afterworld. The house was in the hands of their enemies.

However, the Chalice still shone with a subtle light. LeBlanc had not yet activated it and questioned if she was right to delay the full deployment of its magic. It was almost overflowing with power. Its time was coming.

Amanda shook her head and stood up straight. She had overcome the stupefying effects of LeBlanc's spell, though her emotions were still calmer than they'd been. She tilted her head and blinked. "What's that sound?"

Since she had the sharpest ears of any of them, it took another two or three seconds before the other council members and Ezeudo heard it: a faint buzz, growing louder by the moment.

James remarked, "I would have guessed it was your doing. A swarm of bees, maybe? But you were out of it for the last minute or so. Actually, it sounds like a goddamn helicopter."

What could only be described as an air-raid siren went off, causing them to jump an inch.

"Warning," a man's voice, amplified a thousand times, proclaimed. "This is not a drill. This is the Federal Emergency Signal, Code Oh-Two-Six-Niner. Please await further instructions. Disaster relief is on its way. If you must evacuate the area, directions to the nearest safe zone will be forthcoming. Warning. This is not a drill..."

Ezeudo gaped. "What on earth is that? A trick of the Orthodoxy? Or is your government coming to help us?"

LeBlanc wasn't sure. "Not the Orthodoxy."

The buzz grew louder, and the witches above them began to stomp around and scream curses and orders. Things crashed and zipped about; there was general chaos.

James snapped his fingers. "Drones! It's a fleet of drones dive-bombing the fuckers. Like Amanda's Hitchcockian bird swarm earlier, only better. Who the hell is commanding them, though? I don't know."

He stopped, and so did LeBlanc. And Ezeudo. The three of them—and no one else—heard a woman's voice respond to James' implied question.

I am. I sent them to help you, not that I'm a big fan of yours. What the hell are you doing? Hiding in a basement?

LeBlanc moved closer to the table. Her hand closed around the Chalice.

"Okay," James commented in a shaky voice. "I don't know who that is. Ezeudo? LeBlanc?"

Ezeudo looked as though he had gone into a trance. LeBlanc, too, was stunned. "It was not Anezka. As I said, we still have friends in the world, but now is not the time to discover their identity. Get everyone together. We need to—"

The hatch leading into the cellar exploded into fragments, the magical detritus of the many layers of shields they had sealed it with dissipating into the astral ether.

"Go!" LeBlanc shouted.

Everyone bolted, Josiah and Hugh carrying Lauren between them and the others following. LeBlanc hesitated; she felt as though she *should* remain and let the others escape first, but if she was lost, so was the Chalice, and with it, their last hope.

Anezka's voice shrieked into her brain again. *What is that? What are you holding in your hand, LeBlanc?*

LeBlanc conjured the strongest shield she could muster, blocking off the staircase from the rest of the cellar as witches jumped down to attack.

Nothing you would understand, she replied.

James pushed past her. "Someone needs to delay them while everyone else gets away. It might as well be me."

"No." Mary Mitchell stepped up. "It should be me this time. You had your chance to foolishly risk yourself before, James, and I had to spend weeks taking care of you thereafter." She smiled. "It's your turn to suffer for a similar length of time, resuscitating me after we win."

The shield was already cracking. It was difficult to see in the darkness and disorder, but LeBlanc perceived that Anezka had descended after the initial wave of her troops, not trusting the role of breaking through their defenses to anyone but herself.

LeBlanc seized James' hand. "Come." She pulled him along, ignoring his confused protests, as Mary raised her hands for battle, feeling the roots and seeds in the ground around them. "There is a chance they will capture and interrogate rather than kill her."

James sputtered as they stomped toward the tunnel exit. "You mean to leave her to be *tortured?* What's wrong with you, LeBlanc? You've never been this goddamn coldhearted."

Then the Chalice, in LeBlanc's grasp, glowed white, and part of its power wafted toward Mary.

"She will be all right," LeBlanc stated. "But we must go."

Ahead of them, Ezeudo moved fluidly, only half-conscious of what he did. Everything was beginning to resemble a dream.

It is you, he said in his mind, not sure if the person he was addressing could hear him. *The vigilante, Motorcycle Woman. Kera. That is your name, is it not? I saw you. I watched you from afar. Who are you in truth, and why are you helping us?*

Josiah Kane opened the hidden hatch, revealing an opening barely large enough for a grown man to walk through while stooped over. Filthy water and muck spilled into the cellar, flowing down the tunnel from the swamp like effluvia through a pipe.

Crystal Green, beside Ezeudo, cast another healing spell on Lauren to help her clamber through the tunnel. Then they all filed in, struggling to keep their balance amidst the flowing water and irregular, muddy footing. Behind them, LeBlanc and James brought up the rear. The Chalice was glowing.

Kera responded to Ezeudo's query. *You guys are the lesser of two evils, or so it seems. Don't prove me wrong on that. I'm exhausted from all the shit I've done to help you after you tried to trick me and stole my friends' powers.*

Good luck, though.

James left spells in their wake to slow the Orthodoxy's advance as they struggled through the tunnel. "Where does this thing emerge again?"

LeBlanc's beautiful dress was, for the first time anyone could recall, dirty and torn. "Far out in the swamp. Ezeudo, I told you to avoid a particular place with a dead tree in a clear pool. We will end up close to that point. This time, ignore what I said before. That is exactly where we must go."

Perhaps five minutes later, Josiah was the first to sight the end of the tunnel. "Up there. Come along, we're just about out of here. Good Lord, the entire swamp is spilling down there into the cellar. LeBlanc, I'm afraid your friend's house will collapse and the whole property will turn into a lake."

"Who cares?" LeBlanc snapped. "We have more important things to worry about."

Behind them, the grandmistress sounded again.

Hugh informed them, "They figured out it leads into the bayou, I think."

A hundred yards or so back, the earth erupted and water formed a geyser. In the gloom of the swamp it was hard to tell, but Ezeudo, trying to look with his mind's eye, perceived figures rocketing up from the depths, blasting the swamp aside. The witches had opted to take a shortcut to the surface rather than follow the length of the tunnel.

The air-raid siren was still blaring in the distance, though it sounded fainter now. Out in the dank wilderness, anything associated with civilization or technology seemed far away.

Amanda waited for LeBlanc. "When is that Chalice going to kick in? *I'm* going to ask it to help us if you don't do it soon. And where is Mary?"

"Soon," said LeBlanc. "Find the clear pool with the dead tree. You must trust me. Go."

Then the ground and water exploded again, this time in the middle of the group. Everything went black.

Amanda awoke, unsure of where she was or what had happened. It came back quickly; she was floating on a piece of sedge amidst the mucky water of the Mississippi Delta. She looked around. "LeBlanc? James? Hugh?"

Two figures approached, whom she recognized as Josiah and Crystal. "Where is everyone?"

Crystal coughed. "We got scattered by that blast. I don't know if the Orthodoxy did that or if it was something from all those government drones. Ugh. Did LeBlanc say where this pool is?"

"No," Josiah confirmed, in a dismal tone. "She did not. Though I'm guessing—*behind you!*"

Crystal and Amanda ducked as javelins of ice, rock, and mud streaked through the dark air, missing their heads by inches. They spun toward the source of the threat.

Advancing toward them through the swamp was a tall, gaunt-faced aging man in dark clothes, whose eyes glinted like small pale stones. On either side of him was a younger witch. "Now," he said in a dry, raspy voice, "is your chance to surrender."

Josiah threw his cane. Vassily deflected it with a kinetic blast, but it worked its way over to one of the warlock's assistants. She reacted too slowly, and the cane whacked her across the face. She slumped over the exposed roots of a mangrove.

The other witch struck the water around the council members with a thin bolt of lightning. All three screamed in pain but dispelled the shock a heartbeat later. They conjured shields around themselves, though swamp water seeped in around their legs.

Vassily flicked his hand and the water by their ankles froze, trapping them. Then he commanded another gout of water to rise above them, freezing it, too, so spears of ice descended toward their shields. Mostly they splintered with little effect, but the shields were weakened.

Amanda concentrated. At her summons, a swarm of mosquitoes appeared from a brackish pool, humming and buzzing around the head of the younger female witch. She jerked in fear and discomfort and tried to dispatch the insects with a firefly spell. While she was busy, Crystal encased her in a thick shell of ice.

"Ah," quipped Vassily. "You too have an affinity for cold. Where are you from?"

Crystal smiled. "Saguenay, Quebec originally."

The warlock bowed. "Arkhangelsk. It stays in the blood."

Josiah reeled in shock as two massive waves of ice crashed against each other. So much moisture had been frozen as part of the two casters' attacks that the water level around him was noticeably lower. "Crystal, do you have this under control?" He raised his hand, and his cane returned to his grasp.

Amanda cried out as another witch emerged from the shadow and pounced on her. The two women struggled in the shallows and black gloom.

Crystal grunted with exertion. She was losing. The Russian warlock was stronger, or at least not as tired and frightened.

Before Josiah could intervene, something like a snake rose out of the water. He assumed it was Amanda's doing, but she was still wrestling with her ambusher—and it wasn't a snake.

Vassily let out a guttural cry of alarm as the thick vine wrapped around his neck, arms, and chest. His ice wall cracked as Crystal escaped from it, her own mass of frozen stalagmites moving closer to the warlock.

Josiah saw no point in waiting. He threw his cane at the gaunt-faced man, putting enough magically augmented force behind it to send a Humvee into orbit.

The cane's end pierced Vassily's throat, and as the warlock gurgled, the hooked portion swept through the rest of his neck. His head toppled off his shoulders, landing with a splash in the shallow water, and the rest of him followed a second later.

Crystal exhaled, allowing the mass of ice to crumble around her. "Thanks."

"Don't mention it," said Josiah, catching his cane as it returned to his hand. "Now, where is Amanda? And everyone else for that matter."

Mary Mitchell's voice announced, "I'm here. I got away while they were blasting their way through the ground. I haven't the slightest idea where anyone else is."

Josiah expanded his mind, seeking his friends. "The pool. Where is it?"

CHAPTER TWENTY-THREE

Ezeudo stopped and stared in awe.

The water of the pool was as clear as crystal, and the tree that rose from its center was white like bone. The nearby trees were denser than anywhere else. Strangely, the sky was brighter, as though it was a dim noon in a dense forest, but it was still early evening unless he was gravely mistaken. Was dawn already upon them?

James and LeBlanc were with him. They didn't know what had become of the others.

LeBlanc stepped past Ezeudo into the pool. "Come along. Do not be afraid. Anezka will be focused on me and the Chalice. Our friends can handle the rest of them without us."

"God," James gasped. "I hope you're right. What the hell is this place? The light is all wrong. It's...eerie. That sounds weird for someone in my profession, I know, but I've never seen anything like this."

LeBlanc turned to face him. "Long ago, when I was a little girl, I thought the same thing. This is Old Jack's resting place. Here, the power of the Chalice is stronger."

Ezeudo frowned. He had lost his connection to Kera, and it disturbed him. The best of his new friends were by his side, yet he had never in his life felt more alone. Dread created a weight in his stomach, a premonition of bad things to come.

He spun. Standing across from him, beyond the threshold of the clear pool between two black and dripping trees, was Anezka, the grandmistress of the Orthodoxy. Her black hair was curiously undisturbed by everything that had taken place since the start of the battle, and like her subordinates, she was using a shield to part the swamp and walk atop the water and mud. But when she stepped into the pool, the shield failed, and the clear water touched her ankles.

The woman glanced down at it in annoyance. Then she looked up, dismissing Ezeudo and focusing on the one she regarded as her equal.

"LeBlanc," she began in her distinctive voice, no longer bothering with the unnatural reverb she had used when commanding her minions. "Let me guess. That cup is a repository of power, and this strange place amplifies its effects. You think it will give you victory."

James looked at his friend. "Mother. Activate it now. What are we waiting for?"

The Creole faced the Ukrainian. "I have faith, Anezka, that all things will be balanced as they should be. That those who seek to upset the balance will regret doing so, and that the residue of wasted magic shall finally be put to good use, correcting terrible wrongs before they can be done. Just ask Old Jack."

She raised the Chalice.

White light blazed from its depths, illuminating the strange pool to the brilliance of a summer afternoon. But the light stayed within the cup; it seemed confused as to where it should go.

Ezeudo cringed. The dread within him had intensified to alarm. *No. LeBlanc is doing something wrong. She is overconfident! She missed something, but what?*

Anezka had tensed, impressed by the blatant aura of the artifact's power. But her mind was working visibly behind her cold eyes, unraveling the riddle inherent in LeBlanc's words.

"Ah, yes," the grandmistress stated. Her voice sounded gentle, almost meek. "So long, so long has magic been unbalanced in your favor. The council has imposed its iron will upon this country for centuries. Lesser witches have had to submit. Those who did not had their memories erased, their powers taken away. Yes? That was what Mindy told me. Yes, poor Mindy, whose husband Dan died for the sake of your glory."

James sputtered. "What the fuck are you talking about, bitch? You burned my house down!" He raised his hand to unleash an attack spell against her, but the light in the Chalice had flared and seemed to be restraining him.

Ezeudo stared.

LeBlanc looked past the dead tree at something in the gloom beyond the circle of light around the pool. "Old Jack! She lies. She is twisting the truth."

"Oh?" Anezka countered. "I was once a poor farm girl, what people would have called a peasant in older times. Everything was weighted against me by people who possessed power, but I have risen since then to liberate those who were good enough to take what belonged to them. This is what I shall do in America. Anyone who can serve me well may do so. *That* is balance."

LeBlanc had focused on the Chalice, trying to assert control over its power, but the white light within shot out like a diamond flare, leaving the cup dark and empty and swirling around Anezka. White flames ringed her feet and a rippling column of energy, halfway between lighting and sunshine, fell upon her from the sky.

"Oh, no." LeBlanc sighed. "James, Ezeudo. I am so terribly sorry."

James leaped forward, no longer restrained by the Chalice's indecision. He hurled a confusion spell at the grandmistress in conjunction with a localized heat spell powerful enough to melt steel, and he felt the power of his magic reflect back on him.

Screaming, he was consumed by a flash of white light that blasted him twenty feet across the pool to land with a splash beside the dead tree.

Anezka laughed and extended her hand, and a bolt of white lightning curled out to wrap itself around James, holding him in place and tormenting him.

LeBlanc stepped back. "Ezeudo. We must get to—"

Another lightning bolt leaped toward her. She caught it in the Chalice, which redirected it into the water at her feet. Sparks and steam rose as LeBlanc struggled to resist electrocution while fighting Anezka's mind and essence as she had done at the Lovecraft estate.

But where they had been evenly matched before, now the clear advantage lay with the grandmistress. Giddy with more power than she had ever possessed, the Ukrainian had no need for subtlety and struck LeBlanc with another bolt and another, driving her back with brute force until at last, one engulfed her. She tossed the Chalice aside in her throes and collapsed into the water, imprisoned and in agony as the lightning wrapped around her body.

Ezeudo watched the cup sail through the air and land in the water beyond the tree. It looked like nothing so much as an old cup, at the moment, worthless for anything except collecting water. He dashed toward it, his hands wrapping around its neck, and got to his feet, backing toward a tiny island on the far side of the pool. Some of the water remained in the Chalice's bowl. It was still clear.

Anezka advanced across the pool. She was floating now, her black dress billowing on currents of power, and her hair flew about her shoulders like a writhing mass of snakes.

"You there," she called, her voice like that of a thunder goddess making a poor attempt at mercy upon mere mortals. "I do not recall your name; you are the new recruit from Nigeria. You have no cause to be loyal to these people. They coerced you into joining them, didn't they?"

Ezeudo stepped back onto surprisingly dry earth; a narrow pathway led up the little island. "As a matter of fact," he called out, his brain going numb, "they did." It would be pointless to lie. He clutched the Chalice to his chest.

Anezka hovered closer. As she passed the dead white tree, it burst into flames, though the fire did not harm it. The water beneath her feet began to steam and bubble.

"Ahh," rumbled the grandmistress, "I can see into your mind now. You always wished to do good in the world. At first, you had the correct idea of resisting these two and the council they represent." She gestured at James and LeBlanc, who were suspended in a state of helpless torment. "But gradually, their lies convinced you. You reached the conclusion that you *needed* people like them to do good. That good only comes from order and stability."

Ezeudo's hands trembled. It was as though she had ripped the veil from his secret thoughts, revealing everything that had consumed him during his time training with the council.

Anezka went on. "In a way, you were correct. But look at these fools. They are pompous and incompetent. Those who are least suited to enforcing order upon the world are the ones who crow about it most strongly. They advertise their good intentions to people like you, but you have *real* potential. I would hate to have to destroy it. It would be a waste. I have lost many excellent witches in this fight. Someone will need to replace them."

His knees wobbled.

Old Jack, whoever you are, he begged, wondering if Anezka could hear his thoughts, *if LeBlanc was right about you, tell me what to do. And if she was wrong, then may I die now, knowing I tried my best.*

Someone answered, but it wasn't Old Jack.

Ezeudo, said Kera. *That's your name. I heard everything. I heard what she said. She's half right, but what she is proposing is not the solution. You know that. It's obvious to us humans, even if whatever power she's seized hold of can't figure it out yet. Gods and spirits don't always understand us, but I think you and I understand each other. We're the same. Until the council found you, you did things your own way. You followed your conscience.*

Anezka's eyes blazed, and an angry reddish tint appeared in the crackling white light that surrounded her. "What? Who is that? *Kera!* You are condemned to death, you little whore. How dare you compare yourself to this fine young man! You and he are nothing alike! You are a scavenger. Ezeudo, do not listen to her. Set the Chalice down and come with me. I will not harm you."

Ezeudo froze. Anezka's new powers had cut across his mind, sealing it off from further communication with Kera, but the girl's words resonated in the core of his being.

He glanced down at the Chalice. A few specks of white light, faint but sparkling, were growing within the water he had brought from the pool.

He stood up straight. "I will come with you and give you the Chalice," he declared, "if I have your word that you will never again harm anyone with your powers."

Anezka floated another meter closer to him. "You are not in a position to make demands of that nature. Everyone must defend themselves at times."

"Yes," Ezeudo agreed. "Innocent people like Mindy and Dan. People like Damian and Zacharia, or those poor souls I read about not long ago who had their blood drained in strange rituals. People like the man imprisoned on the other side of this swamp who warned me to flee this place or those whose throats were cut not an hour ago, to power a spell that hardly required their sacrifice."

The light around the witch crackled again and began turning

from red to black, though it was still shot through with streaks of white. "Do not be ridiculous," she said. "The council could have avoided all of that if they had submitted at once. Their resistance is to blame."

The white light within the Chalice was growing stronger.

Ezeudo set the cup down at his feet. "So be it then. I give it to you in the understanding that people like the council—or whoever is to blame for such things—shall never be able to wield its power."

Anezka's lip curled. "How clever. You think you can still escape reality through trickery. The imbalance the council represented was weakness. They had no right to rule, and that is why I defeated them. I begin to question whether you are worthy to join me after all."

Ezeudo kicked the Chalice into the pool, where it floated halfway between them. The white light seeped into the clear waters. "Take it then, but you had better be certain. I hope you are as confident in your principles as I am."

Anezka threw a bolt of lightning at him. It struck him in the chest, knocking him back, and he howled in pain. His muscles spasmed, and he struck the dirt behind him hard. But the blast dissipated; it did not encircle him as it had James and LeBlanc.

He rose to his knees and watched as the grandmistress of the Orthodoxy knelt to retrieve the Chalice.

"There," she said, lifting it. "All things are as they should be."

The sky darkened. The pool and the water turned jet-black, and the light surrounding the witch winked out. The spells that held James and LeBlanc in stasis vanished, and they collapsed into the water in exhaustion.

Her head jerked around in shock. She tried to drop the cup, but it refused to leave her grasp. Above her head, the darkness coalesced into a cloud and a voice, deep and ancient, rippled up from the pool.

"You have proven yourself unworthy," it proclaimed.

Ezeudo saw Anezka's face, contorted with rage and confusion, for a split second before another bolt of blazing light fell upon her from the sky. She screamed as brilliant fire rose in a column around her, and her charred skeleton shrieked in time with the roaring of the flames. Then it dissolved into ash, which sank beneath the water and was claimed by the mud.

The darkness receded as quickly as it had come, and the grove returned to its strange perpetual twilight. Silence reigned.

Ezeudo put his face against the earth and breathed in and out, his respirations shuddering in his chest as sweat poured from his brow. Then he got to his feet, walked into the pool, and helped his friends to their feet.

James clutched his arm. "Oh, God. Oh, fuck. Thank you. It's over, isn't it? I knew it. I knew you were the right horse to bet on all this time, man. Jesus. Shit."

Ezeudo patted the man's back. "Thank you."

LeBlanc, more haggard and pitiful than he had ever seen her, recovered from her ordeal quickly. "Ezeudo. Where is the Chalice?"

They both looked around. It was nowhere to be seen. LeBlanc stepped past him and looked at the tiny island beyond the tree. "Ah. It has returned to its place. You know, it has traditionally had a guardian but has managed without one for some time now. You might be well-suited to the job."

James, calmer now, looked up. "What? You mean, leave Ezeudo *here* to spend the next hundred years watching a cup?"

LeBlanc shrugged. "It would prevent the sorts of misunderstandings that nearly killed us all. Old Jack is wise, but humans are craftier. He believed Anezka's lies...at first. You managed to draw out the truth."

Ezeudo paused. "I do not think most of humanity needs the Chalice. I can do more good working with you, particularly if you would be open to making changes. Anezka's lies were intertwined with the truth."

LeBlanc flinched. "I suppose that is…possible."

CHAPTER TWENTY-FOUR

Kera held out her hand. "Hit me."

Chris slapped a bottle into her hand. "My own special blend," he explained. "I more or less figured you'd be running on empty at some point during the night, so I mixed strong coffee, energy drink shit, whole milk, and as much sugar as I could fit into the bottle while keeping it a liquid rather than a paste."

Kera unscrewed the lid. "Perfect. Best boyfriend ever." She chugged half the bottle in one swig.

She sat, legs crossed, on the ground. In addition to Chris, Pavla, Stephanie, and Lia were there too. After fleeing Montecito, they had taken a back road into public land in the mountains and stopped at the most out-of-the-way, godforsaken spot they could find, surrounded by rocks, crags, trees, and shrubs.

It seemed like the appropriate place for what they were about to do, or rather, what *she* was about to do. They had all agreed that she should handle it alone, with them by her side to help if necessary.

Steph asked what they all wanted to know. "Did they win? Kera? Pavla? One of you two must know."

Pavla gave one of her small, sad smiles. "I cannot say for sure, but Anezka is dead. I felt her die. It was...it was not pleasant, but neither was she. She brought it on herself."

Kera nodded. "I felt *something*. And that Ezeudo guy has a good head on his shoulders. As for the rest of them, well, that's what we're about to find out."

Snapping her fingers, Steph quipped, "You'll teach me how to astrally project later, right? I want to try it out on Regina sometime. Just to mess with her."

"Of course," Kera vowed. "Now, give me a minute in peace."

They shut up, and she closed her eyes.

First, she found Ezeudo. It was not him she wanted to speak to this time, so she did not intrude upon his mind. Instead, she expanded to those around him, seeking them out via their memories of and emotional connections to him. Once she had a firm grasp of who and where they were, she would send her message.

The two people to whom he was closest were a nerdy white guy and an attractive, eccentrically-dressed black woman. Kera's hands formed claws, but she made herself relax. His best friends were "the Duo"—the two thaumaturges who had come after her months ago and had depowered the Kims.

She took a deep breath. *All accounts will be settled. All misunderstandings will be cleared up.*

Then she was ready.

Kera recalled what she knew about scrying, about psychic messages, and about illusions. Combining those with her activity on the astral plane as when she'd melded minds with Pavla and Stephanie was the key to astral projection, one of the most advanced of all magical skills. Pavla had given her pointers, but the task was ultimately hers.

She concentrated and felt the purplish void spinning beneath her. Though her body was inert on the ground off the side of the road in the coastal hills, her spirit traveled hundreds of miles across deserts, mountains, plains, and swamps. It knew exactly where to go.

Once it arrived, it created the proper image for itself, much like the one she had used half a year in the past to threaten Lia and Johnny and Sven into abandoning their life of crime: a terrible but majestic figure in black leather and a nice bike helmet.

Kera opened her eyes. Around her, she saw a humble farmhouse somewhere in rural Louisiana. It was not the place she had expected. The council had relocated to a house near the one they had recently occupied.

The thaumaturges, who had been clustered around a table, stood up, some of them knocking over their chairs. In addition to the council and Ezeudo, there was also an elderly black couple and a youngish white woman who were clearly not members. They had the gift, but only a touch of it.

The lady in the multicolored dress who was one-half of the Duo was the first to speak. She seemed to be their leader or the closest thing they had to one.

"Who are you?" she asked. "I have my suspicions, as do we all. If you are going to appear before us in this fashion as we are about to relax after the longest night of our lives, you should be polite enough to introduce yourself."

Kera hesitated. "My name is Kera. Most people know me as Motorcycle Man or Woman. Whatever. We *almost* met before. You came looking for me."

The other half of the duo, the mild-looking guy with the glasses, nodded. "I remember that. Somehow I didn't think we'd seen the last of you. No hard feelings, especially since you saved us all. And not just us. All of North America."

The others chimed in, agreeing and thanking her. They all introduced themselves. Mother LeBlanc. James Lovecraft.

Ezeudo, of course. And others with names like Amanda, Lauren, Samantha, Crystal, Mary, Josiah, and Hugh. The old couple was the Grandises, and the sad-faced woman was Mindy.

"Okay, great," Kera stated, and she heard the ghostly echo of her voice in the room. "So what happened to the Orthodoxy?"

LeBlanc cleared her throat. "With your help, not least that fleet of drones, they were defeated and driven off. At least half their members perished in the battle, including much of their senior leaders and their grandmistress. The others have fled. I do not think they will remain in America. Weakened as they are, they'll have trouble retaining the territory they held in Eastern Europe before they began their invasion."

Kera wasn't sure Pavla could hear her, but if not, she could fill her in later. "Good, but let's get one thing absolutely fucking clear here. I saved your asses not because I'm a big fan, but because you were the less terrible of the two groups. Your council is pompous, overbearing, and wants to control everyone else's magic. At least you're not murderous, human-sacrificing gangsters, right? But my aid doesn't come for free. You owe me."

James grimaced. "Sounds about right. What are your terms, O mighty biker chick?"

"You cannot," Kera went on, "go back to your old shenanigans. You have no right to erase the powers of anyone who doesn't join you or submit to you. Maybe you think you're doing the right thing, but you're not. People have the right to flourish on their own terms. Make a few changes in how you do business, and we'll get along."

Ezeudo folded his hands in front of him. "She is rude," he observed, "but it is a good point."

LeBlanc glared at him, then looked at the illusory specter of Kera. "We are indebted to you, Kera, and you are clearly a force to be reckoned with. Of course, we also possess knowledge handed down through many generations, which you do not, and we are not accustomed to being threatened except by our enemies."

Kera had expected something like that. "I don't want to be your enemy, but if you come after me again, or my friends, then let's just say I won't get what I want. Either you run a more laissez-faire system from now on, or we're going to have problems. I would rather have allies than foes, or at least people who are, you know, neutral. I'll be in touch. Let me know when you make up your minds."

With that, she receded into the astral murk, banishing the illusion and flying back to her own body in the mountains of California.

She opened her eyes and saw her friends around her.

Steph asked, "How did it go?"

Kera groaned and got to her feet. "The projection went off without a hitch. As for the negotiation, well, I told them what I had to say. They're going to think it over."

Pavla took her by the arm. "They will think you a cocky upstart and try to dismiss you, but you have not allowed them to do so. That was wise. I know you only wish to be left alone to practice magic as you see fit for the greater good of your home city. They would be smart not to interfere."

Chris chuckled. "People do love interfering, though."

Lia glanced at the Jeep and back. "Pardon me, but weren't you talking about dealing with the book before we went home?"

"Yes," said Pavla. "I know you are tired, Kera, but we must destroy it before anything else. Psellus will try again unless he is exorcised. As for the book, it may be possible to save it, but I am not sure."

Kera shook her head. "I skimmed it and noticed something. All the spells are part of a super-spell that encompasses the entire grimoire. It's like a really high-interest loan. To learn any of the spells, you have to pay in the form of letting Viator Psellus cast them *through* you, and he'll hijack your body while he's at it. The crafty bastard preserved his existence all this time by playing on people's curiosity and desire for power."

Pavla's shoulders slumped. "Ah, that is tragic. His knowledge might have been incredibly beneficial if it had been a normal spellbook. But yes, it is too dangerous. And the world of magic is changing."

Stephanie added, "I hate the thought of burning a book. Who the hell does that? But I'll help you anyway. This particular one sounds like an exception."

The three sorceresses brought the grimoire out from where it had rested, wrapped in a blanket, in the back compartment of Chris' Jeep. Kera thought she could hear Psellus' voice whispering through the leather. He was getting antsy again.

They tossed the book on the ground and surrounded it, forming a circle and linking hands.

What? the wizard's disembodied voice asked. *What are you doing?*

Kera replied, *Sorry, Psellus. In your day, you were probably one of the greats, but you've had your day and a bunch of other days that you stole from other people. It's time for you to move on to the next world.*

No! he protested. *Think about what you're doing. The world will lose a vast store of spellcraft.*

They said nothing in response. To her friends, Pavla stated, "I will handle the exorcism of his spirit. You two focus on destroying the book and resisting any effort by Psellus to leap out at any of us."

Chris took Lia's hand and led her to the other side of the road. "Might be good to stand back if there's a risk of random demonic possession involved."

Lia shook her head. "I cannot *believe* the shit I've let you guys talk me into lately."

Pavla began speaking in Latin, urging the soul of Viator

Psellus to relinquish its hold on the world and progress to the next plane of existence, ignoring his pleas and protests, as Kera and Stephanie shielded them and collaborated on a heat generation spell.

The grimoire burst into flames, groaning and spitting as its leather and vellum turned to ash. A faint dark form leaped out but was rebuffed by the shields. Then Pavla swept her arms upward and the shadowy silhouette was gone, leaving behind nothing but a vague mental echo.

"It is done," she declared.

"Did you hear that?" Doug asked.

Mia, scowling, did not bother answering at first. "No. What?"

He glanced at the side road they'd just passed. "A weird-ass voice begging people to reconsider or something like that."

His partner looked at him. "The hell? I didn't hear anything. I'm curious, though."

She pulled over, turned around, and sped down the back road, which led into the hills on state land. After a minute or two, they spied a tiny spot of glowing light. A Jeep was parked nearby, and five people stood around what looked like a burned-out campfire. Four women and a man, all of them in their twenties to early thirties.

Mia brought the car to a stop and rolled down the window. Two of the women looked at her.

"Hi," she greeted them, trying to sound friendly. The disappointment of not making it to Brimes' place before the feds had put her in a shitty-ass mood. "We're reporters. Don't worry, you're not in trouble. We thought we heard something. Is everything all right?"

While she spoke, Doug surreptitiously filmed the group.

A slender young white woman wearing black leather stepped forth. "Yeah, we're fine. Had a smoking accident. I keep telling my dipshit boyfriend not to flick cigarette butts out the window. Thanks to our quick intervention, yet another California wildfire was prevented."

She gave them a thumbs-up, then turned away. They all stomped out the remaining glowing embers of the tiny fire and piled back into their Jeep.

Mia rolled up the window, turned around, and drove away. "Well, that was a waste of time. Smartass college kids were probably hitting a bong, and one of them dropped their Zippo in the chaparral."

Doug cleared his throat. "No, it wasn't. I got footage of *her*."

Mia snorted. "Who? That girl? She's not your type and probably a little young for you. Wait, is she a celebrity?"

"Of course," he confirmed. "She's Motorcycle Woman. The ass was the same. The leather rode up the crack in just the right way for me to confirm it. I'll show you later when we examine the video."

Mia slammed on the brakes and pulled the car to the side of the road.

"Doug, shut the *fuck* up, okay? There never was a Motorcycle Man, Woman, or whatever. It was an urban legend. We kept chasing it because we *wanted* it to be true, but it was just a bunch of copycats emulating a bunch of coincidences that happened for a bunch of reasons that aren't even reasons. Mass hysteria. We wasted our time. Let's go back to doing human interest stories. I'm tired of superhero crap and fairytales."

Her partner was silent for nearly two minutes, so she fired the car up and started back down the highway.

Doug rolled his shoulders. "If you say so." He wasn't so sure, though. Still, thoughts of mozzarella sticks were beginning to eclipse thoughts of MM. "In any event, it was fun while it lasted."

Everyone thought Kera was the one with the most cause to celebrate, but she had been the quietest and the most serious through the whole gathering.

She and the rest of her friends—the agency—had congregated at the Kims' place, squashing themselves tightly around the modest dinner table in their none-too-spacious kitchen. Knowing they were coming, Mrs. Kim had pushed her kitchen to its limits in preparing a vast feast.

Lia stared down at her clean plate, wiping her mouth and smiling in half-embarrassed gratitude. "You know," she commented, "my mother stopped making, um, Korean food when I was six. It's...nice to get a home-cooked meal like this again. It's been a long time."

Mrs. Kim, her face as warm and pleasant as usual, took the younger woman's hand and helped her to her feet, saying something to Lia in her native language. Then she glanced at Kera.

Kera waved a hand. "You can have her for now. Go have a private conversation about Korean stuff. But I'd like both of you back later."

Mrs. Kim chuckled, and she and Lia walked into the living room. That freed up some elbow room around the table.

Chris rested his hands on his stomach. "As usual, that was amazing. My compliments to the chef when she gets back."

Mr. Kim flapped his hands. "Yes, yes, she knows she is a good cook. She is very arrogant about her culinary skills. But you're welcome. Now, how the hell did you get rid of those Orthodoxy people from half the country away? And what is this nonsense about the book?"

"Drones," said Chris. "I'm not allowed to reveal the details. State secret. Otherwise, magical stuff, but you'll have to ask the ladies about that part."

Stephanie volunteered, "The book was possessing people, but

we got rid of it. Threw the feds off at the last minute, too. Just hope they took the bait. If they show up at any of our doors later, we'll have to enchant the hell out of them and hope for the best."

Mr. Kim nodded and grinned broadly. "Ah, excellent. That shouldn't be hard. Feds do not usually have much imagination or sense of humor. It should be easy to make them go away and catch aliens or something instead."

Pavla added, "We are not certain the Orthodoxy is gone for good. Some of them might wish to continue Anezka's vendetta against me or Kera, but they were badly weakened. LeBlanc, the leader of the council, seems to think that they'll choose to consolidate their turf around Moscow until they can recover. Hopefully, they never will. Some of them were my friends, but the world is better off *without* the risk of them reigning over half the magic users on the planet. I would know."

Kera did not feel she had much to contribute. She laughed occasionally, listened, and ate and drank enough for three people. Her exertions last night had left her feeling drained all day.

Finally, Mr. Kim got her alone on the landing of the stairs.

"Kera," he began. "What is wrong? If anything."

She looked at him, struggling with how to answer the question. "I'm not sure. Nothing is bothering me; I just feel...I don't know. Like this is the end of an era. I guess I'm wondering what comes next. Where we go from here."

The old man nodded and stared vacantly out the window. "Hmm, yes. That makes sense. Well, do you still want to run a detective agency?"

"Yes," she affirmed.

"And do you still want to be with Chris? Still want to be friends with all of us here tonight? Still want to live in LA?"

For a second, she wondered if he suspected her of dissatisfaction with them and thought she had said or did something wrong.

No, she reassured herself. *He's just putting things in perspective.*

"Yes," she said again. "I don't plan on making any major changes in the foreseeable future."

Mr. Kim chuckled. "Well, then. That's most of your future right there, but I know what you mean. You accomplished many things, and now they are done and over with. But other stuff will come. Maybe more boring, but less risk of dying. Give it time. If there are other things you have in mind, they will come to the surface when they are ready."

She sniffled and looked up, feeling a little better. "Yeah, I think so. Thank you, good sir."

They hugged. "Of course. Don't hold onto me for too long. Chris will start getting jealous."

She laughed and released him. "Right. I'm going to grab him and wander out back if that's okay."

He nodded and waved his hand, strolling back toward the living area to join his wife and Lia.

Chris was still in the dining room. Kera grabbed him by the arm and hauled him outside.

"So, then," he began. "What's up?"

She kicked at the gravel. "Absolutely nothing. Having done all the stuff we did this past half a year, I feel like there might not be anything else worth doing. And in the meantime, here I am, waiting for those council pricks to get back in touch with me. Ugh. I don't like waiting for people."

Chris took her by the waist and kissed her. "Understandable. As for 'stuff worth doing,' we'll *invent* new stuff if we have to. Not for the job—we don't want to make up crimes just so we can investigate them—but, like, vacations. Hobbies. Maybe, at some indeterminate point in the future, a normal family life. Maybe."

She raised an eyebrow. "Oh, really? Well, it's worth considering. We'll see."

Her phone rang.

"Fuck! It's my fucking mother. God-fucking-dammit. What

the fuck is she doing calling at this hour? It's, like, 10:30 in Connecticut right now."

Chris shook his head sadly. "For a minute, it seemed like you were getting back into a good mood. Alas."

Kera hesitated as the phone buzzed. "I should just let it ring and call her back tomorrow. No, the hell with it. I don't have anything better to do. But what do I tell her? After *yesterday?* Ugh."

Her boyfriend gave her one of his serious looks. "You could try telling her the truth for once."

She paused, then hovered her finger over the green icon. "Maybe."

James had finally allowed himself a drink. Much of his memory of the flight from New York to Louisiana was hazy since he'd been incapacitated, but to the best of his recollection, his last drink had been in his house.

Back when his house still existed.

"Drinking in public," he told himself, "is healthier anyway."

Ezeudo had noticed him leaving and insisted on coming along. "I would like a drink too. I hear New Orleans is an excellent place to be drunk."

James shrugged. "Okay. Most places are, really, but Mardi Gras and all that. Though I think that's in the spring. It's, like, October now."

"Yes," Ezeudo agreed. "It is. A beautiful month in Geneva, and perhaps in New York."

They walked together down the streets, bright with artificial lights, and ducked into the first decent-looking pub they came to. Within, a couple of morose characters looked at them briefly, then turned back to their beverages, while an animated younger couple joked between themselves and ignored the two men.

James ordered a whiskey on the rocks, and Ezeudo had the same.

Sipping his drink, he smiled. "I love this crap," he confessed. "But it's not a substitute for...anything. Can't take the place of life. It's just booze. Bad for your liver."

"Only when you drink too much," Ezeudo pointed out. He sipped his whiskey. "So, our situation is odd. I am about to be promoted to full member of the council, but LeBlanc and Mitchell are also saying that they might *disband* the council. It does not make much sense."

James glowered into his glass. "Yeah. It doesn't. My home used to *be* the council in a manner of speaking. Weird that I would get to be host and master of ceremonies despite being the youngest, newest member. At least until you came along, and your membership is mostly because of me. *Everything* since last Christmas, when I first pitched the book idea, is because of me. My idea of how to save the council led to its destruction and a worldwide revolution in the order of magic and the deaths of three of my friends and colleagues as well as other poor schmucks. Oh, and I'm homeless. If the council disbands, I'm left with...nothing. Absolutely nothing."

Ezeudo caught his gaze and held it. "James. That is not true. You have us, your friends. Oh, and everything is *not* your fault. Even if there is no council, the people who made it up will be around. You still have some of your family fortune in banks and investment accounts, do you not?"

"Yes." He rubbed his nose. "Lost all the family heirlooms and priceless magical paraphernalia, but I still have money. I can go back to being rich if I pretend to be *nouveau riche* and buy a horrible yuppie McMansion in a suburb in Florida or something. I guess it's not that bad. I'll manage."

Ezeudo looked into the distance. "I think I might go back to Europe, though I should like to visit America as often as I can. We will all manage, with the council or not. We each have free will and the power to exercise it. What happens tomorrow is up to each of us each day."

James was silent for a long moment. He drained his glass.

"My friend," he intoned, "I truly hope you're right."

THE END

CHECKOUT KERA'S COMPLETE STORY ON AUDIO

Kera MacDonagh's story is also available on Audio beginning with book one, *How to be a Badass Witch*. The series is narrated by the wonder Holly Adams!

Click here to hear the adventure on audio.

CREATOR NOTES
JUNE 24, 2021

Thank you for not only reading this story but these author notes in the back as well!

Our girl Kera is all grown up. This is the last of the three trilogies we planned for her, but one can never know the future.

I hope you enjoyed where we took Kera, her relationship(s), and her purpose in life.

While I'm not sure we will see or hear from Kera again, you should expect to see another Badass <something> book in the future.

I really like the premise and believe we can do more with the concept. I have to admit, I'm partial to something like a shifter in the next story. Maybe a dragon shifter?

Or you know, we could do the ol' faithful and do a werewolf. My personal favorite is a vampire.

I started my career writing about vampires (Bethany Anne in *The Kurtherian Gambit*) and they hold a special place in my heart.

As a publisher, I am well aware that werewolves are more popular (by sales figures) than vampires. I'm not sure why that is; perhaps women just connect more with a hot, sweaty, hairy guy than a pale dead guy who has an iron deficiency and needs sun and a tan.

Ok, I think I just answered my own question.

AH HA! That explains why I need to do a *How to be a Badass Vampire* book: the vampires need to get their mojo.

If you enjoy these Badass stories, you will probably like just about anything I've done with Martha Carr (if you haven't looked into those). Look also for books by Judith Berens, a combined pen name for Martha Carr and Michael Anderle.

If you are ready for a change of pace, try out the *Witch of the Federation* stories. A young girl grows up in a future that is sci-fi with aliens who remind you of either orcs (the Dreth) or elves (The Meligornians).

Thank you for reading my stories!

Take care of yourself, enjoy your week or weekend, and talk to you in the next book!

Ad Aeternitatem,

Michael Anderle

BOOKS BY MICHAEL ANDERLE

Sign up for the LMBPN email list to be notified of new releases and special deals!

https://lmbpn.com/email/

For a complete list of books by Michael Anderle, please visit:

www.lmbpn.com/ma-books/

CONNECT WITH MICHAEL

Connect with Michael Anderle

Website: http://lmbpn.com

Email List: http://lmbpn.com/email/

Social Media:

https://www.facebook.com/LMBPNPublishing

https://twitter.com/MichaelAnderle

https://www.instagram.com/lmbpn_publishing/

https://www.bookbub.com/authors/michael-anderle

www.ingramcontent.com/pod-product-compliance
Lightning Source LLC
LaVergne TN
LVHW041625060526
838200LV00040B/1446